A HIDDEN ROSE

LINEN AND LACE - BOOK FIVE

ROSIE CHAPEL

A Hidden Rose
Linen and Lace - Book Five

Rosie Chapel

First printing 2018
ISBN: 978-0-6482797-2-3 (e-book)
ISBN: 978-0-6451116-5-1 (paperback)

Ulfire Pty. Ltd.
P.O. Box 1481
South Perth
WA 6951
Australia

www.rosiechapel.com

Images courtesy: Period Images and Deposit Photos
Cover Artwork: JF Holland

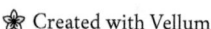 Created with Vellum

~

To Melody, Julie, Lilly, Jackie and Amy ~
thank you for suffering me generally being a nuisance.
Even though we are separated by many miles, I feel you right here
beside me, offering your love, support, and endless patience.
I appreciate it more than you will ever know!

~

ACKNOWLEDGMENTS

Thank you to Janet for her discerning eye.
To Julie for creating this beautiful cover.
To Graham at *A Fading Street Publishers* for his editing skills,
and to my hubby for his technical wizardry.
I could not do this without you!

~

~

The Linen and Lace Clan

An exclusive club, only accessible to the fortuitous few. Those who - no matter their differences in money, titles, background or position - marry for love.

In an era when status, influence, and wealth are bolstered under the guise of marriage, you are like rare gemstones - admired and envied.

Let your mutual respect and true affection for one another be the beacons by which you navigate the rough and the smooth of life's journey.

Whether your clothing be of the cheapest linen or the finest lace, may the blend of either or both bring the richest and happiest union.

~

A Hidden Rose
Linen and Lace - Book Five

PROLOGUE

NORTH SEA ~ MAY 1819

*G*ale force winds shrieked around them, sailors struggling to control the schooner as it was tossed relentlessly. Icy rain lashed at already drenched bodies, and chilled fingers fought to hang onto sheetlines on a dangerously slippery deck.

Nicholas Drummond, along with his crew had been battling the storm for hours and it showed no signs of abating. On his port side, through the grey gloom, he could make out a bay, offering a modicum of shelter and the chance to save both crew and vessel.

He knew they were north of Whitby and running his mind's eye over the navigational charts on the captain's desk, Nick guessed it was probably Runswick Bay. At this point, risking shallower waters was better than trying to ride out the storm on open sea.

They managed to turn the ship, so the wind blew through the sails not across them and were in the process of heaving to when disaster struck.

There was a curious roar. Nicholas turned to see what on earth could be louder than this tumult, to behold a monstrous wall of black water rearing higher than the masts, a split second before it crashed over the hull.

The men desperately grappled for anything that might save them from being swept into the treacherous sea, the dark rise of the cliffs looming ominously closer.

Nicholas, or Nick as he was known to all and sundry, clung to the wheel, until the wave subsided, then, pulling himself upright, moved across the deck accounting for all his men. He worried manning the lifeboat would be useless, he could tell by the white swirls of water, they were nearly on the rocks, the little wooden boat would probably be smashed to pieces before the crew could pull around into the bay.

He needed to get the men to safety, they were paramount, the schooner, well it was likely already lost, but Nick was determined not a man would suffer the same fate. Thankfully, this was a sea trial, so they weren't carrying any cargo other than their own supplies.

Hanging on to whatever he could, he made his way cautiously across the deck to Captain Richards, long time employee of Trentams — the Drummond's shipyard — one of Nick's closest friends, and about as an experienced a sailor as you could get.

"Captain, do you think we can risk getting the men off?" Nick bawled over the thunderous noise, watching as Richards ran all potential scenarios through his head. None had a positive outcome, but some would be less deadly than others.

"If we can get the boat down before the wind bashes it against the hull, we might have a chance," Captain Richards yelled back, dashing water off his face, and the two struggled to the waist of the schooner, where the boat was lashed.

Working together they untied the gripes, which tethered the little boat while underway — cold fingers and sodden ropes hampering their efforts, while the remainder of the crew continued in their attempts to bring the ship around. It was clearly a losing battle.

First mate, Mr Dillon and Able Seaman, Mr Lamb, appeared through the deluge and, deciding it would be too dangerous to use the tricing pendants to manoeuvre the boat into position under the davit, the four dragged the boat to the stern and began attaching the frapping lines.

Once completed, Captain Richards struggled along the deck to tell the remaining three they must abandon ship. Despite their desperation to save the schooner, the captain's word was law, so using the rail as support, they slipped and slithered to where the boat, now attached to the davit, was ready to be lowered.

Already aboard, Mr Dillon directed each sailor to the optimum place, distributing their weight evenly.

Nick and the captain stayed to operate the davit. Normally one person could manage, but the heave of the swell, and the buffeting wind was making everything twice as difficult. Nick realised the current angle of the ship might prevent the winch from working properly, but by now it was either take the risk or they would all perish.

At least this way five of them had a chance.

"What about you Cap'n, Mr Drummond?" demanded Mr Marshall, the second mate, as the boat began to drop below the deck.

"Don't worry about us, just get to safety," hollered the captain, as the little vessel, see-sawing rather wildly, finally hit the water. It tipped with the swell, but righted itself, the built-in cork serving its purpose.

Mr Dillon and Mr Jones grabbed the oars, fighting the waves, but slowly, slowly it looked as though they were pulling away.

Nick exhaled a long-held breath, praying they would get around the ship, and into the calmer waters of the bay, knowing his fate, and that of Richards' was out of his hands.

The ship creaked, rivets and planks beginning to give way, while he and the captain moved towards the main mast, intent on coming up with a way of escaping a watery grave. Just then, he noticed a dark shape coming alongside the starboard side.

It was a large, wooden boat, in which four men wearing oilskins gripped solid oars. A gravelly voice hailed them.

"Come on, you fools!" Notwithstanding the imminent peril facing them, Nick and Richards grinned at each other — a lifeboat. Rescue!

Praising all that was holy, the pair, tiring now, gathered the last of their energy to toss a heavy length of rope over the side. A few seconds of argument ensued while Captain Richards tried to make Nick go first.

"No, Michael!" Nick shouted, deliberately using his friend's given name rather than his nautical title. "At the end of the day, I am responsible for this ship and its crew. I cannot in all conscience let you wait until I am in that boat. Go on, man! I'm right behind you."

Richards hesitated, but Nick gave him a shove to the shoulder and dropped him a wink. There was a sudden respite in the wind and the captain slid down the rope, long years of manning the rigging coming to the fore.

"Your turn!" barked one of their rescuers. Nick turned to begin his descent when above the tempest came an horrendous cracking.

Raising his eyes, Nick saw the foremast snap like a twig, tearing through the foresail, its downward journey in slow motion, as rigging and sails tangled together.

The last thing Nick recalled with any clarity was his captain's bellow.

"Jump!"

CHAPTER 1

*T*he silence was deafening. *Where was he?* It had been so noisy. *Why was that again?* Nick tried to work out what was going on, but he couldn't concentrate. Maybe he was dead, that was why it was so quiet. *Well, damn it, that wasn't very convenient, not when he was in the middle of... wait... what was he in the middle of?*

While ruminating on whether this was indeed his demise, Nick became aware his whole body ached, his head was throbbing like the devil, and he had a raging thirst. Leaning towards not being dead, he surmised it might be an idea to get up. He tried to move, only to feel a gentle hand rest on his chest.

"Lie back, sir. You have a fever. You need to rest." The voice was that of a woman, soft — her accent unfamiliar. Nick groaned and tried to sit up again. "Please do as I ask. I daresay your head is thumping and looking at these bruises, you likely feel as though the ship landed on you, which it nearly did."

Nick frowned. She was making no sense. "What ship?" he croaked, the two words enough to spike agony in his throat.

He gasped in pain, and felt a cup pressed against his lips. He tried to gulp its contents.

"Slowly, sip it slowly, it will help." Cool, sweet liquid slipped over his tongue, easing his inflamed throat. "A little more," when he tried to pull away, "please just for me."

Nick was trying work out who 'me' was when everything grew dim, and oblivion claimed him.

Rose Archer, sat for a few more minutes, wiping a damp cloth over the man's face, neck, and wrists, trying to cool the fire burning through him. It was five days since the ship ran aground on the rocks, five days since the lifeboat rescued the last two sailors from the ship just as it gave up its argument with the storm. This man, the only one still bedridden was causing her father, the local doctor, serious concern.

Incredibly, all seven crew were safe. The locals came out in force, risking their own lives to save the hapless seafarers. The five in the little boat managed to row their way into the bay, to be picked up by one of the fishing cobles.

The Zetland lifeboat from Redcar, several miles up the coast — dispatched immediately upon receiving the signal a ship was in trouble, long before the crew realised how dire their situation was — arrived in the nick of time.

The villagers, as was their habit, took the men in. Drying, warming, feeding, and clothing them, discovering that although soaked to the skin, the worst injury except for the man lying on the bed was a broken arm.

The storm raged well into the following day, but in the late afternoon, had blown itself out, and as the sun began to set, it was as though it had never happened. The sky was clear, the breeze light, and the sea calm.

Captain Michael Richards who, fortunately, received only

a few lacerations and a good drenching, had been up and about the morning after the shipwreck. Determined to get out onto the rocks to see whether anything was salvageable, he was persuaded to wait until at least the next day. The tide would be at its lowest around noon, giving them a good couple of hours to forage.

Rose heard his heavy footfall coming up the stairs to check on his friend, and she felt a smile tug on her lips at his harried knock.

"Come in," she called quietly. The catch on the door lifted, and the captain poked his head around.

"Is he still lying abed?" he grumbled. "What that man will do to get out of hard work."

Rose chuckled; he said the same every day. "He has stirred but seems confused."

The captain bit down on a snort of laughter. "That's nothing to worry about, he's always confused. Spent too many hours in a stuffy office instead of out at sea. It addled his brain." Coming to sit at the opposite side of the bed. Running an experienced eye over his friend, Michael's brow creased. "He's not getting any better, is he?"

Rose shook her head. "Worse, if anything."

"I need to contact his family. They will not yet know of the wreck. Mr Drummond, his brother, must be informed, and if Nick is as sick as you say …" he did not finish his sentence. Life on the open ocean was unforgiving, all who sailed knew the perils associated therewith, in whatever nautical sphere you travelled. Even so, that Nick might die was difficult to accept.

Michael — as he asked everyone to refer to him, eschewing his formal title with these kind souls — had known Nick over a decade, and the two were firm friends.

He had watched Nick grow, maturing from a young lad, totally uninterested in the shipping industry to one wholly vested in its success.

He knew how many hours Nick had spent under the tutelage of Mr Holland, Trentams' Master Shipwright. Months and months, learning everything he could about the business. He was trained in navigation — both map and sky — how to steer a ship, how to trim a sail, how to climb the rigging, the importance of maintenance, and what to do in a wild storm.

Nick worked hard, did all that was asked, even going so far as to swab decks, sand and paint wood — chafed by the constant motion of rope and canvas — and repair sails. Most tasks he would never normally be required to undertake. He argued if he wasn't prepared even to attempt to understand what his crew was expected to do, how on earth could he command their respect; and respect him they did.

This was supposed to be a routine sea trial. They had taken every precaution, checked all available information on weather patterns, and this time of year, the unpredictable waters around the English coast were supposed to be relatively calm.

Two days ago, the storm hit.

It came out of nowhere. One minute it was blue sky, and bright sunshine. A stiff breeze granted, but that was nothing unusual. Within half an hour, the sky darkened until blacker than a moonless night, the storm bursting over them with terrifying ferocity. Richards, in all his years at sea, had never seen anything like it and had been moved to question whether the world was about to end, so apocalyptic did it seem.

Grateful none of the crew was killed and, acutely aware of the hazards faced by their rescuers, Richards was quick to thank everyone involved, and intended to inform Hugh Drummond of their efforts. From a long seafaring family,

Richards understood their response, had the tables been turned he would have done the same — that didn't make it any less heroic. Now it appeared as though Nick might succumb to his injuries and resulting fever.

Nick was about to follow his friend when the mast snapped in half — as though little more than a twig. He scrambled to get out of the way, only to have a massive chunk of wood slam into him, toppling him over the railing and into the turbulent waves.

Those in the lifeboat pulled him out quickly, but he sustained several piercing wounds from the splinters, not to mention being knocked unconscious and swallowing half the sea. It was another, very long, half hour before they got to shore, where willing hands carried him to the doctor's house, since when Nick remained in a stupor.

Michael studied his friend, taking in his shallow breathing, the dark circles under his eyes and the dryness of his skin — worried the doctor had missed something. Were there minuscule splinters of wood festering, or was this simply a fever brought on from being soaked over a lengthy period? He believed the latter less probable, the rest of the crew got equally as wet, yet none fell ill. He was about to comment on this when Rose spoke again.

"I think Papa is concerned there may be tiny shards of wood deep in one or more of his wounds. He was waiting until today to see whether there was any change for the better, and as there isn't, I think he will likely dig about some more. Might you stay? You could hold Mr Drummond, so he doesn't jerk, and cause more damage."

Michael nodded, "I am happy to, but first I need to send an urgent letter to London. How often does the mail coach come through?"

Rose grinned as she said, "Once a week, if we are lucky." Michael gaped at her. "'Tis the country. We are not so busy with letters as you city folk. Most hereabouts do not know how to write. What would be the point of a regular mail coach?" Michael began stammering about important missives, but she interrupted him, adding. "If you write your letter, Adrian Baxter, Walt the butcher's son, will go over yonder, probably to Whitby. He'll make sure your letter is on the next mail coach."

"Thank you, I shall do that right away. Please come and get me should your father need my assistance prior to my return." Michael was staying at the cottage of Sam Tucker, the baker, two doors down. Squeezing Nick's shoulder, he took his leave, and stumped down the stairs.

Rose chuckled to herself, for all these men were sailors, they hailed from a city used to more conveniences and luxuries than were available in the middle of nowhere, so far north. They were fortunate there was doctor.

Her father loved this idyllic little hamlet, living here since his arrival in the district not long before his marriage. His practice covered a large area, and it might have been easier had he settled in a more central spot, but he was adamant, making his rounds on Nellie, his beloved mare. It wasn't ideal, but he made it work. Something Nick would be grateful for, if he regained full consciousness.

Two hours later, Dr Joseph Archer was frowning over his patient. His thorough examination uncovered what he believed to be the source of the infection. An unmistakable odour, and signs of poison in at least two of the larger cuts, supported his theory. Nevertheless, to be absolutely certain, he would need to treat each cut, gash, and laceration with the same care, just in case. He could not risk ignoring the possibility any others of the man's wounds harboured a stray shard.

It would take no little time, and Joseph did not want to attempt it until the morrow. Starting early with long hours of daylight was better than beginning his task now, the afternoon already half over.

"Rose." The doctor stuck his head out of the bedchamber, calling to his daughter, who was cleaning bowls, cloths, and instruments, as well as sifting out those soiled bandages unable to be reused, and placing them in a heap to be burned.

"I'll be there in a minute, Papa." Her voice floated back up to him. He could hear familiar sounds of domesticity as Rose banged about in their modest kitchen. Unbidden, a wave of sadness washed over him, remembering Abigail, his wife, doing much the same.

It was four years since Abigail died, slipping quietly away, none of Joseph's prodigious knowledge or medicine able to save her. A bright and cheerful soul, her loss had left a gaping hole in the lives of her husband and daughter, and for a while it seemed they might never recover.

Time worked its magic, and slowly they began to adjust. The villagers rallied around to ensure their grief did not swamp them. Now just the two of them, Joseph relied on Rose more than he realised. In turn, she loved helping her father and they worked well together. A woman's presence often calming some of his more crotchety patients.

CHAPTER 2

*R*ose appeared bearing a tray on which stood two cups of hot tea, one each for her father and her, along with some of the sweet honey mixture for Nick, who hadn't woken despite the doctor's ministrations. As they sipped the strong brew, Joseph explained his plan, Rose nodding, adding a comment here and there. Halfway through their conversation, Michael returned, and Joseph updated him on what they intended to do.

"I have sent a letter to his family, telling them what happened, suggesting Hugh come with all haste," Michael said, glancing at his friend who was shifting restlessly. "Has he woken since this morning?"

Rose shook her head. "No, but mayhap if we sit and talk with him, tell him you and his crew are safe, that his family know what happened, it might help. Papa says even those deeply unconscious can register conversation."

He could hear voices, at least two, maybe three different voices. Their words were indistinguishable, blending together. He was thirsty, and his head was pounding. Waking up seemed too hard but he wanted to know what was going on, so forced his lids open.

"Water," he croaked through dry lips. A cool hand tilted his head, and a cup of sweet liquid, the taste of which he vaguely recalled, was held allowing him to sip its contents. He swallowed several mouthfuls, the effect of the drink almost instantaneous. Groggily he looked around to see Michael leaning against the window frame, as well as an older man, and a young woman — neither of whom he recognised. *That was odd, what were they all doing in his bedchamber?*

He began to ask, but the cool hand patted him on the arm, and a feminine voice told him not to try talking.

"Mr Drummond, please rest and, if you feel up to it, listen. You are in Runswick Bay. Your ship ran aground in the storm. Captain Richards has sent a letter to your family, and you feel ill because you have a serious infection."

Nick tried to focus, but everything was swimmy. He remembered the storm, but what about his men. He made to get up, muttering something completely unintelligible about the crew, and the rain, and rescue.

"Please lay back, sir. You are unwell, and must rest," the woman repeated her plea. He ignored her, pushing to lift himself, when a heavy hand pressed down on his shoulders.

"Nick," a deep voice rumbled. "Do as you're told for once. These people are trying to save your life and I would appreciate it if you would let them."

"Michael?" Needing to be sure he wasn't dreaming. If Michael was there it was all right, he was in charge.

"Yes, 'tis me. Now if you lie still, I will tell you what happened."

He fell back against the pillows, wincing at the pain in his head. He became aware Michael was now sitting beside him, but it hurt his eyes to keep them open. He smiled a little in acknowledgement and let his friend talk.

Michael calmly and quietly apprised Nick of everything from the moment the storm hit to five minutes ago. He explained how they got the men off in the little wooden boat, and that another vessel braved the sea to rescue them both, but he, Nick, was thwacked by a piece of mast just as he was about to shimmy down the rope.

Adding, it was now five days later, and this was the first time he had shown any signs of waking. He had a fever and the doctor needed to remove a few tiny splinters from at least two of his injuries.

Michael concluded his account, and it was clear Nick was fading again.

"I have written to Hugh, Nick, but I do not know how long it will take for the letter to get to London. Please don't go and die on us, at least until he gets here."

Nick's eyes flickered open and, ignoring the discomfort, held Michael's gaze. "I promise." The ghost of a grin accompanied his whispered reply, and Michael knew his friend would not give up without a fight.

"That's it, you will be fit as a fiddle in no time, at which point you can help to repair the ship."

"Sounds good," Nick croaked, his eyelids drooping once again.

Nick drifted back to sleep. Joseph checked his pulse, pleased to note it was not quite as erratic as it had been.

"We shall let him sleep, hopefully this is the turning point. Rose, please will you bring him some more soup shortly? At least he swallows that without realising," Joseph asked his daughter who nodded, affirming there was already some heating on the stove, in preparation for the evening meal.

"Would you like to join us, Captain Richards?" she smiled at the burly man who dwarfed her in the cramped bedchamber, the sloping eaves making him hunch. "There is plenty, and you will be here when Mr Drummond wakes again. He might feel up to another chat, and a familiar face makes such a difference."

The captain accepted graciously, saying he would be happy to sit with Nick if they had matters to which they should be attending. Appreciating the man's offer, Rose and Joseph hurried downstairs to complete the rest of the day's tasks awaiting them.

The evening passed uneventfully, Nick woke enough to swallow some soup, and have a brief conversation with Michael, but it wasn't long before he fell back to sleep. His rest was not too disturbed, and the doctor, checking his patient periodically, surmised Nick's temperature was lowering. This gave him cause to hope the fever was abating, but affirmed the operation scheduled for the morrow would go ahead.

"I cannot risk ignoring the possibility it is more than a simple chill brought on by the accident. Moreover, his wounds should be examined and redressed. I would rather be safe than sorry," he elaborated, when Michael asked whether it would be necessary.

Michael nodded his head, sagely. "You know best, Doc. What time will you begin? I can be here if you need a strong arm to keep him still."

"I was thinking nine. Earlier is better, for the day will be cooler."

Michael saw the sense in this and, as the evening was

drawing on, thanked Rose for a lovely meal, and them both for their generous hospitality, before taking his leave. His long stride bringing him to his lodgings in less than a minute.

∼

The next morning dawned bright and sunny. Joseph, up since first light, made sure his instruments were clean, and his cloths, ointments and bandages, laid out. In the small surgery at the back of the house, Rose scrubbed a wooden table within an inch of its life, covering it with several old, but clean sheets.

Although it would prove a challenge to bring Nick downstairs, Joseph preferred to operate in this room. The light was better, and it was too hard to operate on someone lying on a mattress, unless there was no alternative. He hoped two or three of the villagers would assist him in this endeavour.

On the dot of nine, Michael knocked on the front door. Rose showed him through to the back room, whereupon Joseph explained his predicament. In quick understanding, Michael made haste along the street, and collected the rest of his crew. Used to lugging heavy items around the awkward interiors of ships, willing hands lifted Nick, who had yet to wake, down the narrow stairs, and through to the clinic.

At the same time as they laid their employer carefully on the table, Nick opened his eyes. Scanning the men around him, he offered a rare smile.

"Now I know how sack of coal feels. Hard to believe you lot are capable of such fine seamanship," he rasped. "Might I ask why you dragged me from that comfortable bed to drop me on a cold, hard table?"

"We need to check your wounds for splinters, sir." It was that feminine voice again and, turning his head, Nick saw a young woman. Odd, he was sure she had been a dream. She smiled at him, and despite feeling utterly wretched, he was aware of a lift in his spirits. She was still speaking, and he tried to concentrate. "Your men carried you down here because 'tis easier and safer to operate in the clinic than in your bed chamber. Do not worry, soon you will be back upstairs where 'tis warm."

Concerned Nick did not recall their conversation of the previous afternoon. Rose glanced at her father who shook his head. She patted his hand, covering him with another sheet. Joseph shooed out all but Michael, affirming he would let them know as soon as it was over.

"This is going to hurt isn't it?" he queried, into thin air. *Where did she go? Was she a dream after all?* Her face reappeared, hovering over his. She squeezed his hand.

"I'm afraid it will, but Papa will be quick, and Captain Richards is here.

"To hold me down no doubt," Nick groused.

"Well, no use you squirming, while the doc here wields his scalpel." Michael's rumbled response confirmed Nick's suspicions.

Joseph re-entered the clinic, washing his hands in a bowl of clean water. "I think we'll begin," offering Nick a sip of laudanum, which he swallowed, gratefully.

Nick gritted his teeth in anticipation. Even half-conscious he knew how excruciating this would be. A cool hand grasped his, and that gentle voice spoke again.

"Look at me, Mr Drummond, sir."

Nick shifted ever-so slightly, and his gaze locked with hers. He felt the doctor unwrap the bandage around his head and, determined not to make a sound, concentrated on her features.

Her eyes were the most incredible blue, and to distract himself from the unpleasant sensations the doctor was causing, he tried to think of what they reminded him. Corn-flowers maybe, no, more like bluebells — the faint purple hint in their depths, reminiscent of his sister's favourite flower. Her lightly tanned skin made them even more startling.

Nick could see his reflection as she stared back at him and was shocked at his unkempt appearance.

"I beg your pardon," he murmured, "had I known I would be in the presence of a lady, I would have shaved," he hissed a breath, his words slurring. A combination of the opiate taking effect, and a dowel probing one of the lacerations on his skull.

"I do believe I will let it pass, just this once."

He heard the amusement in her voice, and quiet though her reply, it demanded his attention. He swung his eyes back to her face, ignoring the disorientation the movement elicited, and resumed his scrutiny. Her nose was neat and straight, with a smattering of freckles flowing out over high cheekbones.

Following the curve of her face around her jaw line to her chin, his eyes drifted to her lips. Not too thin, not too full, and currently she was chewing the bottom one. An abstracted gesture, but one, which prompted him to wonder how it would feel to rub his thumb over the bitten flesh.

He blinked in an attempt to banish the image, but it floated, tantalisingly, at the edge of his mind. Forcing his gaze away, his eyes tracked upwards to her hair. Silvery blonde, with an occasional darker streak, it was plaited and twisted up into a tidy chignon, one or two strands already escaping to frame her self-possessed face.

He did not know how tall she was, only having seen her sitting beside him, but she seemed diminutive. Her delicate features, slender hands, and light touch giving her a fairy-like quality.

"I am losing my mind," he groused inwardly, or so he thought.

"What do you mean, losing?" A muffled bark of laughter from where Michael was sitting by his head, large hands gripping his shoulders, while the doctor continued his investigation.

"Damn, did I say that out loud?"

"No matter, 'tis the laudanum speaking. Close your eyes and sleep. When you wake all will be done." The fairy wiped a cool cloth over his hot face and down his neck.

"I fear if I close my eyes I will not wake again." The words out before he could stop them. *Well don't you just sound like a grown man in charge of a ship?* Cursing silently.

"Trust my father, Mr Drummond. He is a skilled surgeon. He trained at St Bart's in London and saved many men during the war."

St Bart's, he knew that name. Jessica, his sister, worked there before her recent marriage. Two names swam into his fuddled mind.

"I know Dr Napier and Dr Elliott," he grunted, becoming aware of a sickly sound and the impression his brains were being sucked out. "Urrgghhh ..." Before he could ask, agony lanced through his skull and darkness staked its claim.

"Daniel and Theo, eh? What a small world. Who would have guessed? Several years behind me but good men. Came across 'em on the Peninsula." Joseph Archer mused absently — seemingly oblivious to Nick's theatrics — dropping a second splinter into the bowl by his elbow before rinsing the tiny metal pincers in another on the bench top alongside him.

Holding a candle close to Nick's head, he peered intently for several minutes tilting it this way and that, shedding as much light on the injuries as he was able. "All clear there, now this last one on his chest." He stood, pushing back the chair, and rolling his shoulders to stretch out tired muscles.

Folding back the sheet, and removing the nightshirt, Joseph peeled away the wrappings around Nick's upper body.

CHAPTER 3

*D*espite knowing it was not appropriate, Rose found her eyes straying to the expanse of skin, again and again, while her father operated.

She was supposed to be cleaning way the bloodied cloths and bandages, but she could not help herself. Nick's upper torso was broad and muscular, but lean, not an ounce of excess fat; his skin deeply tanned, presumably from being at sea.

Whilst monitoring his progress, Rose had spent hours studying his face and his hands. She reckoned Nick had artist's hands. Large, but not spades like those of a farmer, his fingers long and slender.

This however — this honed physique was something else entirely, reminding Rose of the marble statuary depicted in one of her father's old books on Ancient Greece. The regular rise and fall of his chest as he breathed was hypnotic, and she itched to place her hand over his heart, to feel its rhythm.

"Rose," her father's voice snapped her attention back and, acting on instinct rather than instruction — which she missed — handed him the ointment he used to keep infection at bay. With his index finger, Joseph pushed a large dollop into the laceration, coating it thoroughly before covering it with a swatch of clean cloth, and bandaging it securely in place.

Straightening up, the doctor spoke. "I hope I removed everything. I cannot find any more, and continuing to poke around might risk further damage, especially in those head wounds. Now 'tis up to Mr Drummond. He seems healthy enough generally, I think he should pull through."

"You mean there remains some question, even after all this?" Michael demanded, standing, to pace to floor.

"There is always a chance infection lurks in his blood, too entrenched for him to throw it off. Mr Drummond's skin is cool to the touch, today. His pulse is regular, and his breathing no longer laboured, all good signs. All we can do is keep the injuries clean, make sure he drinks plenty of water, and if Rose here can persuade him to swallow some food, your friend has every chance."

Michael nodded slowly, the doctor's words made sense, but the slightest prospect Nick might die, tore at him. He prayed Hugh would not tarry in his travels, once he received his letter, but, notwithstanding any holdups, it would be days before he could get here. Running a hand through his neatly tied-back hair, Michael muttered something about updating the rest of the crew and stomped out.

"Papa. Tell me the truth. Are you preparing the captain for the worst, or do you believe Mr Drummond will survive?"

Joseph barely glanced at his daughter, then seeing her expression, turned to face her properly. Resting his hands on her shoulders, he looked her in the eye. "I believe he will survive, pet. Now get along, and make your old Papa a cup of tea, would you? That was hard work."

Rose smiled and hugged him before hurrying through into the main house to make hot drinks.

Meditatively, Joseph watched her go. He had noticed a change in Rose's behaviour while caring for this man from London. He did not think she even realised it herself, but not only was he was her father; he was also trained to detect subtle alterations in people's demeanour indicating ill health.

He was aware Nick affected her but guessed she didn't know why. He hoped she wasn't going to do anything as juvenile as to develop a *tendre* for Mr Drummond. Soon the man would leave. Runswick Bay and all therein, naught but a hazy memory.

Sighing, and knowing there was little he could do about it and having no intention of interfering … yet … he turned his attention back to his patient.

The hammering in his skull was tortuous. He wished he was at Whiteoaks. Billie always had the perfect remedy for every ailment, and this headache was the one to end all headaches. *Why the devil was it so painful?*

Nick shuffled, trying to settle his head more comfortably on the pillow. That brought a fresh wave of splintering agony and he could not prevent a groan slipping over his dry lips.

"Lie still, here sip this, it will ease the pain."

That voice, it was the fairy again. He didn't think he was dead. Surely, being dead wouldn't hurt so much? Why was the fairy here? Was he hallucinating? Laudanum, yes, someone gave him laudanum… ahhh… that explained it. He was definitely hallucinating. He didn't think there were such things as fairies.

He heard a stifled giggle. He made a concerted effort not

to frown, vaguely aware this would exacerbate his headache, but to open his eyes was beyond him.

"Why would you think I am a fairy?" a lilting voice asked.

"You are not?" *Was he really having this conversation?*

"Silly, of course not, 'tis me, Rose."

"Rose? I don't know any... wait." *Was there a Rose at Whiteoaks? That must be it.* "Am I at Whiteoaks? How did I get here? No matter, Rose, please ask Billie for one of her brews."

Another giggle.

"Mr Drummond, sir, do sip this. I promise you will feel better." He felt the rim of a cup rest against his lips, and a cool liquid slid over his tongue to moisten his parched throat. It tasted peculiar, but not offensive. "You are in Runswick Bay, do you not recall?" The voice sounded perplexed, concerned even.

Images reared up in his mind. A schooner, a storm, and his men trying to keep the ship from being smashed on the rocks.

"My ship..." he husked.

"Is aground. Captain Richards says it can be salvaged, so do not fret about it. The crew have done what they can to ensure the damage is limited, but there's a hole in the port side that will require some patching." Her voice was practical, no emotion about the loss of a vessel. Well it wasn't her ship was it? He groaned. How would he explain this to Hugh? He tried to get up.

"Mr Drummond. Stay put, 'tis only hours since your operation you—"

"Where's Giles? I need to get to London. Hugh must be informed," he interrupted.

"Who is this Giles?"

"My brother's brother-in-law. He's an earl," as though that made all the difference.

"Well he's not here, so he cannot help. Please..." when

Nick made another attempt to get up, "…lay down… your head."

Nick dropped back on the downy pillow, wincing because it sparked a fresh onslaught of those damned hammers. He endeavoured to open his eyes and looked up into a worried face.

A cool cloth was applied to his brow, while gentle fingers tucked the sheet back around him. Heavy footsteps approached, and a burly man filled the doorway.

"You're awake, finally. You really need to stop lolling about, Nick, leaving all the hard work to the lads." Michael grinned as he stepped over the threshold. Nick tried to return it but couldn't quite manage.

"He keeps trying to get up," the fairy — *what was her name? Rose?* — informed his visitor.

"Bloody telltale," he griped. Nick's tones were harsher than he intended, frustrated by the weakness pervading his body, and he sensed rather than saw her reaction.

Stiffening, *she did not need to sit here and be insulted*, Rose stood to leave.

For reasons he could not fathom, Nick did not want her to. Regardless of her insufferable insistence he stay abed, her presence soothed him. Her gentle voice dulled the agony in his head and chest. He reached for her hand, which was just above the covers. "Please don't go."

Startled, Rose met his eyes. He blinked once and his lips curved in the barest hint of a smile.

She squeezed his hand and resumed her seat. "Only if you do as I ask. My father's instructions are not for my benefit. I care little whether you live or die, but the captain here seems to think you are a worthy friend. One whom he would like to have around a while longer, if only so he can bait you. I think 'tis only fair you let him." The warmth in her lilting voice, belied her apparent indifference.

Nick smiled again, but the hammering was increasing, and the room was slewing at a most precarious angle.

"Rose…" it hurt even to speak. *Hell, and damnation.* "Pain…" he bit out.

Gently, Rose slipped her arm under his neck, and steadied his head, allowing him to sip the strange tasting liquid. He swallowed the contents of the cup, and before he could think of anything else to say fell back into oblivion.

Michael watched; his brow creased. "Is this normal?"

"Yes, I think so. I will not leave him unless you or Papa are here. It is because of the operation this morning. Papa had to delve deeply into the wounds to extract the splinters. That, on top of the fever still lurking has knocked him insensible. I reckon after a night of undisturbed sleep he will feel much better, although, I suspect his head will hurt like the devil for several days."

Michael chuckled at Rose's turn of phrase. No city refinement here, among the farmers and fishermen. Yet for all that, Rose was polite and poised. She dressed neatly, and her accent was not quite as broad as some in the village. He mused over how this could be. He knew the family had lived here for years, since before Rose was born. Shaking his head, it was no business of his anyway.

"Take a break, Miss Archer. I will sit with Nick for a while. You must be exhausted."

Rose only left Nick's side if she absolutely had to, sleeping on the floor, in case he woke in the night and was either in pain or disoriented. She argued her father needed proper rest. He was the one with patients across the district, not her. She was young and healthy; she could sleep when everything went back to normal.

"Thank you, Captain. I shall return shortly."

"Get some rest. I am quite capable of looking after this recalcitrant for a couple of hours. Go." He shooed her out as though she was a child. Smiling gratefully, she tiptoed down the stairs to her bedchamber. Truth be told she was so tired, she could barely stand. Without bothering to undress, lay on her bed fully clothed, falling straight to sleep.

∾

Nick gave everyone a few more sleepless nights before he turned the corner. His fever continued to spike, causing grave concern, and Joseph was beginning to despair his patient would recover.

In the early hours of the fourth morning after the operation, to the relief of all, it broke, and Nick's naturally healthy constitution took over. Weak for several days, he struggled to get out of bed and could not negotiate the stairs at all without the assistance of Michael or Joseph, but gradually his strength returned.

Within the week, he was able to get as far as the wooden bench at the front door. Here he could watch the world go by, such as it was in a small village, enjoy the sun on his face, and the smell of the sea air drifting by, much more refreshing than London's docklands.

His crew, well Michael's crew, paused to chat as they went to and from the shore, where they continued to monitor the ship. The breach in the port side was now repaired, and they hoped to float the vessel on the next high tide, in order to patch the smaller holes, as well as inspect the underside of the hull for any further damage.

In her spare time, between helping her father and doing her domestic chores, Rose sat with Nick, ostensibly to prevent him from rushing at life while he recuperated. In reality, she wanted to get to know him. Without appearing to, she encouraged him to talk about life in London, his family, his work at Trentams, and why he chose to oversee the sea trials of *The Diligence*.

Nick, who was for the most part a taciturn young man, found himself opening up to this diminutive young woman, her sparkling blue eyes inviting all manner of confidences. He asked questions in return, listening to her chattering away guilelessly about her life here in Yorkshire, her father's job, and what his crew were up to.

Her voice soothed him, for he suffered an outsize in headaches, and when they struck, he struggled to focus on anything for more than a few minutes. Rose's gentle tones washed over him like a lullaby, and he frequently dropped off to sleep while she was in mid-sentence.

Rose wasn't offended in the slightest. It was what he needed, and in truth, her gossip was probably boring enough to send anyone to sleep. Since the greatest excitement in Runswick Bay for the last five years was the wreck of his ship, her tales tended to revolve around minor misadventures involving the locals.

Little did she realise, Nick was fascinated. The livelihood of these people was far removed from his own. Slower maybe, quieter definitely, but no less interesting. It could be a harsh environment, because although the summers were milder than further south, the winters were often severe, and trying to make ends meet was a constant battle against the elements and the isolation.

CHAPTER 4

*W*hile he convalesced, Nick began to explore a little further afield, accompanied by either Rose or Michael. The day he managed to walk up the steep track to the top of the bank above the village, was the day he fell in love with Yorkshire. It was clear and sunny, and the view in every direction, spectacular.

Spread out in front of him, as far as the eye could see, a vast swathe of moorland, broken here and there by cottages and farms. Below, the red rooftops of the village, its inhabitants bustling specks going about their daily business. Behind, the bay and the glistening sea — calm today, its glassy surface only marred by a few ripples as the tide changed.

Seagulls wheeled above him, their sharp cry cleaving the peace. The air was fresh, with a hint of saltiness. Nick breathed in deeply. His chest heaved from the exertion, and his legs were trembling, but he was endlessly glad he survived to see this, and oddly grateful his ship had wrecked — he would not think to visit such a place voluntarily.

Rose sank down onto the ground to pluck daisies,

threading them together to make a chain. Nick watched her. She wasn't wearing a hat, in fact except for an odd occasion, he could not remember Rose ever wearing one, despite the number of times they sat in the sunshine.

Convention, it seemed, was not quite as strict so far from London. Her silvery hair shone in the sunlight, a few strands unravelling from the neat plait. Carefully twisting the fragile stems, Rose bent her head, concentrating on her task, and Nick was beset by an almost overwhelming desire to stroke his fingers along the smooth, slender curve of her exposed neck.

Startled at an emotion he did not recognise, Nick forced his gaze out to sea, then down, to admire *The Diligence*. No longer wedged against the rocks, the schooner stood proud and tall in the middle of the bay. Michael informed him it should be seaworthy within the week, and he hoped to join his crew for the trip back. That would likely depend on Hugh, if he ever arrived.

His eyes drifted back to Rose who, sensing his scrutiny, lifted her head, and beamed at him. Her bright smile tugged a responding grin from his lips, and throwing caution to the winds, he dropped down beside her.

"How long is it since Michael sent for Hugh?" His mundane query an attempt to keep his mind distracted from what his body wanted to do.

Rose contemplated that for a moment, working out how long it had been since the missive was dispatched. "The day before your operation… hmmm… ten days past."

"When do you think they might arrive?"

"If Adrian caught the mail coach, and it wasn't delayed, and your brother set off as soon as he could make the arrangements, and *he* had no delays, I expect they might be here in a day or two. If any of those things didn't happen in a timely manner, it could be a week or more."

Rose shrugged; time and distance meant little to her. She got up with the dawn, went to bed at nightfall and worked hard during the hours of daylight. This was the first time in her recall anyone from further afield than Redcar or Whitby, had visited her village.

"Are you in a hurry to leave, to go home?" she ventured, a curious melancholy sweeping through her at the notion she would never see him again. Determined not to dwell on what she could not alter, she continued. "Sorry, of course you are, you must miss your home, and your family. That was a silly question." Focusing on the daisies, cursing the flush blooming over her cheeks.

"I believe I will miss y... this place," he caught himself before saying something he could not retract. "I had no idea such beauty existed so far north." An unusual tone in Nick's voice prompted Rose to glance up. Their eyes collided, and a peculiar frisson trickled along her spine. All around them quieted.

Unable to stop himself, Nick angled his body forward, rested a light finger under Rose's chin and brushed his lips to hers.

Eyes fluttering closed, Rose heard her breathing stutter, but she had no intention of pulling away. This might be her one and only chance to kiss him, and she was desperate to know how it would feel. Oh, and it was sublime. His lips, cool and firm, moved leisurely over hers, the stubble shadowing his jawline scratching her soft skin.

His other hand curved around her nape, fingers entwining into her hair, at the same time as Rose, to prevent herself leaning too close, and landing in an ungainly heap against Nick's chest, placed her hand just above his knee, his muscles flexing under her touch.

Nick's head was screaming at him to stop. This was Rose, his doctor's daughter, and he had no mind to place her in an uncompromising position, but it was as though she had him be-spelled. From the moment he heard her voice, gentle tones penetrating his pain, entreating him to rest, she entranced him.

She was dainty, delicate of feature, reminiscent of the *contes de fées* — fairy tales — his sister Jessica read over and over again when a child, yet he had watched while she worked, her strength and endurance undeniable. She was irrepressible, intelligent, funny and, from the brief time they had spent together, he surmised her to be unfailingly loyal. *She would make a good wife.*

Nick jerked backwards. *A wife? He wasn't looking for a wife, he was a sailor. The last thing he needed was a wife.* Life on the high seas was hazardous, this past month attesting just how hazardous. Even if he bore an affection for Ro... a woman, he had no intention of marrying. It was hard enough saying goodbye to his family when he set off on these sea trials.

To leave someone you loved for weeks, possibly months on end with no certainty of return was unconscionable. *Wait... loved? Don't be asinine, Nick,* he admonished himself. *You have known her scant days, you cannot be in love with her. 'Tis merely gratitude for her care while you recovered.*

Rose was staring at him in bewilderment. One minute he was kissing her in quite the most delectable fashion, the next, glowering as though she had given him the plague. An ache, somewhere in the region of her heart, stirred and she turned away, determined he would not see.

"I think 'tis time we walked back. We don't want you to become tired," she said over-brightly, standing up, the daisy chain falling onto the grass, as she brushed dust off her skirts.

"Rose, please, I apologise for kissing you. It was unthinkably rude. Forgive me. I had no mind to frighten you."

'Tsk, you didn't, Mr Drummond. I am not easily frightened. It was a nice kiss, but I expect you are still suffering from the effects of laudanum, and forgot it was just me and not one of your London ladies." High colour washing her cheeks, Rose stood rigidly, waiting for him to fall into step beside her.

Keenly aware she had reverted to his formal address, rather than his name, which he had invited her to use days previously, Nick allowed the matter rest for now.

For a man usually insensitive to a woman's emotions, he experienced an inexplicable sadness at her cold shoulder, and wondered how to regain their lighthearted cordiality.

He spied the daisies, a crumpled heap and without thinking, scooped them up, tucking them into his pocket.

They descended the steep path in uncomfortable silence. Upon reaching the edge of the village, Rose halted and rested one hand on his arm.

"Mr Drummond, 'tis me who should apologise. I behaved like a spoilt child on yon moor. It was just so lovely to be kissed. I've never been kissed…" artlessly, "…and I want it to be a fond memory, not one of disquiet." She held his gaze when she spoke.

The innocence of her words caused Nick to bite his lip in chagrin. He should be honest with her. He *had* initiated the kiss. "It was not disquiet prompted me to break the kiss, Rose. I wanted to kiss you for days."

She glanced up at him, eyes wide with surprise. "Me? What on earth for?" The question tripping off her tongue. "No, don't say any more, I might not like the answer."

"Rose, my life is far removed from yours. Here 'tis uncomplicated, the days slide by under a familiar rhythm. My life has no rhythm. One day I may be working in the shipyard, the next running sea trials through treacherous waters. Nothing is the same from one day to the next and, while I cannot deny it sounds exciting, 'tis also dangerous. I decided long ago, I would never subject someone I cared about to that worry."

All Rose heard was 'cared about.'

"You care about me?"

It was barely a murmur, but Nick's sharp ears caught it.

"Of course, I care about you. I don't kiss every woman I meet."

"I thought mayhap it was a city habit." She grinned suddenly, a wicked twinkle in her eyes.

Nick sucked in a breath. It was all he could do not to drag her back against him. *Control your urges man* he chided himself, *you will be leaving soon.* Instead he chuckled. "Not everything in London is decadent. 'Tis unfortunate you live so far away. I think you might enjoy a sojourn there."

As this was impossible, he felt safe suggesting it, yet at the same time a strange bleakness circled the edge of his mind knowing soon he would leave, never to see her again. *Dammit, this would **not** do.* He contrived to shove all nonsensical, feminine sentimentality out of his head, and instilled a practical note into his voice.

"We should not tarry, doubtless your father is waiting to prod and poke at me again. I will be glad when I no long require these bandages, or his daily examinations." Thinking to divert Rose's attention. It worked.

"Oh, sir, are you in discomfort? We should not have attempted such a long walk today. I knew it was too far."

Before they set out, she had tried to dissuade him from going all the way to the top of the cliff, fearing he was exceeding the limits of his current capabilities. Typically, Nick wanted to go that little bit further, push that little bit harder.

Perhaps it was his competitive nature, or maybe it was because it took him longer than the majority of his contemporaries to decide upon a career.

Until recently, Nick had shown no interest in the family business, but during the previous year when circumstances required he shoulder some responsibility, he had developed an unexpected passion for all things shipping, and as with everything he attempted, threw himself into it, with vigour.

"Do not fret Rose, I am fine. Simply wearied of restrictions. I hope it will not be too many more days before I am allowed to inspect my ship."

Thus far, Michael had refused to let Nick anywhere near *The Diligence*, knowing once aboard he would scour the vessel from top to bottom. Although the exterior was thoroughly patched, the interior had yet to be repaired, and Michael had no mind to put his friend at further risk of injury.

Rose chuckled. "Captain Richards is eminently sensible, Mr Drummond. I am sure he will row you out to *The Diligence* with enthusiasm once Papa gives you a clean bill of health." They were almost at Thistle Cottage, abode of the Archers. On their approach the door was flung wide, and Joseph peered out.

"About time you two. Mr Drummond, if you please?"

Nick turned, dropping a slow wink, Rose burst out laughing, and ignoring her father's quizzical brow, went through the adjacent door into the main house to prepare dinner.

CHAPTER 5

The evening passed cheerfully, and when her father, Nick, and Michael — who, as had become his habit, joined them — became engrossed in a discussion about politics, Rose excused herself. The kitchen set to rights, she removed her pinafore and, collecting a raggedy old wrap, sauntered down to the water's edge.

Brightly painted fishing boats bobbed on their anchors as the waves lapped the shore, shadows lengthened, the sun dipping to the horizon over the moor behind her. Sounds of laughter and chatter floated on the still air.

All was tranquil.

Rose pondered her life. She loved it here but since the precipitous arrival of the men from *The Diligence* and hearing their stories of what was beyond her doorstep, she had developed a hankering to see a wider world. *What would London be like?* To see the hustle and bustle of a big city must be wondrous. She had been to Whitby, but that was as far as she remembered travelling, remaining sheltered here in this quiet backwater.

She heard footsteps. Wishing it was Nick, she turned, a

ready smile on her face, to see Adrian strolling towards her. By sheer force of will she held the smile as he came to sit next to her on the sea wall.

"Good evening, Rose. I haven't seen you for several days." His tone… reproachful.

"I have been helping Papa with Mr Drummond, and the other sailors, Adrian. It isn't easy for him on his own, with all the extra work."

Her reply, sharper than she intended, but of late Adrian had begun to treat her possessively, as though he had some kind of say over her future and it was irksome. When they were children, she didn't mind being bossed about, but she was twenty years old. She could think for herself, and had *no* desire to be ruled, or managed.

"Well, they'll be gone soon and can't come quick enough for me. Good riddance, I say."

"What do you mean?" Rose was confused by his belligerent tone. Normally, Adrian was a placid soul, not much seemed to rattle him.

"All their city ways, complaining about the lack of luxuries. 'Ain't no place for that kind here. As for that Drummond, posh accent and foppish attitude."

Rose frowned. "Don't be so narrow minded, Adrian. The poor crew were nearly drowned and all you can say is good riddance. I have not heard a single complaint, and as far as I can tell, they have enjoyed their stay. Moreover, how you can consider Mr Drummond to be foppish is beyond me." The man in question being broader and taller than Adrian and, decidedly *not* foppish.

"You like this man? Rose you are *my* girl. I forbid you to see him again."

"*Your* girl, since when? Wait… you forbid me? **You forbid me!**" Rose was in a fine temper. If it wasn't men kissing her and then saying it could never be more, it was childhood friends declaring they owned her. "Adrian Baxter if you *ever* say that again, I'll... I'll..."

"What will you do Rose," he stood, towering over her, his attitude intimidating.

She bounced off the wall to glare up at him, hands on hips. "I'll box your ears, if I have to stand on a table to do so. How *dare* you? I am no one's 'girl.' If, and that is an *enormous* if, I am beset with the, arguably lamentable craving to bind myself to a man, we shall be equals. I will *not* be dictated to and I am not, nor will I ever be anyone's possession! Good*night* to you." Tossing her head, Rose stormed along the path to her home.

She entered the parlour where the three men were chatting over pungent cigars — retrieved from the ship's hold, and amazingly still dry. Joseph, glanced up, and casually asked her to make them a hot drink.

"I *beg* your pardon?" Her voice was dangerously calm.

Joseph repeated his request.

"Is it not enough I cook, and clean, and assist you in the surgery with your patients? Has it *ever* occurred to you, I might be tired, and would appreciate someone taking the time to offer me a drink?" Her tones becoming shriller with every word.

The three men gaped at her; mouths open in astonishment. Who was this virago and where was kind, mild, little Rose?

"No, I don't suppose it has. Make your own bloody drinks. I'm going to bed." And with that she marched through the room, banging the door on her way out, thudded up the stairs, and slammed her bedroom door behind her for good measure.

Shocked silence reigned in the parlour.

"I do apologise for my daughter's behaviour, gentlemen.

'Tis unlike her, I hope she's not sickening for something." Rubbing his chin, Joseph ruminated on the notion.

Nick pursed his lips. Rose seemed happy enough before she disappeared half an hour ago. Something or someone must have goaded her — her father's request, the final straw. The image of her as she railed at them, flickered into his mind.

She looked magnificent in full flood and, her slight stature aside, in her ire, Rose dominated the room. Her hair crackled around her head, her eyes flashed blue fire, and there was nothing remotely fairy-like about her while she vented her spleen. He could not prevent a smile from curving his lips.

Michael, seeing it, groaned inwardly. This was a complication he did not need. The ship was close to being sail worthy, and if young Nick went and fell for the chit, it could only lead to heartbreak, probably for Rose more than Nick. He didn't want to leave the village on a sour note. He made up his mind to have a quiet word the next day. First things first, however.

"Perhaps she feels taken for granted," he interposed gently. "She's barely slept the last week or so, what with looking after Nick..."

Nick, who had no awareness of the hours Rose spent tending to him, swivelled in his chair, to stare at Michael in surprise. The latter nodded at his friend's unspoken question.

"... and keeping house here, not to mention all the other chores she does. She never complains, but I imagine she is weary. Mayhap we should make her the hot drink she desires, and you could take it up for her, sir."

"Eh... what... capital idea man, hot drink... yes that will help." Joseph agreed, making no move to the kitchen, bewildered by his daughter's outburst.

Michael heaved his bulk out of the chair and, following his own suggestion, set about heating a pan of milk, while readying four cups. In a tin at one side of the stove he found some chocolate, already grated, adding it to the milk when it came to the boil. A sprinkle of sugar to sweeten, and the drinks were ready. Placing all four drinks on a tray, he carried them through to the parlour.

"Dr Archer, might you take Rose's hot chocolate?"

Joseph stood, shaking his head. "Thank you Captain much obliged to you, sir." He took two cups and climbed the stairs. Knocking softly on Rose's door, he entered at her quiet invitation.

"How about a nice cup of hot chocolate, my dear?" he said, lowering himself gingerly onto the rickety chair next to his daughter's bed.

"Thank you, Papa," she muttered, not all that graciously. She was sitting on her bed, fully clothed, legs out in front of her, absently lacing two ribbons together, then doing it all over again.

"Want to talk about it?" Her father coaxed.

"Not really." She huffed a sigh. "I'm sorry, Papa. I'm just a little weary. I hoped a walk might help, but Adrian came to join me. First, he complained about the continued presence of the sailors, and then became possessive. I did not take kindly to either sentiment. I refuse to be owned. I will only marry a man who will love me for me, not as a chattel or someone to tame.

"You and Mama had a loving relationship, you shared things. I want that, not to spend my days being ordered about by some oaf who cannot lift a finger to help me. I know it is contentious, but I will not be swayed." A red stain flared up her cheeks, but she was resolute.

Joseph patted her hand. "I want that too, pet, and I apologise for being thoughtless. Shall we start afresh on the morrow?"

"I'd like that, and thank you for the chocolate, 'tis delicious." Sipping the steaming beverage.

"The captain made it." Joseph's astonishment at Michael's expertise in this matter, clear in his tone, making Rose giggle. "I'll leave you to your rest, Rose. I hope you have a proper sleep tonight. And thank you for all your hard work around here. I do appreciate you, you know."

Rose caught her father's hand. "I know, Papa." She squeezed his fingers. Bending to kiss her cheek, the doctor left, slowly descending the stairs to join the two men in the parlour.

At their raised eyebrows, he confirmed she appreciated the gesture. "She admits to feeling tired, not helped by young Baxter assuming he had the right to dictate her life," he elaborated.

Both men nodded sagely, but didn't comment, other than to say it was probably time for bed. Michael strolled off to Sam's where no doubt a tasty baked delight and a nightcap awaited, while Nick went quietly to his room at the top of the house.

It wasn't long before the last carousers from the tavern rolled home, and the village slept.

To Rose's relief, no one referred to her tantrum, Michael and Nick behaving as though it never happened. When she bumped into Adrian, as she stepped out of the grocer's, he apologised for being crass. Rose accepted graciously but didn't waste any time with idle chitchat.

His behaviour rankled, and she did not want to give him any reason to assume she was more than a friend. It floored her that he considered her to be 'his girl' — she had not given him any reason to think such a thing. Yes, they had known each other for many years, but all she felt for him was mild affection. To assume it was anything more was preposterous.

Michael tactfully cautioned Nick not to toy with Rose's heart, reminding him, once they left Runswick Bay, it was unlikely they would ever return. Nick agreed, but Michael surmised his friend's affection for the doctor's daughter went deeper than even Nick himself realised.

Praying it was a fleeting *tendre*, Michael put it out of his mind, and turned his concentration to organising the last of the ship's running repairs.

On a cool and blustery afternoon, as the week drew to a close, there was a flurry of activity, and a coach rattled down the steep track into the village. Anyone addled enough to risk such an endeavour attracted people into the street, where they watched four huge black stallions — manes and tails rippling in the breeze — clip clop majestically between the houses, guided by an immaculately liveried coachman.

The entourage reached the slipway and halted. Jumping down, the coachman dropped the step and opened the door. An extremely tall man with dark blonde hair stepped out and turned to offer his hand to the second occupant.

A lady, and clearly, she was a lady — for all her exquisite travelling attire appeared plain, it probably cost more than the monthly income of all the villagers put together — placed one leather clad foot on the step and stopped. Stretching her arms above her head, she gazed around, breathing in the salty air.

"Oh Hugh, this is perfection," she was heard to cry, smiling at the man holding out his hand to assist her down.

His responding grin lit up a face that seemed familiar. "I agree. If Nick could plan the most idyllic place to wreck one of my schooners, this would be it."

They both stood, and soaked in the view, eyes drawn to the vessel rocking at anchor in the bay. A voice hailed them from the street opposite the track by which the coach had entered the village.

"Lady Helena, Mr Drummond, I am mighty pleased to see you." Pumping the hand of the gentleman, up and down, rigorously.

"Michael, my good man. 'Tis glad we are to see you too. Your letter was cause for great shock, and we made haste with our journey. Unfortunately, the weather was inclement on much of the route, hence our tardiness…" the man referred to as Mr Drummond — Hugh — paused, his throat working, unwilling to voice his question. Michael's letter had indicated Nick, his brother, might not survive his injuries, and Hugh found himself at a loss.

"Captain. How is Nick?" Lady Helena interjected, modulated tones masking her fear.

"He is well, and currently over on yon ship, checking my repairs." Michael chuckled in amused resignation. "Anyone would think I was a mere cabin boy not a sea captain with more than two score years' experience."

Reassured, the two visitors relaxed, visibly, and Helena hugged the captain.

"Thank you for taking care of him, Michael. His mother wanted to come with us, in case…" Helena didn't complete that thought, "…but she has been unwell of late and 'tis a long journey."

While they were chatting, several of the villagers, and a couple of the crew approached. Michael made introductions where appropriate, after which followed many handshakes and curtsies. Most had never met an actual lady, and Helena, radiantly beautiful, was a most refined example of feminine nobility.

She was not one for standing on ceremony and greeted everyone in a warm and friendly manner. Years of putting people at their ease came to the fore, as she asked each person about their lives, their families, between singing praises of the moor, and the sea and how glorious this place was, immediately endearing herself to all and sundry.

CHAPTER 6

The news about the new arrivals spread, and the crowd grew. More and more people spilled out of their homes or joined the throng as they returned from wherever they had been working, all eager to see who the visitors were.

First a shipwreck, now nobility — for a sleepy village this was cause for great excitement, and the noise could be heard right around the bay. So preoccupied were they, no one noticed the rowing boat approaching the shore, its four passengers confused at the milling mass of people.

Teddy Lamb, crew member of *The Diligence*, jumped out as they rowed into the breakers. The sound of the boat grating over the shingle caught Hugh's attention. Politely excusing himself he strode down to the shore, and all but yanked Nick out of the skiff.

"God, Nick. When we got Michael's letter…" Hugh pulled his brother into a bear hug. Overt demonstrations of affection were unusual in the Drummond household, but this was an extraordinary circumstance. Nick allowed himself a moment of comfort, before pulling back

"Sorry Hugh, your sloop… she… it need—"

"I do not care about my ship. 'Tis you who is most important, you and the rest of the crew. To think…" he stopped again. "The letter said you were gravely injured. What happened? Wait, before you tell me…" Hugh walked down the slipway to meet the rest of the crew, shaking hands and chatting with each one, reassuring himself all were hale and hearty.

He was a fair and considerate employer, his employees were aware of their importance to him, over and above the contributions they made to the continued success of his shipyard. The wreck of his latest schooner was a blow, but any loss of life would have been far harder to bear.

The four men, including Nick, explained the damage sustained, detailing the repairs already completed.

"I believe the ship will be ready to sail in less than a week Sir," Teddy said. "We've been working every day since she were re-floated. Mind, young Mr Drummond here spent all of it lying abed. Lazy tyke." He grinned, being great friends with Nick, who chuckled sheepishly.

"Trust me, I'd rather be banging nails into the hull of a ship, than having someone digging them out of my skull," he retorted. Teddy slapped him on the back, and calling a hello to several of the villagers, he and the other two crew who worked on the schooner that afternoon, traipsed off to the tavern for a much-needed ale.

"Do you have lodgings arranged?" Nick asked, aware the evening was drawing in.

"Not yet, there is a boarding house about a mile back on the moor road. We should get rooms there," Hugh replied, absently. He hadn't planned that far ahead, knowing when they arrived in Runswick Bay, all he would think about was getting to Nick, and hoping he was still alive. They had availed themselves of rooms at coaching inns on the journey north. Today, a place to sleep was the last thing on his mind.

"I am sure there will be rooms in the village, the tavern I know has two or three, but maybe Helena..." Nick left that dangling. Helena wasn't averse to putting up with a few less luxuries than she was used to, but he had no mind to assume.

"Maybe Helena what?" That young lady appeared, placing her hand on Nick's arm. "Nick, we were so worr—" she didn't get any further. Nick drew her into a brotherly hug, in much the same way he would Jessica, his sister.

"I'm sorry, Helena, it was not my intent to cause such upset. Thankfully, I wrecked in a place where they have a decent and very thorough doctor. I have been cared for as well as at any hospital in London." Nick hooked Helena's arm through his and they walked up the slipway to where the crowd still buzzed.

It took several more minutes before the newcomers were able to extricate themselves, but eventually the hordes started to disperse; a cool beer or an evening meal calling, allowing Helena, Nick, and Hugh, to wend their way to the doctor's home.

Rose, who had already informed her father of the imminent arrival of two more Londoners, was busy organising a hot meal. She heard them enter, but remained in the kitchen, her emotions in upheaval. She knew this day was coming. Nick had a life, a home, elsewhere.

This was merely a temporary hiccup for him. He would leave for London and forget the few weeks of enforced recuperation here in the north of England. No doubt he would be attending parties and soirees, where he would meet beautiful women, more suitable than she could ever hope to be.

The ache in the region of her heart returned, and she blinked away treacherous tears. Her life was here with her father, a prospect which suddenly seemed dreary.

Straightening her shoulders, Rose prepared the meal, and while the stew was bubbling on the stove, ran up to her bedchamber for a hasty wash, changing her dress, and brushing her hair, making herself presentable.

Stealing back down the stairs, intent on checking the stew, Rose was halted when Nick stuck his head out of the parlour, the rumble of voices from within echoing along the narrow hallway.

"Rose, there you are, please come and meet my brother and his wife." Unthinking, he reached his hand out to grasp hers, to draw her into the room, but she shook her head.

"You can't," she whispered. "It's not right." Brushing past, she slipped into the parlour, and dipped a perfect curtsy to their guests. Nick followed, momentarily perplexed, soon forgotten as Rose was now the one swept into hugs from Helena and Hugh, who ignored her squeak of surprise at the unexpected familiarity.

"Thank you for helping your father to look after Nick," Helena said, holding Rose's bewildered blue eyes with her penetrating violet gaze. "I suspect he was an ornery patient, and one you will be glad to wash your hands of."

Rose smiled shyly. "He was an exemplary patient, Lady Helena, except of late when he thought he knew better than Papa and balked at the daily examinations." Grinning at Nick, whose cheeks reddened. "He was brave too." She threw this last in, with studied nonchalance.

Helena, who had been about to say something to Nick, heard something in her tone, and glanced at Rose sharply. The younger girl's expression was bland, but Helena was nothing if not astute and decided to see whether her intuition was on the mark.

"Please come through to the dining room, I have a meal ready to serve," Rose added, leading the way through to the spacious dining room. The newcomers were astonished at the size of the house, which from the front appeared no more than a cottage typical of the rest of the village.

Spotting their confusion, Joseph explained that when he bought the property, he was able to afford the slightly smaller adjoining abode, giving him a sizeable home.

With the help of the locals he converted the adjacent cottage into a clinic and small surgery, a kitchen, parlour and this dining room.

They also knocked the upstairs through and were able to create four bedchambers. Nick was not the first necessitating around the clock monitoring and having the patient under the doctor's own roof was most convenient.

Rose served the meal. It was plain fare, but she was a good cook, and all at the table tucked in with zest. Apple pie with cream for a second course, rounding off the meal with a glass of port, when they retired to the parlour.

Assuming the visitors would be staying with them, Rose had aired the guest room as soon as she heard of their arrival and mentioned it now.

"We couldn't take advantage of your hospitality any more than we already have. You have been so generous, looking after Nick and now this." Helena opened her hand in an encompassing gesture. "We shall return to the coaching inn we passed, not far back along the moor road."

"You will do no such thing," Joseph interrupted. "Lady Helena, we could not in all conscience allow you to rattle back up that hill, when we have a perfectly adequate bedchamber, ready made up. Please, stay. I'm sure Nick would like you to."

Helena's hesitation was prompted by her awareness extra

guests meant more mouths to feed, but she could see the doctor was adamant.

Acquiescing, gracefully, she said. "Thank you, I had no mind to add to your already busy workload, but I should very much enjoy staying here." Relaxing back into the comfortable chair, she smiled. "This means I get to see the sunrise over the sea. How wonderful."

Hugh and Nick chuckled. Helena's love of open water, be it river or sea, was well known among her family and friends. Many's the day she turned up at Trentams just to watch the traffic plying up and down the Thames.

Lively chat went back and forth, as though the company had known each other for years. The four men — Michael, his suggestion that his presence was one mouth too many being pooh-poohed by both Joseph and Rose — discussed the ship, and what needed to be completed, while the two women talked about their lives.

Helena found Rose, enchanting. Her quiet poise and obvious intelligence, making her an interesting conversationalist, and in turn Rose was fascinated by Helena's work at a women's refuge in London. After several minutes, Helena changed tack, asking Rose about the shipwreck, and its aftermath.

"Please tell me what happened to Nick. How bad was it? 'Tis unlikely he will share that information with me, and maybe not even with Hugh. He tends to keep things close to his chest, and as he looks to be healing well, he will tuck it away never to be spoken of again. I need to know whether any of his injuries are likely to cause recurring problems."

Rose read concern in the woman's face. It was clear the Drummonds cared deeply for each other, and oddly warming that Nick belonged to such a family.

"He was badly injured when brought here. The mast broke, and part of it hit him, tossing him into the sea. The lifeboat was already there and the crew, along with Captain Richards, got him to safety as quickly as possible. He was unconscious for five days, and when he did regain his sense, seemed confused as to his whereabouts."

Rose went on to provide Helena with all the details: the infection, the fever, and the operation. She half-expected a lady of her guest's status to faint at the gruesome nature of her description, but Helena barely paled.

Unbeknownst to Rose, Lady Helena Drummond was not easily discomposed, having seen, and experienced, her fair share of the ugly side of life. A few poisonous wounds were naught in comparison.

Her voice low, to keep their discussion private, Rose concluded her report, by saying Nick still tired easily, but could walk to the top of the bank.

"I think given one or two more weeks of rest, interspersed with proper exercise and fresh air, he will soon be back to the Nick you know. I know Papa does not anticipate any of the wounds Nick sustained, to have long-term complications. He will be fit to return to London whenever you decide to travel."

Her voice took on a melancholy note, and Helena noticed Rose's gaze kept drifting to Nick, who was engrossed in all things shipping with the other three men.

An idea began to blossom at the back of Helena's mind. She meditated on it, determining to suggest it to Hugh in the privacy of their bedchamber. It would serve two purposes if she could pull it off. Pushing it aside for now, she asked Rose about the area, listening as Rose's tone became one of joyful enthusiasm, while describing the village and surrounds.

CHAPTER 7

*R*ose strolled along the path circling the bay. It was early morning, dawn had scarcely broken. The air was cool, but pleasant, and the birds were at full song, determined no one should sleep on so beautiful a day.

She walked as far as the rocks, the same rocks upon which the ship had run aground. Finding a dry one, she sat down, bunching her skirts under her legs. Ostensibly admiring the view, her gaze had turned inward.

It was three days since Lady Helena and Mr Drummond had arrived in Runswick Bay. Three days since she was able to orchestrate any time alone with Nick. It was both tearing her apart and giving her the chance to prepare for his departure.

Their brief acquaintance aside, Nick had become more important to her than she anticipated. She was acutely aware when he was nearby, her ears straining to hear his voice, her eyes desperate for a glimpse of his craggy face.

Despite his remarks of almost a week ago — goodness was it that long? — Rose suspected Nick said them in justification of his actions. She in no way regretted their kiss. She would not spurn him should he attempt to repeat the gesture, but she imagined, to Nick, she was an amusing diversion, forgotten the moment his carriage reached the moor road.

Lost in reverie, she didn't hear quiet footsteps approaching. Nothing, until a voice spoke behind her, prompting a surprised squawk.

"My apologies for disturbing your thoughts. I saw you sitting here and wondered whether I might join you?" It was Lady Helena.

Rose nodded. "I would be glad of the company, Lady Helena, my thoughts are not particularly uplifting this morning."

They fell into easy chatter. Over the preceding days, Rose had assumed the role of guide. Showing the visitors everything there was to see around Runswick Bay, as well as shielding them from the more effusive members of the village who tended to let their excitement overwhelm their good sense.

Of Nick she had seen little. He spent most of each day on *The Diligence*, with the rest of the crew, ensuring the repairs would transport them safely back to Trentams.

"I love this time of day," Helena spoke quietly. "Before the world is awake, the only sounds, birdsong, the soft whoosh of the waves, and the wind in the trees. 'Tis incomparable."

Rose twisted on her rock to study her companion's face. "I feel the same. To be alone abroad is a boon I delight in. To take a moment in the peace before chores, and my other tasks intervene. 'Tis a memory I draw on when I feel weary or irritated. It never fails to calm me."

The two women shared a smile of complete understanding.

"Rose, Hugh and I would like to thank you and your father for everything you have done for Nick. Hugh has something organised for your father, but we wish to invite you to accompany us back to London. I wanted to discuss it with you before we spoke with Dr Archer in case it is of no interest.

"Should your father be agreeable, and can spare you, I am hoping you might stay with us, at the very least for the remainder of the summer, better still until the end of the year. I do believe you would find six months in the city, a refreshing change and quite convivial."

Rose gawked at Helena. There was no other way to describe her astonished expression. Her jaw dropped, and her eyes nearly fell out of their sockets.

"Y-you would like me to c-come to L-London... with you?" she stammered. *Her, a country bumpkin, visiting London.*

Closing her eyes, Rose shook her head, concerned for a moment she was at home in bed, and this was a dream. Opening them again, she was pleased to note the scene in front of her had not changed. Helena was regarding her steadily.

"I do beg your pardon, my lady, but might you repeat that?"

Helena did so, adding, "...of course, we would arrange a new wardrobe for you. I do not expect you have cause to attend several balls a week here in the bay." The truth in Helena's words, made Rose blush, but the other woman's tone was not patronising, she was stating a fact.

"Really? I am not refined or elegant and am aware my accent is coarse. I do have one ball gown, but I expect 'tis woefully unfashionable. It was my mother's," she said by way of explanation. Her voice dropped to a whisper. "Are you sure? Oh, to see London..." Rose trailed off. *Would Papa agree?*

This was an answer to her prayers. She might get to see more of Nick. Even though common sense adjured this was prolonging the agony of their eventual parting, she would give everything to extend it, even for a day.

"I am certain. You shall stay with us, and we will enjoy the variety of amusements London offers at this time of the year. 'Tis not just balls. There are picnics, shopping, visits to the museums and art galleries, carriage rides, taking tea at Gunter's, oh so much. Even when the Season is over, most families of the *ton* continue to organise all manner of events, and we never lack for entertaining diversions."

Helena beamed at Rose, who became caught up with her enthusiasm, the two discussing what they might do while in the city.

"If you do not think I would be a burden, and Papa agrees, I cannot think of anything I would like better." Rose grinned suddenly, her face transforming into that of the vivacious young woman she usually was, and her beauty struck Helena almost speechless. A beauty, Rose had no idea she possessed.

Helena's mind went back to the previous evening, when she had taken a moment to study Nick, covertly, during dinner. It was obvious Nick was entranced by Rose, but was it to him an enjoyable interlude or did his feelings run deeper?

While the offer to take Rose to London was, first and foremost, by way of thanking the Archer family for their care of Nick, Helena wanted to see whether whatever was growing between these two was worth them exploring, or naught but a brief flirtation. She could contrive to have them attend the same events while in London and then let fate, and perhaps a little human interference, decide.

Ignoring all this for now, the two women gossiped about this and that, meandering back to Thistle Cottage, where

Helena helped Rose prepare breakfast. This was another facet of Helena, which astonished Rose.

The morning after their arrival, she appeared in the kitchen, on cue to assist her hostess with every meal. Politely, Rose tried to shoo her out, but their guest refused to leave, saying it was hard enough having Nick to look after without worrying about two more people.

Admitting she couldn't cook, but was willing to do everything else, Helena suited her words to actions, laying the table, serving food, and washing the pots. Rose was astounded, but inordinately grateful.

Nick might not need round the clock attention, but there was always a steady queue of people requiring the doctor, and Rose was expected to be on hand to assist her father should the need arise.

After breakfast, Helena and Hugh asked Joseph whether he might spare them a few moments before his rounds. Ushering them into his study, he invited them to take a seat, and waited.

"In a gesture of our appreciation for your tireless efforts in caring for Nick, we would like to offer Rose a holiday in London. Should you be agreeable, she could travel back with us and remain, hopefully until the end of the year." Helena outlined her plans for the summer and beyond, if the doctor was amenable. Hugh interjected here and there, and they took pains to assure Joseph, Rose would be properly chaperoned at all times.

Helena concluded, "I realise this might seem unexpected, but I have been pondering the prospect since our arrival, and I hope you will consider my, our, request favourably." She sat back, worried she may have overstated their case.

Hugh patted her hand and grinned, confident Joseph would agree.

The room fell quiet while the doctor contemplated the generous offer. The ponderous tick from the old grandfather clock in the corner seemed to become slower the longer they sat. Helena forgot to breathe. Until this moment, she did not realise how much she wanted the doctor to approve her proposal.

Joseph Archer leant back in his chair, ruminating over everything his guests said. It was a wonderful opportunity for Rose, but could he manage without her for six months?

Unbidden, the image of her tired face the evening she shouted at him about making hot drinks sprang to mind. It would be selfish to deny his daughter this chance. It wasn't so long. Rose would be home before he knew it, ignoring the whisper at the edge of his mind, insisting she might never return.

"Lady Helena, Hugh, this is an extraordinary offer, and on behalf of Rose, I am most grateful. If my daughter would like to travel to London, I cannot in all conscience object."

Helena released the breath she wasn't aware she held. Inhaling another, she thanked the doctor, in a surprisingly calm voice, and that all being well — weather and Nick's recovery permitting — they would like to begin their homeward journey, three days hence.

"'Tis unfair to take up any more of your valuable time, and hospitality, and Michael informs us the ship is ready to sail."

Joseph acknowledged her consideration, assuring the Drummonds, Nick was fit to travel.

"He may suffer some residual soreness from his injuries, but what he needs now is time. He can get that in London as well as here. I expect once he is back in the hustle and bustle of the city, a country doctor's instructions will be all too easily forgotten. I beg you to watch him, and do not let him overdo things too soon. I daresay Rose will keep him in line." Chuckling at the recollection of his daughter lecturing Nick on his reckless attitude where his health was concerned.

"If someone can keep my brother in line, I will be eternally grateful," Hugh said, laughingly. "He throws himself at life with little thought of the consequences. I am hoping this accident might prove a jolt, making him consider his actions rather more than he has been doing." Although his tone was light, Hugh continued to be concerned about Nick, and for more reasons than the wounds he sustained in the shipwreck.

Not only a brother for whom Hugh cared deeply, but Nick was an invaluable member of Trentams. The shipping industry was inherently risky, as this latest accident attested, and he had no desire to lose one of his siblings. Pushing that aside for now, he took Helena's hand and they excused themselves from the study, leaving Joseph to his thoughts and the rest of his day.

Joseph found Rose in the clinic, where she was making sure everything was clean and in its place.

"Rose, my dear, might I speak with you?"

"Of course, Papa, is there something you need?" Placing bowls and instruments on pristine cloths. Covering each with another cloth to keep off the dust.

"I need to you to stop what you're doing and listen." He walked over and stilled her hands, catching them in his, before turning her to face him. "Rose, Lady Helena and Mr Drummond have offered to take you to London for a time." His heart sank a little when her face lit up.

He gave her the abbreviated version of their conversation,

reiterating their assurances she would be chaperoned at all times. Rose was quite sure she didn't need an escort, but it was easier not to argue. Maybe she could persuade Helena to relax her vigilance and allow her some freedom.

What about you, Papa? Will you manage without me? I do not want to leave you to cope alone. We have never..." she was unable to say the words.

In all her life, she had not spent a single night away from her father, save the occasional evening he returned home late because of a medical crisis, and even then, he was always back before first light. The thrill at embracing new experiences aside, the enormity of what she was about to embark on was suddenly daunting.

Joseph drew Rose into a hug, patting her back as he had done when she was still a young girl, upset over some childish game gone wrong.

"You will have a marvellous time my dear. London is a magical, if somewhat chaotic city. To be brutally honest, it has more than its fair share of deplorable areas. The slums and docks are no place for a young woman, but the rest is worth seeing. I believe you will find it beneficial, and 'tis generous of the Drummonds to invite you."

Releasing her, he stepped away and said in a practical voice. "Now, time later to ponder this, for I must get on. Where is my bag?" Scratching his head.

"By the front door as usual, Papa," smiled Rose. Her father, for all his medical expertise was quite the scatterbrain when it came to mundane matters. She bit her lip. Would he cope without her? He'd never find anything. As though sensing her thoughts, Joseph turned around, his hand on the door.

"Do not start coming up with excuses not to leave me. I will be fine. Plenty of people hereabouts to help. Go and start packing." He grinned and pushed the door, whistling as he strolled down the street.

Rose stood there until the door swung closed, then a bubble of joy so enormous she feared she might burst with it, had her clapping her hands and spinning around.

London, she was going to London!

CHAPTER 8

*T*he coach rumbled along the road. They had been travelling for six days, and Helena assured Rose they would be in London within three.

Long hours in the carriage had proved too much for Nick. At the end of the first day when he had succumbed to a violent headache, admitting he felt as though the carriage had run over him, they slowed the pace of their journey.

Ongoing discomfort, and the interminable swaying of the coach aside, Rose was captivated by the changing scenery, and the towns they passed through or alongside, declaring travel to be exhilarating.

To make the exercise less gruelling for Nick, they took frequent breaks, and by mid-afternoon had halted at a convenient coaching inn. Each night, following a hearty meal and perhaps a refreshing beer, Rose slept soundly and without dreams.

That all this lay outside her quiet little village amazed Rose. She was not ignorant; Joseph had taught her from an early age. She could read, write, and was relatively competent in mathematics. Whenever she had a spare moment, her father encouraged her to study geography and history.

Thus, she had a fair grasp of the world beyond her doorstep. It was one thing to read about it, another matter entirely to actually see it. She peppered the three Drummonds with numerous questions about everything, from the different species of trees and flowers to names of towns, and rivers.

Her enthusiasm kept them entertained on what was normally an arduous and boring journey, but as they approached London even Rose fell quiet. She was beginning to feel apprehensive about being a country girl in a big city. She had no knowledge of what was expected or how she should behave and didn't want to embarrass the Drummonds.

Helena was not insensitive. That same evening, while enjoying a hearty meal of game pie and hot vegetables washed down with a glass of ale, she tried to reassure her new charge.

"Please do not fret about your time in the city, Rose. I want you to enjoy your time with us, not be anxious."

"Yes, but I'm not elegant or refined and my accent is—" she started to say.

"Rose, trust me, you will be comfortable among our family and friends. They will love you as we do."

Rose had to stop her mouth from falling open. She blushed, thanking her hostess, shyly. "In truth, I am more than a trifle excited. 'Tis that I do not want to let you down."

"You could not do so, even if you tried, now we shall say no more about it." Helena diverted the conversation to an upcoming ball they would be attending. "We will have a day with my modiste to organise you a new wardrobe. It will be so much fun."

Her bright tones doing the trick, and they began a gentle

argument about materials and colours and styles. Well the two women did, the men preferred to discuss the shipyard.

Nick found his gaze kept straying to Rose. Since the day on the moor, they had not shared a single private moment, and until Helena informed him of their plans, had experienced an unexpected sorrow at the thought of saying goodbye.

Blessed with little in the way of romantic notions, Nick did not perceive the reason for so puzzling a sentiment but had become aware of an inexplicable warmth in his heart, knowing his acquaintance with Rose was not over.

In the dim light thrown by the pitiful number of lamps in the, euphemistically titled, dining room, Rose's hair, no longer confined in its neat chignon, shimmered like pale silk. Her eyes, darkening to midnight blue, reflected the flickering candles, and her skin seemed to glow.

She was regaling Helena with ludicrous tales of various mishaps in the village, the pair consumed with mirth, their spontaneous laughter attracting the attention of other patrons.

Several observed the ladies for longer than might be deemed appropriate, and Nick felt his gut tighten at the lewd expressions of a group of men leaning on the bar.

"Hugh," he murmured in an undertone. His brother leant closer to hear. Nick nodded towards the four men troubling him. "I think we might be in for a spot of bother."

Hugh glanced around, his brow furrowing. "Do not even think of challenging them, Nick. I did not travel all those miles, as though the hounds of hell were after me to ensure your well-being, only to have you beaten to pulp on the way home. Mother would never forgive me. Let me handle this."

Hugh stood, his immense height and muscular stature enough to give most with ill-intent second thoughts. Moreover, he exuded power, honed over many years. First in the army, now in the cutthroat business of shipping — one could not show weakness to the competition when your livelihood was at stake.

As he stepped out of the booth in which they were sitting, Hugh stilled his features and glared at the four plainly inebriated men who threatened to be nuisances, until they began to squirm under his gimlet gaze. Satisfied they understood his tacit message, he swung around to face the rest of the room, which had fallen silent.

"Good evening, gentleman, and ladies," tipping his head to the few women seated in the taproom, his deep voice reaching the farthest corner. "I imagine you are weary either from a long day on the road, or a longer day's work. Perhaps a round of ale, or maybe port for the ladies, would help lift your spirits?" He smiled genially over the crowd. Mutters of appreciation began, and one spoke up.

"That's mighty generous of you, sir. Happen we'd all enjoy a cool drink. Thankee kindly."

Hugh strolled calmly over to where the barkeep was polishing glasses with a less than clean rag. A muttered conversation, the chink of coin, and Hugh returned to his seat as though naught was amiss.

The atmosphere eased, chatter resumed, and the awkward moment was forgotten, but almost immediately, at a nod from the barkeep, two burly farmer-types, quietly and without fuss, escorted the drunken louts off the premises.

Rose watched this unfold in astonishment. While she had known Hugh only a matter of days, he was never anything other than affable. This stern side to him was a revelation.

Helena caught her stunned expression, and chuckled. "That is Hugh's 'do not mess with me' face." She reached out to catch her husband's hand where it lay on the table, his fingers tapping out a tuneless ditty. "I admit it can be quite off putting when not expected. He only uses it when absolutely necessary."

Hugh smiled at his wife and, turning his hand, squeezed her fingers while dropping a slow wink at Rose, who suddenly saw the funny side, and burst into giggles.

"Perhaps this a timely reminder. Rose, London is not like Runswick Bay. There are many who do not treat ladies properly and if by chance we become separated while out, please do not try to make your own way home. Stay where you are, and I will find you. I know the city, and it is easy to take a wrong turn, becoming lost in the maze of streets, where unscrupulous people lurk."

Then Helena changed the subject, unwilling to frighten her guest before they had even arrived in the capital.

Early evening, three days later, two carriages rattled to a halt. As they approached their destination, and despite her best intentions not to miss a thing, Rose had nodded off — the rocking of the carriage, soporific. Helena shook her gently, and she came awake with a start, full of apologies.

"It is of no matter, we are all tired. I do believe I shut my eyes for a little while too." Smiling at the younger woman. "Come now," she helped Rose step down from the carriage.

For the first few moments after the coach stopped, she tended to feel rather wobbly, as though the ground was shifting under her feet. Hugh assured her, when this happened on the first day of their journey, it was not unusual and was rather like being at sea. The swell of the waves under the ship had the same effect.

Rolling her shoulders and flexing her limbs to ease aching muscles, Rose stared around. The street was quiet. Tall trees, blossoms filling the air with heady fragrance, were planted at regular intervals, their leafy spread offering a green barrier between road and footpath. The path itself was wide and swept clean of any debris.

The houses were three, four storeys high, and all along the terrace were similarly faced with, Rose was to discover later, yellow-grey bricks, made from London clay. Narrow, elaborate, wrought-iron balconies overlooked the street. Front entrances, embellished with decorative cream-coloured stuccoed centrepieces or slender Romanesque columns, on an alternating basis, broke up the monotony. Tall, sash windows, some of which glowed from the candles lit within, were spread evenly over each facade.

The overall impression was of genteel refinement.

Gazing up at the one they were standing in front of, Rose sighed with delight. "Lady Helena, your home is exquisite."

"Thank you, Rose. Welcome to Stanton House. We are rather partial are we not, Hugh?" Smiling at her husband who was waiting patiently in the doorway while the two women discussed his home.

"We are." He grinned a reply. "Come along, you can admire the street on the morrow, it will still be here. We should go in. Standing outside is not getting us our meal."

A hive of activity was going on around Rose. Smartly uniformed men and women hurried to convey the luggage indoors, allowing the coachmen to take carriages and horses along the passage to the stables in the mews at the rear of the house.

The rest of the evening passed in a kind of blur for Rose. She was shown to an enormous bedchamber, where her clothes were already being unpacked and tidied away, much to her humiliation. The maid was wearing better quality attire than any of the items Rose had brought with her.

Penny, said maid, didn't seem to notice and in fact commented on how pretty her special dress was. Rose thought it probably more a sympathetic assurance, but she appreciated it all the same.

"Now, Miss Rose, let me brush your hair," Penny waved aside Rose's remark that she could manage on her own. "'Tis relaxing after a long day in a carriage, to have someone brush your hair, and yours is so beautiful." Rose blushed but acquiesced, admitting when Penny had finished, she certainly felt less weary.

A thorough wash in the basin, rid her of some of the dust from the road, then she slipped into a clean gown. Used to dressing herself, Rose had no wish to upset Penny, and stood quietly while the maid fastened the buttons.

"There you go, miss. My you do look lovely."

Rose stared at her reflection, amazed at the effect the young girl had achieved, with so small a change. Instead of her habitual long plait, or chignon, Penny had divided her hair into several thin plaits, before twisting them into a deceptively simple-looking style, a few strands left loose to frame her elfin face.

"Why, Penny, thank you. You are a miracle worker." She turned her head this way and that, blinking at the image of the woman gazing back at her. *Could that truly be her? Mayhap she wouldn't embarrass Lady Helena after all.*

Penny grinned in a friendly manner, before escorting her downstairs to the parlour, where the family gathered prior to their evening meal. Hugh was already there and offered Rose a glass of sherry.

"Maybe a very small one," she assented. "'Tis such a treat. Papa allows me one glass a week with our Sunday dinner."

Hugh, fascinated by how others lived, asked an innocuous question regarding Runswick Bay, prompting Rose to chatter artlessly about her home and the countryside surrounding it. Soon Helena and Nick joined them, and they moved into the dining room, whereupon Rose bit her lip so as not to exclaim at the sheer beauty of the space

Tastefully decorated in pastel shades of blue and cream, the room was light and airy. Three windows, currently hidden behind heavy silk drapes of a slightly darker blue would, during the day, offer a view of the garden.

A large table covered in a snowy white cloth, graced the centre of the room, and was laid for four. Fine china, delicate blue flowers adorning the rim, was placed between gilt-edged silver cutlery, and the tablecloth was besprinkled with tiny rainbows as the multitude of candles caught the facets in the crystal glasses, the colours swirling and changing when a footman poured the wine.

Hugh led Rose around to one of eight mahogany chairs, and she sank on to the cushioned seat, attempting to behave in a manner of which her father would approve.

Nick took the seat opposite, and spent the entire meal observing Rose, something, which did not go unnoticed by Helena. At the end of the sumptuous repast, they returned to the drawing room, where Hugh and Nick had a nip of whisky, while Helena and Rose enjoyed a drop of Madeira.

"I thought perhaps we should spend tomorrow quietly here. Mama Drummond has invited us to join her for dinner, but I do believe we would benefit from the restorative of a day doing nothing, expect perhaps a short walk in the afternoon."

"Nick and I will be at Trentams for most of the day, my love. There will be any amount of work to deal with, and we need to prepare for the return of *The Diligence*. Both the dry and wet docks have vessels moored in them at present, and we need to ensure at least one is available when the damaged ship arrives."

Nick felt warmth creep up his cheeks. Even acknowledging there was absolutely nothing he could have done to prevent the damage to the schooner, he continued to feel responsible. Spotting his discomfort, Hugh sought to alleviate it.

"Nick, please, the wreck was not your fault. Michael told me what happened, every last detail. You did everything humanly possible to save my ship, but sometimes Mother Nature is unforgiving. As I informed Lord Faversham last year, prior to his untimely demise, 'tis the people who make Trentams not the ships.

"Without my construction team those ships cannot be built. Without my crew they cannot be sailed, they would be simply random pieces of wood and canvas. Moreover, you are my brother, do you think I would be happy if you saved the ship only to die the process? You nearly were killed."

His face darkened. "Your life is worth more than all the ships plying the oceans combined, so please stop blaming yourself."

"Such a tempest occurs maybe once in a decade, if that," Rose chimed in, without thinking. "I cannot recall another happening in my lifetime. When I was a child, I pestered the fishermen for stories. They told tales of violent storms, but although during autumn and winter we are battered by some terrible gales and driving rain, 'tis rare at this time of the year. The last one destroyed the whole of our fishing fleet, and the tide flooded the houses near the shore. I overheard old Walt telling Captain Richards he was shocked any of your crew survived, and 'twas only quick thinking by you and the captain saved them."

She smiled brightly at both men, and her practical tones seeming to persuade Nick as nothing else had.

"Thank you, Rose. I suspect Nick needed to hear that from someone other than his brother," Hugh grinned. "Now, we shall make no further mention of the matter. What occurred cannot be changed, you were not at fault and all are safe."

Dismissing the subject, Hugh returned to a more neutral topic and the rest of the evening flew by in light conversation about nothing of any import at all.

CHAPTER 9

*I*t did not take long for Rose to become comfortable in her temporary abode. The day after they arrived, Helena showed her guest through Stanton House — named, her hostess explained, after the village attached to Whiteoaks, her family's country estate — and introduced her to their staff. Later in the afternoon, the two enjoyed a promenade, but the weather turned inclement, forcing them to shorten their constitutional.

Unperturbed by a bit of drizzle, Rose would have walked further. Living in the north east of England, if you went home every time it rained you never accomplished anything. Still, she was a guest, so kept her peace, and they enjoyed the remainder of the afternoon ensconced in the cosy parlour, chatting about upcoming balls and soirees.

A convivial evening followed at Drummond House. Mrs Drummond, aware Rose had lost her own mother several years previously, was especially welcoming of her guest. Nick joined them for the meal, disappearing almost straight afterwards, saying he was meeting friends. Rose had the strangest notion he was avoiding her, at a loss to know why.

She made no comment, but Helena noticed the slight droop of her mouth when Nick said goodbye.

~

The visit to Helena's modiste was an eye-opening, jaw-dropping experience for Rose. There were so many different materials, and designs, and trims, not to mention the accessories. By the end of the day, Rose was in flat spin. She had suffered being pinned, twisted, and posed, encouraged to try on numerous styles of gowns, day dresses, and goodness knows what else. Then came the shoes, evening slippers, boots, and coats.

It was entertaining, exhilarating, and utterly exhausting, with Helena completely ignoring Rose's plea not to throw her money away on so many clothes.

"I will have no reason to wear such fine dresses in the village, Lady Helena." Horrified at what this must be costing.

"Rose, my dear, you cannot be seen more than twice in the same gown at a ball. Then we have picnics, calls, shopping, afternoon tea at Gunter's …" Helena ticked them off on her fingers, listing a veritable plenitude of social events, until Rose was tempted to question her sanity at agreeing to come to London at all. Moreover, this was only the first of several visits until the modiste, Madam Thibault, was satisfied.

Resigning herself to the inevitable, Rose stopped worrying, and eventually began to enjoy the exercise of trying on the beautifully made clothes. She *was* relieved when no longer required to spend hours standing on a box while people tutted and frowned at her.

Her sparse wardrobe was now almost overflowing, and Rose had to admit, Helena possessed a keen eye for colours and styles. She had to be careful not to trip over or tear any of them, which for a girl used to running along the beach barefoot, presented somewhat of a challenge.

∼

A week after arriving in London, Rose danced down the steps to a waiting carriage, Helena close behind. They were going to Sanctuary House, where Helena spent most of her days when not chaperoning a guest, and then on to Trentams. Rose had expressed great interest in seeing both places, requesting she be allowed to visit.

The morning was bright and sunny, bathing the city in a welcoming light. The carriage was open, a pleasant breeze keeping the women from becoming too warm. They chatted while the coach rattled through busy streets, now at ease with each other, Rose calling her hostess Helena without the accompanying 'lady.' Something Helena had asked her to do before they left Whitby.

"It isn't proper. You are a lady, nothing you can do about that, and it isn't right my being so informal," was Rose's considered opinion

"Yes, but 'tis my prerogative to ask people to drop my title. After all, I am also Mrs Drummond, and you never think of calling me that. Rose, you are my friend, and my friends call me Helena."

Rose had stuttered a feeble argument to the contrary, but in the end, gave up. Helena could be very persuasive when she chose and, as Rose did not expect to see her, or any of the Drummond family again, once she returned to the village, she acquiesced.

The carriage rolled to halt in front of a large building. Helena explained a fire had gutted the original refuge, this new structure — erected on the same footprint — completed only a few weeks previously. So new in fact, the staff was still in the process of organising everything into its place. There were many willing hands, and soon it would be set to rights.

Constructed from brick, rather than wood, with a set of double doors reached by six wide stone steps, it stood three storeys high. Its simple frontage, impressive without being intimidating.

Initially, there had been talk of towering columns and fancy iron balconies, more suited to a bank or museum than a refuge. Thankfully, the haven's benefactors preferred the building to appear welcoming not formidable, dismissing the more elaborate design suggestions.

Leading Rose up the steps, and into the quiet entrance hall, Helena gave a comprehensive tour of the facility. The stone-flagged ground floor housed offices, kitchens, and a huge laundry. Situated up the first flight of stairs, fifteen bedchambers, neatly furnished with a bed, wardrobe, chair and washbowl.

There were even three rooms set aside for bathing, a luxury few were afforded in this area of the city. On the upper floor — several storerooms, and five extra bedchambers. All manner of items were regularly donated to the refuge, and those in charge were delighted to have an area cordoned off, specifically for stock of any kind.

In a small annexe on the ground floor at the rear of the building, the clinic could be found. It was quiet here, away from the hustle and bustle of the main refuge. A place where those requiring minor treatment could rest without being disturbed. Sanctuary House had a resident doctor, and a few of the women were training as assistants.

The tour took over an hour. Rose was interested in the day-to-day workings of the refuge and asked many questions. She wondered, out loud, whether she might be able to help while she was staying in London, her medical knowledge, not inconsiderable.

"You are supposed to be enjoying a holiday, Rose, not tiring yourself out working," Helena chided gently

"I know, and 'tis wonderful not to worry about getting up at dawn," something she still did, "or getting through all my chores. Please do not think I am ungrateful for this opportunity, but I am used to my days being full and busy. I fear if I am idle for any length of time, I may go mad."

Rose spread her hands, apologetically, hoping her comments did not upset her generous hostess. "Lad… Helena, if you think I have anything to offer here, I would be honoured, nay I would love to help. Even if 'tis nothing more than washing up after meals."

Helena ruminated over Rose's request. In truth, it answered her concerns about leaving Rose alone on the days she normally attended Sanctuary House. She would ensure the girl did not overdo it, and they would not miss any of the social events already arranged. Yes, the more she thought about it the better it sounded.

"I cannot think of a single reason why you shouldn't, Rose," Helena said after a few minutes of silence. "I usually come three or four days each week, and 'tis always congenial to have company."

Rose clapped her hands with delight, the sound echoing through the lofty hall, making her blush.

"Oh, I'm sorry, I did not mean to make so much noise." She grinned not looking particularly repentant. Her joy was infectious, pulling a responding chuckle from Helena. Poking her head into one of the offices, Helena had a few words with whoever was within, and then introduced Rose to Mrs Parry.

"Mrs Parry administers this huge place, along with Mrs Forester," Helena explained. "After what happened last year, we need to know who comes and goes, so we can account for people in an emergency."

"An unenviable task, I imagine," Rose dipped a curtsy, smiling at the iron-haired lady who came around from behind the desk. "I am very pleased to meet you, Mrs Parry. I hope I am not upsetting the smooth running of your refuge by asking to assist in some small capacity."

"Certainly not. Helena tells me you have some medical knowledge?" She raised a brow and Rose nodded. "That is a boon for us, even if only for a brief period."

The three women discussed the refuge. Mrs Parry updated Helena on anything pertinent since she was last there, agreeing Rose could come on Helena's regular three days, starting the following week.

"That gives us a few more days to be social butterflies," Helena smiled, tucking her arm through Rose's, the pair strolling back out to the carriage. It was warm now, and despite the space around the refuge, the narrow roads between it and Trentams were stuffy and airless.

"This is why it is so easy for fire to take hold," commented Helena, smiling at Rose's appalled expression.

"How do people live in such confined surroundings?" she whispered. "I think I might die if I struggled to see the sky or smell fresh air." For a girl used to wide open spaces, the realities of London's overcrowded neighbourhoods came as an unpleasant surprise.

Helena shrugged. "You become accustomed to it," she replied. "Yes, I agree, 'tis a harsh world, but for the most part the people here do not miss what they have never experienced. They work hard for their living and do what they can with what little they have.

"You must be watchful though, Rose. There are unsavoury characters roaming these streets on the lookout for easy prey. Those down on their luck, or who take a wrong turn might easily end up in a precarious situation. This is what I meant, at the coaching inn. To get lost in these districts is not something I would wish upon anyone." She held her friend's gaze, until Rose nodded her understanding.

Shortly thereafter, the carriage drew up in the great receiving yard at Trentams. As they stepped down from the carriage, two young boys tumbled out of the large, red-brick, office building.

"Lady 'Elena, Lady 'Elena," one of them cried. "Oh, 'tis glad I am to see you 'ome safe 'n' sound." The taller of the pair, a tow-haired boy of maybe ten and three years, ran over and, removing his cap, swept an elaborate bow.

"Timmy, how marvellous to see you. How is your dear Mama? Has she shaken off that nasty cold yet?" The two chatted about the lad's family for a minute or so.

"Rose, please let me introduce you to Timmy, our most trusted messenger."

Timmy sidled over to where Rose was standing, bowed over her gloved hand, and dropped her a cheeky wink as he straightened up. "Mighty pleased to meetcha." Grinning in delight when Rose dropped a curtsy.

"The honour is all mine, Sir." She smiled back.

"Ohhh, are you from up North, Miss?" Her unusual accent immediately marking her origins as being far from the city. At her assent, he continued, "Is it cold up there? Does is snow all year 'round? Are there wolves and bears?" He peppered her with questions, until Rose held up her hands in mock submission.

"Goodness me, Timmy where to start. The village I come from is on the coast. It is warm in the summer, and chilly in the winter. We do get snow, but so close to the sea, 'tis not usually too bad, because the salty air keeps the worst at bay. No wolves or bears though."

His bright face drooped at this.

"I am sorry to disappoint you." Rose bit her lip to control her mirth at his doleful expression. "Were you, mayhap, thinking of visiting?"

Timmy slapped his leg, laughing uproariously. "Thinkin' of visitin'? Like I'm some kind o' lord. Oh, Oh," he held his sides, guffawing. "Lady 'Elena, you found a one here, she'm be very droll." It took him a few minutes to sober up, at which point he introduced the other young lad.

"Where's me manners? Tsk. Lady 'Elena, Miss Rose, this 'ere is Roland. I'm training 'im." Puffing out his chest with importance.

Knowing Timmy, Helena raised a brow, giving him permission to expand.

"Now we're so busy up at Sanctuary 'Ouse, I can't manage on me own. Roland is me best friend, and nearly as trust-wurvy as me." Clearly, Timmy didn't lavish praise lightly. "Ai bin gettin' 'im familiar wiv me duties, like wots to be expected an' all. Ai fink he'll be suitable."

Rubbing his hand over his chin, while he studied a squirming Roland, in thoughtful consideration.

Rose did not dare look at Helena for fear of bursting into laughter. Timmy was so serious. Helena, with the aplomb honed over years of maintaining her composure, greeted the boy with warmth.

"It is lovely to meet you, Roland. Thank you for assisting Timmy. You boys are very important to Sanctuary House, as well as Trentams, so please take every care."

Roland smiled shyly and bowed to both ladies.

Unable to help it, Rose reached for his hand and shook it. "May I add, how pleased I am to meet you too, Roland? You are both fine young men."

The two boys preened under the praise of this petite newcomer with the peculiar accent, who seemed as though she had stepped out of a storybook. She and Helena were such contrasts. Helena — fair skinned, violet eyed, with glossy black hair, next to Rose — lightly-tanned skin, eyes the colour of the summer sky, and hair like spun silver. Both extraordinarily beautiful, and neither aware of it.

Timmy bowed again, saying he would see them soon, "'Opefully at the 'Ouse," his voice floated back to them, he and Roland dashing off to complete whatever task they had been assigned.

CHAPTER 10

"*T*immy is thoroughly indispensable," Helena commented, watching the boys rush out of the gate, before ushering Rose towards the main office.

"He has proved his worth, more times than I care to count. He knows this area of London like the back of his hand. Seems to hear and see things most would miss, is loyal, honest, and utterly reliable."

"I imagine the appreciation goes both ways, Helena." Rose said in her quiet way. "Would I be right in assuming you and Mr Drummond ensure Timmy's family, and probably Roland's now, are provided for by the subtlest means?"

Helena's cheeks went a little pink. "You *are* astute, Rose Archer. Yes, we pay them good coin and, keep an eye on Timmy's mother, and his two younger brothers. There is no father, and we have not asked his whereabouts, 'tis not our business. Mrs Ward takes in mending, so we have to be careful with how we boost their coffers. Timmy carries messages, runs errands, and is allocated small manual tasks, a job he now apparently shares with Roland."

Helena smiled at Timmy's brazen cheek. "He's a funny one, but we wouldn't change him."

In the next few minutes Timmy and Roland were forgotten, when Helena led Rose up to Hugh Drummond's office. It was a large room, brightly lit by the sun streaming through numerous windows.

Tables, strewn with maps and papers, were dotted about, and navigational charts lined the walls. Hugh was sitting behind an enormous, polished wooden desk, talking to a pretty woman who was taking notes. They looked up at Helena's light knock, their faces creasing into smiles.

"Helena and Rose, how delightful to see you." Hugh stood. "Mrs Collins, this is Rose Archer, the lady who took such great care of Nick when he was injured."

The woman stood also and dipped a curtsy to the newcomers. "Lady Helena, 'tis lovely to see you. May I say how glad I am, we all are, that Master Nick recovered so quickly." She turned to Rose. "A pleasure to meet you, Miss Archer. Master Nick told us all about you and your father. How are you enjoying London? I expect 'tis very different from your village."

"I find London to be exhilarating. It is vibrant and noisy, and so many people. In truth, I did not realise such an enormous number of people existed, never mind lived in one city." She grinned at Mrs Collins who laughed merrily.

"I can only imagine," amusement lacing her tones, "and please call me Lynette. Mrs Collins makes me sound as though I am in my dotage." Rose smilingly agreed, on the proviso Lynette might return the favour. They chatted for a moment or two, then Lynette hurried away to organise refreshments.

While talking with Lynette, Rose noticed out of the corner of her eye, how Hugh greeted his wife. Even though there were others in the room, he did not hesitate to take her hand, and kiss her forehead.

That Lynette appeared oblivious indicted this was his normal salutation. An image of Nick greeting her in a similar fashion sent a stab of yearning through her. She forced it aside. Nick had barely spoken to her since their arrival in London.

To be fair, he lived with his mother at Drummond House, which was some distance from Stanton House, but Rose could not shake the impression he was deliberately staying away.

Mayhap he deemed her suitable for a dalliance while far from home, but much too unsophisticated for London society. *She missed him.*

Rose rubbed her forehead, as though to dispel unsettling thoughts, but they refused to be banished. Determined not to let a man spoil her time in London, she ignored them.

Ecstatic to be shown through into the main shipyard, Rose duly admired the docks, both and wet and dry, in one of which was moored a vast Indiaman. Rose had never seen a ship so enormous, craning her neck in order to see the top.

In the second dock, *The Diligence* rocked gently; even damaged she was elegant and streamlined. Rose stared at the vessel for long moments. Memories of the storm and subsequent days flooded her mind, and she had to wrest her concentration back to what Hugh was saying.

"She arrived three days ago. The journey took longer than usual as they were unable to travel at full sail," Hugh explained as they walked around the yard, taking care not to trip over bollards, random lumps of wood, or pieces of equipment.

Shouts from men working, rhythmic banging of hammers, the grating whoosh of saws, the smell of hewn wood, tar and the river, all familiar to Rose. Admittedly, on a much smaller scale, but these were sounds and smells she grew up with.

"Thank you, Mr Drummond, for taking time out of your day to show me Trentams, 'tis most impressive. Papa would have appreciated this," she flung her arm wide, "ships fascinate him. He relished being able to discuss the shipping trade with Master Nick, and Captain Richards."

Rose felt her lips tremble, acutely aware of the distance between her father and herself. Controlling the urge to cry, a childish reaction she had no time for, Rose asked another pertinent question, and the moment passed.

When they arrived back in the office a familiar figure was angled over one of the tables. He turned as the group entered, a grin lighting his face. Rose felt her heart flutter. *Really? This was ridiculous. Clearly, he had no desire to be in her company, now he was healed and home. Why did he insist on lingering in her thoughts?* Mustering up an excuse of a smile at his greeting.

"What do you think of Trentams, Rose?" Nick enquired cheerfully.

"I think it is marvellous, and I am so glad *The Diligence* is safely moored. It must have been a concern for you all while she was at sea even though much of the damage was repaired in Runswick Bay." Her response, coolly polite.

Nick frowned. *What was going on in her head?* He ran his eyes over her petite form. She was breathtakingly beautiful. Her hat had slipped back, revealing her silvery hair, braided neatly in a long glimmering plait, hanging down her back.

She was wearing one of her new dresses. He rarely took notice of what the womenfolk wore, but the spring green hue complemented her features so perfectly, he found he could not tear his gaze away. She reminded him of a flower garden, just before it blooms.

Hell Nick, what is wrong with you? Flower garden indeed.

Mentally shaking his head, he asked whether they would like more coffee. The two ladies declined, but Hugh accepted, prompting Helena to remark it was time to leave them to their day.

"Thank you again, Mr Drummond. I have enjoyed today immensely. First the refuge and now your yard. 'Tis generous of you giving up your time to show me around, both of you." Rose included Helena in her warm smile.

"It is our pleasure. I am glad you found it interesting, most women I know would have a fit of the vapours should they be shown either." Helena grinned.

"Ah, but Rose is not most women," interjected Nick, willing Rose to look at him. She spun slowly around on her heel, unaware Helena had grabbed Hugh's arm and was all but dragging him out of the office, muttering fiercely in his ear.

"Pray tell, how would you know that?" she demanded, her tones chilly.

Nick stepped closer.

"You forget, I chanced to observe you for many days. I know you are able to stomach the sight of ugly wounds without flinching yet have a gentle touch and a kind manner. You have experienced the harsh life of an isolated village, but you are not hardened. You remain tranquil, as though such things are a minor inconvenience. You are both strong and delicate, tenacious yet fragile. You are well named, Rose.

Rose gaped at him. *My, my, this was an interesting development. Where was her fan?* She opened her mouth to respond but all she could summon up was a rather pathetic croak.

Nick smiled and took one more step. He was so close, she could see the tawny flecks in his eyes, swallowing a gulp when his hand slid around her nape, his thumb coming to rest on her wildly fluttering pulse. Giving her no chance to stop him, Nick bent his mouth to hers.

. . .

The sound of Rose sighing against his lips encouraged Nick to curve his other hand around her slim waist and draw her tightly against him. Letting their kiss deepen, his heartbeat quickened when he felt her respond. This woman, barely more than twenty, enchanted him.

He had tried to keep his distance, but it was torture. Every time Hugh mentioned her name, an image of that afternoon on the clifftop at Runswick Bay popped into his mind. Rose sitting on the sparse grass, making a daisy chain.

He still had it, the daisy chain — well most of it — pressed into the back of his favourite notebook. He expected to say goodbye, never to see Rose again and it would be his only tangible memory of her.

Little did he realise, even had she not come to London, he would never be able to forget Rose. She hovered at the periphery of his consciousness, no matter how hard he tried to banish her.

Nick continued to clutch at the notion he would not marry, would never be so stupid as to fall in love. Before he met Rose, he considered such emotions, nonsensical and frivolous. Despite both his siblings marrying for love — deep, abiding, and unquenchable love, Nick was not interested.

Until Rose.

Now his mind was a chaotic mess. Worldly in many ways, in this Nick was at a loss; unable to distinguish whether his feelings were merely infatuation — which would pass as surely as night follows day — or something more. Rose was the only constant during his recuperation, tending to his every need, mayhap it was gratitude, and he was confusing it with affection.

Even as he thought this, he knew it to be erroneous. Gratitude did not increase your heart rate. Gratitude did not make your chest ache at the thought of not seeing someone. Gratitude certainly did *not* send an embarrassing rush of blood to particular areas of your body, at the most inopportune moments.

While his head persisted in rejecting what his heart had accepted weeks previously, he pushed it all aside and concentrated on kissing Rose.

In her turn, Rose was floored. Since the afternoon on the moor he hadn't shown any romantic interest her, oh, except the night of his brother's arrival when he inadvertently grasped her hand. That, she put down to the excitement of seeing Hugh and Helena. She luxuriated in the kiss for what seemed a lifetime, although it was mere seconds, then remembering where she was, broke away.

"Mr Drum— Nick, you should not… this is not… 'tis your workplace… Hugh and Helena… staff… Lynette, oh dear…" she could hear the words tumbling out of her mouth. They made no sense, but she could not think straight.

They stared at each other, both breathing heavily, eyes slightly glassy. It was evident the kiss affected them more than either might like to admit — yet.

"Oh Nick…" his name whispered off her tongue like an endearment, and it was only by sheer force of will, Nick controlled his urge to repeat that sublime kiss.

"Forgive me, Rose. I have tried to stay away from you, but I do believe you have enslaved me." He grinned, taking her gloved hand, dropping a kiss on her knuckles, before turning it, peeling back the cuff, and dropping another on her wrist. Rose sucked in sharp breath.

"Nicolas Drummond, you are the most audacious man I have ever met. Enslaved you indeed. If I had a fan I daresay I would swat you with it. Enslaved, pah!" Her brusque tone belied by the heart-stopping smile she bestowed on him.

He chuckled, remarking they should probably find Hugh and Helena. "We have been alone too long, and I have no mind to sully your reputation."

"I am from Runswick Bay, well over two hundred miles away. I do not think any here are interested in me or my reputation," she chuckled, as they made their way downstairs to find Hugh and Helena, waiting at the front door engrossed in conversation.

The couple looked up at the sound of footsteps, and as they approached, Helena — easily recognising what had prompted the glowing expressions on the faces of both Nick and Rose — glanced at her husband. His slight nod, tacit acknowledgement her unspoken message was received and understood.

"I beg your pardon for tarrying, Helena. Nick was kind enough to explain those beautiful navigational charts on the walls. I do believe a voyage to the Americas might prove quite the adventure. Mayhap one day..." Rose allowed that to trail off, hoping her artless comments, offered plausible justification for her delay, unaware both Hugh and Helena had their own suspicions as to the true reason for her tardiness.

"It is no matter, Rose. I always enjoy a moment during the day to talk with my wife." Hugh smiled, and the two women said their goodbyes, climbing back into carriage, waving as it rumbled through the huge gates.

CHAPTER 11

$\mathcal{T}$he following evening was the first of several balls Rose was invited to attend. She remained unsure how exactly Helena had managed this in so short a time but was of no mind to question it.

In the week or so since her arrival in London, she had discovered the *ton* were skilful in their machinations, rather like a game of shadows, and far too subtle for her. It was easier simply to enjoy everything.

The Earl and Countess of Wexford were the hosts of this particular ball and, determined to make the best effort she could, towards the end of the afternoon Rose began her preparations. Taking a bath, she washed and dried her hair, and was currently seated in front of the mirror, while Penny styled her locks into something beginning to look quite exotic.

Eschewing the insipid pastels of current fashion, the gown Helena had suggested Rose wear was an eye-catching creation of azure blue. It was trimmed at the hem, neck, and sleeves in a paler hue, and repeated in the broad ribbon around the high waistline.

By some miracle, Penny had fashioned Rose's straight tresses into a mass of curls, fixing them in an intricate pattern around her head. Woven through the silvery blonde coils, a slender ribbon in the same deep blue as the dress, glinted.

Her shoes, matching her gown, were made from soft kid leather, and sported a low heel. Used to wearing flat boots or sandals, Rose had practised for hours in her new slippers, knowing she was quite likely to fall off them if she wasn't careful.

Penny took a step back and pronounced herself satisfied. Rose stood up and turned slowly — her head heavy under the pile of curls.

"Miss Rose, you look beautiful," murmured Penny, clasping her hands against her breast, releasing a sigh of pleasure.

"Only because you are so clever, Penny. Thank you for being patient with me."

"Go on with you, miss." She shooed Rose out of her bedchamber and down the stairs, following with her wrap. At the bottom, Penny draped the vibrant blue shawl around her shoulders and handed her, her reticule. "Enjoy yourself, Miss. You and Lady Helena will be the belles of the ball."

Rose snorted, at the same moment Helena and Hugh came into the hall from the parlour.

"I beg your pardon. Penny was jesting, and I forgot where I was."

Helena grinned and made no comment, the three walking down the steps to the carriage. Wexford House was approximately a mile away, and it was a balmy evening, so they rode with the top down. On arrival, they joined the line of carriages, steadily disgorging their passengers.

They reached the front of the queue and were welcomed by a smart footman. The ladies, after being handed a small card, sought the retiring room to divest themselves of their wraps, and check they still looked presentable. Upon returning to the vast entrance hall, Rose squeaked with surprise when she heard her name boom out over the throng.

Spinning around she gaped at Helena. "Why did he do that?" Her stentorian whisper heard by the liveried steward who announced her, his lips twitching with amusement while attempting to maintain his impassive demeanour.

"Everyone is announced, my dear," Helena replied, taking her by the arm, as they greeted their host and hostess. The Countess of Wexford, a lovely young lady, obviously knew Helena well, and they chatted for a few moments. Helena introduced Rose, who charmed her hostess with her perfectly executed curtsy, shy smile, and heartfelt thank you.

"I am delighted you were able to join us this evening, Miss Archer. I promise to hunt you down later to hear all about your village and the shipwreck. Poor Nick, it must have been a terrible ordeal."

"He recovered quickly, Marianne," Helena interposed. "Thankfully, with his healthy constitution, and the excellent treatment dispensed by Dr Archer, and Rose here, he managed to avoid serious complications. He returned to work as though naught occurred."

Lady Wexford grinned a most un-countess-like grin, the two friends agreeing to see each other during the evening. One could not hold up the line, and Helena ushered Rose to where Hugh had secured some seats, in a quiet corner near the terrace.

"Once the dancing begins, gentleman will wish to add their name to your card," Helena said, indicating the miniature, decorative folded card, which Rose had slipped on her wrist, for want of somewhere else to put it.

Rose, who hadn't even looked at it, raised surprised

eyebrows. *"That's* what this is? I thought it was the menu for the meal." Her cheeks blossomed with colour, realising how gauche she sounded. "Oh my, this is a bad idea Lad— Helena. I have been to dances, but they were in a village hall, not a stately residence. What if I make a complete cake of myself?"

"I very much doubt that will happen," chastised Helena gently, ignoring Rose's curled lip. "All you need do is smile and enjoy yourself. No one is here to trip you up, literally or figuratively. 'Tis a ball not an execution." Amused at Rose's expression, which indicated the latter might be more preferable.

Adroit at putting people at their ease, Helena turned the conversation to other matters, greeting people as they passed, introducing several to Rose. All seemed genuinely interested to meet this poised young woman from so far north of the city who had been instrumental in saving the life of Hugh's brother.

The evening wore on. Sometime later, after a little food and a glass or two of Negus, the dancing began. Strains of music filtered through to where their little group was sitting, and Rose — who loved music but had little occasion to hear it — unconsciously started to sway.

Spotting this, Helena grasped her hand and hauled her onto her feet. "Come along Rose, time for some fun." Leaving their glasses and plates on the little table, the three made their way along a wide corridor towards the ballroom. Ahead, a set of etched glass doors, thrown open for the evening, the glow from innumerable candles creating a golden pathway, invited guests to discover the delights within.

≈

Rose stepped into the ballroom, her senses assaulted by a confusion of colour, light, sounds and scents, so alien to her she felt almost frightened. She shouldn't be here, this was not her world, and she took step backwards. Helena was there, already surmising how the young woman probably felt.

"'Tis rather overwhelming isn't it?" she murmured into Rose's ear. Rose shot her a quick glance, and nodded slowly, insecurities rising like bile in her throat. This was too much.

"Please do not think I am ungrateful, my lady, but this..." she nodded at the scene in front of them, "...this is so far outside of my ken. I will embarrass you and Mr Drummond." She pressed her lips together to stop them from trembling and fisted her hands.

"I am sure you will do no such thing, Rose. Try to relax, they won't eat you."

Rose did not share Helena's confidence.

"Hugh," Helena turned to her husband, "please escort Rose to the dance floor? One set with you and she shall not want for a partner the rest of the evening." Grinning at her tall, handsome husband, who smiled back, tucked Rose's hand through his arm, and headed for the centre of the ballroom.

Without giving Rose time to panic, Hugh whirled her around the floor with expertise, glad to note she was beginning to enjoy herself. Rose was not wholly unfamiliar with the popular dances. Just because she lived in a quiet village didn't mean she didn't attend a local ball, infrequent thought they might be.

Blessed with a natural rhythm, Rose moved with a grace admired by more than one watching from the sidelines. Helena was correct, as the music died away, a crowd of gentleman surrounded her, eager for the next set, and in seconds her card was full.

Gratified by the attention, there was only one man with

whom Rose wanted to dance, and he had yet to arrive. Despite the kiss the previous day, she knew Nick was not attracted to her — well not for more than a brief dalliance. She had nothing to offer a man like him, a notion reinforced when she saw all the other beautiful women floating around, with their fashionable clothes, cultured voices, and flawless manners.

She was naught but a country doctor's daughter, probably quite fun for a quick tumble but not forever material. Her heart constricted. Once more she questioned why she had agreed to come to London. She was only making things worse. The more she saw him, the deeper she fell, and he had made it plain — marriage did not interest him. Moreover, even though he made no mention of her lowly status, marriage to a nobody was never going to be a consideration.

Determined not to let this spoil her evening, Rose plastered a smile on her face, and danced, and talked, and smiled, and laughed, until she was exhausted. It was very late, the ball almost over when she saw him. He was talking to someone who was half-hidden in the shadows.

Like Hugh, Nick was normally quite solemn, but tonight he seemed full of cheer. His smile wide and his eyes sparkled — clear to Rose as though he was right next to her, not the other side of the room. She wondered who it was caused such joy, her heart cracking in the knowledge it wasn't her.

Her current partner, Lord Archibald, was so intent on demonstrating his proficient footwork, he forgot how petite his partner was, almost throwing Rose off the dance floor in his enthusiasm. Rose felt queasy. Too many couples all swirling together, made it seem as though the room was spinning, and Lord Archibald was pirouetting her around too fast.

The inevitable happened, and she missed her footing, bumping into another couple, certain she uttered an unrefined squawk when she did so. Mortified, she grabbed her partner's arm, the portly viscount catching her before she made a ninny of herself. Regaining her footing, Rose lifted her head. Her gaze collided with Nick's, who had doubtless turned to see what on earth all the commotion was about.

Traitorous heat flushed up her cheeks, when Nick's eyes widened, his jaw dropping, recognising the woman at the centre of the chaos. He had never seen her dressed up, nor seen her shimmering hair in anything other than a neat plait or slightly awry bun, now piled on her head in *the* most ornate style.

Rose wondered what he was thinking but had no time to ponder this because at that moment, the dance came to an end. She thanked her partner, who apologised for his vigorous performance. Rose curtsied politely, assuring him it was of no matter and was about to rejoin Helena, when Nick was there, taking her hand.

"Please do me the honour of this dance, Rose?" he cajoled.

She was flustered; her cheeks hot from her embarrassment, and the exertion. Her feet were sore, the new shoes rubbing, but they could have fallen off before she would deny Nick. Smiling shyly, she let him lead her back onto the polished wooden floor where she lost herself in imagination as he swept her effortlessly around the room.

Nick could not believe this was Rose. She was dazzling, her fairy-like features enchanting him all over again. Tonight, under glimmering candlelight, she possessed an ethereal quality, and he was seized by an irrational fear she might vanish into thin air.

Eyes lowered, Rose let him control the dance, which allowed him to study her classical features unobserved. The lustrous sheen of her lightly tanned skin sprinkled liberally with freckles. Hidden from his view, her vivid blue eyes framed by dark lashes — such a contrast to her white-gold hair — currently a smudged curve on each cheekbone. A pert little nose, he suppressed an urgent desire to kiss.

Her gown, which was surely the same shade as her eyes, clung and flowed as though a silken scarf, whispering when she moved. An image of him peeling the layers away popped into his mind, causing his breathing to quicken. He shook his head, but the picture refused to dissipate, and its tenacity floored him.

What *was* it about Rose? She confused the very life out of him. He had no interest in courtship, this… whatever it was he had with Rose… was naught but a fleeting interlude, a harmless romance. Staring down at her, their kiss of the previous day teasing at his mind, the idea this vivacious woman might walk out of his life at the end of her visit, came like a punch to his stomach.

No, he shook his head again. No, this was not how it was supposed to be. She was just a dalliance, an interesting diversion, he did not need a woman in his life, it was too complicated.

Too late, his heart replied, it is much too late.

CHAPTER 12

The dance came to an end, the music faded, and Nick, thanking Rose, escorted her from the ball-room. Unable to spot Hugh or Helena, Rose headed back to their seats.

Rather than listen to his head which informed him, in no uncertain terms, to walk away, Nick chose to trust his heart which could not let Rose go and followed close behind. The corridor was dimly lit, shady alcoves offering secret seclusion.

Without pausing to consider his actions, Nick caught her hand, slipping into one.

"Nick," Rose hissed in undertones. "What are you doing?"

"This." He kissed her.

Rose stood motionless for one, two, three, four seconds, stunned at his temerity, but the potency of his lips was too powerful to resist, and she succumbed. Her arms went around him, fingers splaying over the fine wool of his jacket.

Innocent in the ways of passion she may have been, but Rose was not naïve. Nick's desire for her was blatant, and she took wicked delight in the knowledge it was she who caused this reaction.

His lips moved over hers, teasing, tempting, tantalising. *This must be what it feels like to drown,* she thought distractedly, her legs buckling. She didn't fall. Nick held her close, his embrace tightening, his lips demanding more, and she opened to him, their tongues, touching, tangling, tasting.

A voice along the corridor pierced their senses, and Nick lifted his head, his breathing erratic, his heart racing. Rose began to panic. This was so bad, so very bad. Helena would send her home and rightly so.

"Hush." He placed a finger on her lips as he peered into the gloom. Seeing no one, he stepped away, and raked his eyes over her diminutive shape. *That dress, oh God that dress.* "The coast is clear. Come, let us find my brother, and Helena."

"Wait," Rose whispered, fiercely. "Nick, as much as I... because I do, I really do... that was...oh never mind." She took a steadying breath, her mind in uproar. "What of Helena? If she heard of this, she would think me abusing her hospitality. I like her, Nick. I like Hugh. I do not want to disappoint them by behaving in an unacceptable manner."

Rather than take umbrage, which she expected Nick to do, he smiled; a slow sweet smile that all but undid her resolve. "I do believe you might discover my sister-in-law to be well versed in matters of the heart. She would be more inclined to toss me in the Thames if she thought my actions exceeded the bounds of propriety. 'Twould be me she would blame, not you."

"Well that is not quite fair is it?" Rose retorted. "I wanted that k—" she clamped her mouth shut. *Honestly Rose, learn when to stop talking... wait did he say 'heart'?*

"Not as much as I did," he admitted, quietly, and Rose saw heat steal up his cheeks even in the low light of the hall.

"Nevertheless, I initiated it, and in a dark corridor no less. I promise not to place you in so compromising a situation again."

"How sad." The words tripped off her tongue before she could stop them. Cursing her recalcitrant brain, Rose slipped past him and, head held high, hurried along to where Hugh and Helena were sitting, talking with Marianne.

As soon as the countess saw Rose, she pounced, pleading with her to tell the tale of the shipwreck. Nick came to stand behind Hugh and, at her questioning glance, nodded his head.

Rose told her tale, narrating it as would a master storyteller, weaving it through with just the right amount of drama and tension. Not that any was needed, the truth was harrowing enough. Nick was unaware Rose had witnessed the actual wrecking of *The Diligence*.

Along with every single villager, she had stood on the shore, in fear and trepidation for the lives of those on board. She had seen the small boat drop down the side of the sloop, the crew battling the waves to reach safety. She had watched as the mast plunged onto the deck, and waited until the lifeboat rowed into the bay, carrying two extra sailors, both soaked, one unconscious.

They heard the tremor in her voice when she skimmed over the extent of Nick's injuries. She had no intention of upsetting the sensibilities of her listeners by describing the gruesome nature of them, but did confirm that for several days, Nick hovered between life and death.

What Rose did not realise as she talked was how much she revealed to Nick regarding her attentiveness. While she held her audience spellbound, his mind drifted back to those early days after the wreck. He recalled thinking he was dreaming and she a fairy, his mouth twitching at such nonsense.

Her lilting voice with its soft Yorkshire burr, the only sound able to soothe him into slumber. Her eyes holding his, while Joseph scoured his wounds for the source of infection.

The long hours she had watched over him, talking to him, refusing to let him give up when the pain became excruciating, when to accept death seemed easier.

Her cool fingers on his fevered flesh as she sought to reduce his temperature with damp cloths and medicinal ointments.

He listened, he heard, and before she concluded her account, he finally acknowledged.

He was hopelessly, irrevocably, in love with Rose Archer.

In the days following the ball, Rose was not given any time to ponder those precious moments with Nick. On Sunday, they went to the British Museum, wandering its lofty halls, discussing the many displays.

Rose was fascinated. She could not believe there was so much history in one place, astonished by the marvels therein, and absolutely riveted by the Parthenon exhibit. Rose studied everything for so long, Helena began to wonder whether she would be able to persuade her to leave at all.

Eventually they managed, assuring their guest there was plenty of time to return, and visit those rooms she had missed or wanted to see again.

From the beginning of the next week, Rose accompanied Helena to Sanctuary House. Used to long, hard days of toil, Rose found her duties less onerous than those at home, quickly finding her place among the staff. The routine was familiar, and she relished being able to help, especially in the small clinic at the rear of the refuge.

Doctor Callard was an ex-military doctor, and very experienced. Coincidentally, he knew Rose's father — both had trained at St Bart's and were stationed with neighbouring units during the early years of the recent wars, often joining forces to tend the wounded.

Rose loved to listen to his tales of her father, for although a loving parent, he rarely spoke of his time on the Peninsula, deeming it too harrowing for his daughter to comprehend.

There was something about Rose, which engendered trust. Almost the minute any patient met her, they became less distressed. Her tranquil personality and unhurried gestures brought an atmosphere of calm to even the most agitated situation.

Before long, Dr Callard was relying on her as more than an assistant. Rose was eminently capable of treating minor injuries or complaints, freeing him up for any serious cases. He also had his own practice to attend every day, and it was a relief to leave his clinic in safe hands.

The residents of Sanctuary House were not the only people to avail themselves of the services offered by the clinic. The locals frequented it also, Dr Callard being well respected in the neighbourhood. As a result, Rose came to know many of the people who lived in the streets surrounding the refuge, the children especially knew she was a soft touch.

Barely a day went by without one of them coming to see her for a sore finger or banged knee, more because she also gave them a treat than because their little hurts warranted any medical attention. Timmy and Roland took it upon themselves to act as sentries; ensuring Rose wasn't overwhelmed with time wasters, however endearing they might be.

Her days were busy and long, and at the end of each one, she fell into bed, so tired she could barely think, offering the added bonus of leaving no time to brood over Nick. She saw him occasionally at family gatherings, and the odd ball, but not once did he ask her to dance.

Neither did he attempt to repeat his actions of the night of the Wexford Ball — much to her frustration, the thrill of anticipation, duly doused. In truth, he treated her with utmost respect and cordiality, but nothing more. His reserve at odds with his words of that magical evening.

Rose, who dared to hope the indefinable something they seemed to share had begun to flourish, was humiliated, acknowledging she must have been mistaken. Presumably, his ardent words and intoxicating kiss, were the result of too much wine.

Nick's odd behaviour puzzled and saddened Rose, causing her to withdraw into herself. Her usual verve was lacking and, although politeness itself, she no longer initiated conversation, and found it an effort to maintain her bright smile.

Helena, as ever, had noticed the change. It was troubling but, for the moment, she decided not to interfere, hoping it would resolve itself. To Helena, it was clear as the stars in the night sky that Rose and Nick cared deeply for each other; their secret glances and awkward formality merely compounding her belief. The shift, the change, the acceptance, had to come from Nick.

Until he met Rose, Helena knew Nick had no interest in commitments of any kind, other than the shipyard. He was amenable to escorting a lady to a ball, if he had to, but that was it. In fact, as she mused, Helena realised the only woman she ever had seen him dance with, was Rose. For some inexplicable reason, he had taken a step back, and Helena was aware of how deeply his apparent rejection confused and hurt Rose.

Usually one to jump in where angels fear to tread, this time Helena was unwilling. Rose was her guest, one who would return to her home miles away in the not too distant future. If Nick's affections were superficial, she did not want to risk causing Rose any more anguish. The distance between Rose and Nick grew, and it seemed as though they were destined to remain forever apart.

~

The days slid into weeks and soon Rose realised it was early August and she had been in London more than a month. To her delight, the miserable weather the summer had so far flung at them, finally relented, giving way to the warm sunny days as befitted the season.

As often as she was able, Rose sought the open spaces of the parks, enjoying an interlude sitting on bench and watching the world go by, or finding a quiet place by one of the watercourses. If she took her constitutional in the afternoon, Helena joined her, but Rose liked to be up with the dawn, when it was coolest and as the park was scarcely five minutes' walk from Stanton House, saw no reason why she could not go unaccompanied.

There was no danger.

~

Very early, one mild Wednesday morning, Rose, awake since the predawn chorus, decided she had stayed in bed long enough and would go for a walk. Following a cursory wash, she shrugged into a pastel pink, fine lawn day dress, and a pair of sensible shoes. Slinging a creamy wrap around her shoulders, she crept down the stairs.

She was opening the front door when she heard footsteps and spun on her heel, guiltily, to see Mr Saunders, the Drummond's butler, coming through from the domestic quarters. Blushing, although unsure why, Rose explained she was going to the park.

"I do wish you would let me ask Penny to come with you, Miss Archer…" he started to suggest, as he did every day.

Rose placed her hand on his arm saying, her tones practical. "Penny has enough to do without waiting on me hand and foot, sir. I enjoy a promenade every morning, and you know I always return before anyone else realises I am gone. I admit I cherish these few moments on my own. I am unused to a constant companion."

"'Tis not my business to prevent you, miss, and please call me Saunders." He smiled genially, and Rose grinned back. It had become their daily repartee. He wanted to send someone with her, she refused. She called him sir, he begged her not to, and he suspected Rose continued to do so because she enjoyed the banter.

Thanking him for his discretion, Rose descended the steps to the pavement.

The butler watched her stroll down the street to the corner, a philosophical smile curving his mouth. Within two days of her arrival, Rose knew all the staff by name, not to mention the three cats and four horses.

Her sunny demeanour, and ability to put everyone at ease, had endeared her to all at Stanton House.

Of late she seemed subdued, and Mr Saunders wondered whether she was homesick. He kept an eye on her until she was out of sight, then turned his attention to the chores of the day, all but forgetting their conversation.

CHAPTER 13

*R*ose walked briskly along the path, the peace of the early morning a balm to her unsettled mind. Her thoughts, inevitably, strayed to Nick, the cause of her inner turbulence.

She was aggrieved a mere man had the power to turn her sensible brain into squashed cabbage. What had she said to Adrian? I will not be owned. She half-smiled, acknowledging that while Nick may not have paid any price for her, he had unwittingly gained possession of her heart and soul, and they would always be his.

"*Bah!*" Rose stomped along to the park entrance, passing through the tall, ornate iron gates, before heading towards the small pond in the centre. Once there, she found her favourite spot — a huge copper beech tree, its broad, leafy canopy offering a quiet nook off the main pathway.

Sinking to the ground, she leant against the trunk, stretched out her legs and watched the ducks foraging in the reeds.

. . .

Time slipped by, the sun rose, turning the sky from soft grey, through iridescent pink to bright blue, a smattering of white fluffy clouds, lifting the tired dullness of the trees and shrubs to a kaleidoscope of verdant hues.

Rose, lost in contemplation, missed this time-honoured metamorphosis, but her reverie was shattered by a startled yell not far from where she was sitting.

Scrambling to her feet, Rose hurried from her hiding place, to see two small children a little distance ahead on the main path. One of them lay motionless on the gravel, the other was dancing up and down and shouting, presumably hoping this would revive the one lying so still.

Without pausing to consider anything — at all, Rose was by their side in an instant. Falling to her knees she checked the unconscious child, a little boy perhaps six or seven years old, carefully.

His face was discoloured and grazed; his bottom lip bleeding where his teeth smashed against it, and his knee, badly scuffed. Concerned these two seemed to be without an adult, or older sibling, Rose tried to extract information from the second little boy, who looked two or three years older than his companion. The pair were alike enough to make Rose think they were brothers.

"We was jus' playin' on the 'ill like allus," he piped, thumbing over his shoulder to the slight rise. The land around this part of the city was flatter than a tabletop, prompting the park's architects to add man-made hillocks throughout, providing a far more interesting, and country-side-like vista, with several places for children to roll hoops — or themselves.

Rose frowned. The gentle undulations did not seem high enough for a child to hurt himself.

"How did he fall?" she quizzed, using her handkerchief to dab at the unconscious boy's bloody cheek.

"'E kinda tripped, tried ter stop 'isself, but it were like 'is feet were going too fast, and 'e went down like a sack o' taters. I fink he hit 'is 'ead." Despite his apparent nonchalance, Rose spotted his trembling mouth, and sought to comfort the older child.

"It looks as though he hit his face and knee on the path and probably bit his lip. I am sure he is not badly hurt, but we need to get him home, or..." she paused. To remove an unknown child to Helena's home was a liberty she did not presume to take, but where else was there? "Where are your parents?"

The lad cocked his head. "There's only me Da. Me Ma died when 'e were born," nodding at his brother. "'E's probably already gorn. 'E works dahn the docks."

Rose felt an unexpected kinship with this little boy, remembering only too clearly what is was like to lose your mother. "First things first. Where do you live?" The boy pointed to the opposite end of the park.

"That way."

Which didn't really help.

"Come along then, let us get... what is your brother's name?"

"Andy, and I'm Mark," relaxing a little now this kind lady assumed responsibility. It was tiring being in charge when you were not quite nine years old. "Are you sure, miss? Don't mean ter trouble yer."

"Of course." Not certain she had the strength to carry a small child what could be miles, Rose was not about to reveal that to Mark. "I think Lady Helena might lend us the coach to go to Sanctuary House," she mused. "The doctor is on duty today."

Mark looked panicked. "Lady? Doctor? We can't afford the doc, miss."

"Do not fret, Mark. There is no charge, and Andy must be

examined properly." While she talked, Rose was checking the unconscious boy's vital signs. Andy's pulse was steady and his breathing normal, but underneath the bruising and grazes, his face had a greyish tinge.

He felt a little clammy, but the damp ground could account for some of that. Rose understood how serious head injuries were, even those which seemed innocuous, and she did not have enough knowledge to treat so small a child. He needed professional help, and quickly.

Decision made, she lifted Andy gently and, cradling him against her, retraced her steps to Stanton House, hoping she wouldn't cause upset with her impetuosity. Mark followed on her heels, wide-eyed when she led the way to the quiet street where the Drummonds lived.

Turning the corner onto Bedford Street, she heard footsteps behind her. A voice called her name. Shocked, she glanced over her shoulder to see Nick striding towards her. Despite her bewilderment over his behaviour, she was inordinately pleased to see him, a relieved smile lighting her face.

"Nick! You have no idea how glad I am to see you. Andy here has taken a nasty tumble. He has not regained his senses, and I must get him to Sanctuary House. Dr Callard is on duty today. I know 'tis early, but do you think I might be permitted to borrow your brother's carriage?"

Assessing the situation instantly, Nick assured her it would be no problem, given the circumstances, lifting the boy from her. Rose sagged, no longer bearing the weight of the child.

"Thank you, I was beginning to worry I might drop him." Chagrin lacing her tones

Nick chuckled. "I cannot imagine what prompted you to carry him. Surely coming for help would have been easier?"

"I was concerned if I left him with Mark, he might come around and the two would run off. Head wounds can be tricky, and he is so young. This was my only option." She shrugged. "I am quite strong you know."

"I know," he placated, "but even the lightest of burdens become heavy if carried for too long."

Rose glanced up at him sharply. His face was bland, but she had the oddest notion he was not simply referring to the child. Unable to fathom his meaning at this precise moment, she pushed it aside, and running up the steps to Stanton House, rapped on the knocker.

Mr Saunders opened the door, his professionalism coming to the fore when he beheld the unexpected sight. Master Nick — a scruffy, bruised, and bloodied child in his arms; Miss Rose — looking somewhat dishevelled, with another little street urchin clinging to her skirts.

"Good morning Mr Drummond, Miss Archer…"

"Saunders, as you can see, we have a little problem. Is my brother breakfasting?" Nick knew Hugh was an early riser.

"He is the dining room, sir."

"Good. Please will you ask John to ready the carriage with all haste. We need to get this young chap to the doctor."

Mr Saunders nodded and rushed off to do as he was bidden, while Nick, without relinquishing Andy, walked into the dining room. Hugh, finishing his breakfast, looked up at his entry, his jaw dropping.

"Good morning Nick. Do you often bring children as gifts, or is this by way of an exception?" Eyebrows arched.

"Oh, is this not all the rage?" Nick quipped with a grin. "Rose found the boy in the park. He has not woken, and she believes a visit to Dr Callard is warranted. Are you almost ready? We could drop them at Sanctuary House, go on to Trentams, then send the carriage back for Helena."

Hugh saw the sense in Nick's suggestion and, placing the napkin neatly by his plate, said he would be back momentarily.

Nick returned to where Rose was talking to Mark, who was agog at the sheer size of the hall.

"My 'ole 'ouse would fit in 'ere," he muttered, eyes like saucers. "'Tis so clean I dare not move."

Rose grinned, moving along the chaise so Nick could sit down.

"Hugh will come with us, and then once we have deposited you, and these two scamps at Sanctuary House, we can go on to the shipyard."

"I am concerned Andy has not stirred. 'Tis some time since his fall." Rose searched the boy's pale face for any sign he was coming out of his stupor.

"His breathing is steady, as is his heartbeat," Nick said. "Try not to worry, sweetheart, nothing you can do until the doc sees him." The endearment slipped out.

Rose narrowed her eyes at Nick through dark lashes. He was leaning against the back of the chair, Andy tucked comfortably against him, nothing to indicate he realised his mistake, nothing save a very slight reddening of his cheeks.

Nick caught her look, saw her nose crinkle in the most adorable confusion, and cursed his wayward tongue. As was becoming a habit, he had distanced himself from Rose after the Wexfords' Ball, but he remained wholly aware of her every move at any gathering they both attended.

He watched her covertly, refusing to bow to impulse and ask her to dance, or accompany him on a walk, for fear he would never let her go. His own bewilderment mirrored hers, and he was at a loss.

He dared not open his heart, knowing she would be leaving soon, yet he was never without her. Every time he closed his eyes, her face floated into his mind, teasing, taunting. Neither could he expect her to keep forgiving his incautious dismissal of her emotions.

Perhaps, at a subconscious level, he was forcing the issue. If Rose was the one to give up on him, he would not be guilty of hurting her. A thought he knew to be erroneous the minute it popped into his head. He had already hurt her, the awareness causing him no little pain.

He loved her, that part was quite simple, but he would prefer not to admit it, and let Rose go than complicate life for her. Ignoring the possibility, Rose might quite like him to complicate her life. *How on earth did one navigate through this mire?* he pondered. *It was more difficult than steering a ship through treacherous waters.*

Hugh appeared, saying the carriage would be at the front forthwith, effectively interrupting Nick's introspection. *A good thing too*, he admonished himself, standing up, careful not to bump Andy. He followed Rose down the steps, climbing into the coach, while Mark hopped up with the agility of a young goat, and they trundled off.

On so lovely a morning, the hood was down. Mark took it upon himself to point out to Rose anything he deemed interesting as they rode along. Rose was amused, and listened with apparent fascination, while Nick and Hugh sat back content to let the boy chatter.

"Yer not from round 'ere are yer, miss?" he demanded, after Rose had asked him a question.

"No, I live many miles north. A small village by the sea called Runswick Bay."

At this, Mark fired questions at her, the remainder of the ride and Rose was grateful for the distraction. Andy, despite the occasional groan and fluttering of his eyelids, had not come around, troubling her. It was well over half an hour since she heard Mark's cries, and long periods of insensibility were cause for grave concern, especially in young children.

The journey did not take long, their haste aided by reasonably empty streets. Nearing the refuge, Rose asked John to take them around to the clinic entrance at the rear. Uncertain whether Dr Callard would be here so early, she was relieved when she spotted the door standing ajar, and the little wooden shingle hanging above.

Hugh jumped down, hurrying to find Dr Callard, while Rose thanked the Drummond's genial driver, before guiding Nick down the steps. Mark followed, sticking close to Rose. Doctors frightened him; the last time they needed one, his mother died, and he did not trust them.

The three walked into the cool clinic and while they waited, Rose talked to Andy. He stirred a little, moving restlessly in Nick's arms, but didn't open his eyes. Studying his face, she discerned the lacerations were minor, but a large lump was forming at his temple. He would have a very sore head when he woke.

Dr Callard came through the door, Hugh in his wake, the cheery medic grinning when he saw Rose, and Nick with his bundle.

"Good morning, Miss Archer, Mr Drummond. Well, bless my soul, what do we have here?" Running his experienced eyes over the child, before glancing across at Rose over his spectacles. "Not content with the patients we have, eh? You are now collecting them from further afield." Rose blushed, as he continued. "Hugh tells me you found this child in a park?"

Diffidently, Rose elaborated. "I didn't know where else to take him, Dr Callard, and he has yet to open his eyes," she concluded.

"Quite right too." The doctor asked Nick to lay Andy on

one of the two long tables standing in the centre of the room. He began a meticulous examination, ensuring there were no broken or sprained limbs.

Removing the gravel and dirt from the child's knee, he cleaned and bandaged it, before gently washing the grazes on Andy's pale face. As he was rinsing his cloth for the last time, Andy finally, and to everyone's relief, regained his senses.

He stared up at the stranger, his frightened expression prompting Mark to step forward, and lean over the bed.

"I'm 'ere, Andy. Don'tcha be worryin', this ere is the doc. You were brought 'ere in a carriage, no less, cause yer fell over."

"Hello Andy, my name is Rose. You hit your head but Doctor Callard is making it better for you. Does it hurt?" Rose held his hand, her soft tones cutting through his fear. Silvery hair coming undone from its hasty plait, fell around her elfin face. Her warm smile and sparkling blue eyes made Andy blink several times.

"'Tis the queen of the fairies, Mark," the boy whispered, his eyes and mouth becoming round in wonder.

Nick hid a smile, memories rising up, as Rose chuckled.

"I am no fairy queen, Andy. Do you remember tripping over?"

Eyes fixed on hers, Andy screwed up his face in concentration. "I was runnin' real fast, fastest I've ever run, I reckon. I could 'ear Mark, he were be'ind me. I turned around to see how close he was, and I fink me foot slipped on a rock or a twig. It felt like I was flyin' fer a minute, and everyfing seemed very slow." He shrugged. "That's it, now I'm 'ere."

Rose glanced at Dr Callard, who was listening attentively. "Would you mind staying here with me for a little while young man?" he asked Andy, his tones persuasive. "Mark may stay too. I want to make sure you do not become sick. Sometimes when we bang our heads as hard as you did, we feel dizzy and we vomit. You do not want to be on your own if that happens, do you?"

He smiled benignly at Andy who was feeling scared and miserable.

"I want me Da." His reedy voice lifted in a mournful wail. Rose frowned, glancing at Nick, both aware it was well past the hour when dockworkers started their busy day.

"You said he would be at work, Mark." Rose looked down at the little boy standing next to her. Mark nodded. "I do not think it is a good idea to disturb him." She knew that if the man left his shift, he would likely lose his job.

"Would you agree to Hugh and I swinging by on the way to Trentams?" Nick asked.

Mark gaped at him. "You'd do that fer us, mister?"

"Of course. We can assure him Andy here, is in safe hands and he can come the minute his shift is over." At Nick's pledge, Rose looked at him, over Mark's head, unable to prevent the love she felt for him shining in her beautiful eyes. His heart thudded, and he responded with his slow, sweet smile.

And just like that — in a single moment, in the most inopportune of circumstances — Nick opened his heart.

CHAPTER 14

"*T*hat's mighty kind of yer, sir. He has enough to worry abaht." The adult phrase sounded odd coming from a child's mouth, prompting Nick to drag his gaze away from Rose, and ruffle Mark's hair.

"Do not fret, young Mark. I will explain everything."

While Mark was telling Nick, their father was called Mr Fletcher, and at which dock he worked, Rose turned her attention to Andy who was snivelling. "Andy, your father will be very busy, and it would be unfair to interrupt his day. How about Mark and I stay with you, I know lots of wonderful stories to cheer you?"

Andy thought about this, then nodded, albeit reluctantly.

"Good lad. Now let's find you a nice blanket and if you will allow me, I might seek some tasty treats from the kitchens." Unable to quash a subdued growl from her stomach, making the others laugh, and reminding Rose, she had missed breakfast.

"Rose, my dear, you have not eaten this morning?" Hugh asked.

She shook her head. "There was no time. Hopefully, they

will not mind if I rustle something up in the kitchen. 'Tis no matter, I will organise something presently."

"Are you sure? I could…" Nick interjected.

Rose laughed merrily, inexplicably light of heart. "You could what? Cook some food? Go on with you, Mr Drummond, I will manage. I do not wish to interfere with your day any more than I already have. Thank you, thank you both so very much," she smiled at the two gentlemen.

"I shall call for you on the way home," Nick said, his expression daring her to decline. Something Rose had no intention of doing.

Dipping a curtsy, she replied, "I look forward to it." Her cheeks blooming a becoming pink.

Watching their interaction, Hugh grinned and stored it away to tell his wife later. Helena would be delighted. All he said was. "I am glad we were able to help. Nick, we must make haste, we have much to accomplish today, and we should tell the lad's father." Bowing to Rose and nodding to Dr Callard, while flipping the two boys a coin, he strode out into the sunshine.

Nick followed but when he passed Rose, he caught her hand and squeezed her fingers. Their eyes met, a silent message flickering between them. Rose inclined her head, returning the gesture, then he was gone.

Rose remained motionless, her head in a ferment. Without either saying a word, that something had shifted between them was unequivocal, a barrier, invisible to all but Nick and her, shattered.

Not naive enough to presume all would suddenly be perfect — she was not prepared to let his peculiar behaviour go unchallenged — Rose felt a weight lifting, a darkness banished, and her lips curved in a secret smile.

"Thank you Rose, you did the right thing. Goodness knows what would happen if this turned out to be a concussion. He might become seriously ill." The doctor's words bringing her back to the matter at hand, and she blushed.

"I never thought. He needed help. I was not far from home and, thankfully, Nick happened upon us, on his way to meet Hugh and... oh no, Lady Helena. Heavens, I hope Hugh apprised her of the situation. I cannot think he would not do so, but she will not know the outcome, and might worry. Should I...?" Rose began pacing.

Dr Callard stuck his head through another door and hollered along the quiet corridor. Moments later, Timmy and Roland appeared, both munching on fresh bread rolls, mouths dropping open when they saw Rose.

"'Ello, miss. Nice ter se yer," they chorused. She greeted them politely, executing a low curtsy, making them chortle with glee.

"Right my lads, I have an errand for you." The doctor, scribbling a note in his execrable hand, interrupted their mirth.

The boys stood to attention.

"Please go to Stanton House and ask that this note be given to Lady Helena with alacrity." Timmy gaped at this last word. Doctor Callard grinned, "Speedily," he clarified.

Right you are sir, miss," Timmy bowed, while Roland tipped his cap, and the two dashed away.

Rose moved one of the chairs to the side of the table and, taking Andy's hand, began talking to him about all manner of things, nothing of any import, just enough to stop him going to sleep.

She knew in cases of head injuries it was important to keep the patient awake as long as possible and if they did doze off, to rouse them at regular intervals. Mark pulled up another chair, to sit alongside, listening to tales of Runswick Bay, and the moors, and her friends.

Andy was mesmerised by this pretty lady whom he

continued to believe was a fairy queen. In fact, except for the fact his head ached like the dickens, he was not entirely convinced he wasn't fast asleep in his bed and this was all a dream.

~

While Rose held Andy and Mark spellbound with her stories, Timmy and Roland arrived at Stanton House. At almost the same moment, John, after dropping his two passengers at Trentams, also returned, driving the carriage into the mews at the rear of the residence.

Lady Helena, informed of the incident by her husband, had hurried through her morning routine, intent on following the party to Sanctuary House. On the verge of requesting the second carriage be readied, she was fore-stalled by two things, the first being a loud rap on the front door. Mr Saunders opened it and Helena, crossing the hall, was surprised to see Timmy and Roland on the doorstep.

"Goodness, Timmy. What are you doing here so early? Good morning Roland." She smiled a greeting at the youths.

"Doc Callard asked us to bring this." Timmy handed over the note, which was now rather crumpled. Helena smoothed it out and tried to read the doctor's script. Squinting, and twisting the sheet this way and that, she even turned it upside down thinking she must be reading it the wrong way up. Nothing helped.

"Timmy. Is this to do with Miss Rose?" She waving the note, distractedly.

"Prob'ly. She's at the 'Ouse wiv two little boys. One of 'em 'urt 'isself, I reckon."

"Mr Hugh told me as much. Do you know whether the little boy is badly hurt?" Helena asked, not really expecting them to answer either way, she just needed to ask.

"He was awake afore we left, bit bashed up, but he were talking, so I s'pect he's all right," Timmy replied, unconcernedly.

"I wonder how Miss Rose became involved in that?" Hugh had told her nothing more than Rose and Nick came in with an unconscious child.

"I dunno me lady, but she came over all flustered when she realised you might be worried."

"I am sure she would not intend to cause upset. Let us organise the carriage and discover what has been going on."

Then, and fortuitously, the second thing happened. Barnaby appeared at Helena's elbow to inform her, John had returned and was at her immediate disposal, negating the need to prepare the second carriage.

Before setting off, Helena pressed Timmy and Roland into refreshments. Always hungry, the two lads fell on the poached eggs and fresh toast greedily, thanking her profusely after mopping up every last morsel. Soon, the three were rattling along the bustling streets. Timmy and Roland chattered nineteen to the dozen about all and sundry, and almost before they knew it, the carriage rolled to stop outside Sanctuary House.

Helena thanked John and hurried up the steps into the cool quiet of the refuge; Timmy and Roland scurried off to begin whatever errands they were fulfilling that day. Mrs Parry, ensconced in her office, going through a mound of paperwork, glanced up when Helena stuck her head around the door.

"Lady Helena, good morning. We did not expect you today. Is something amiss?"

"Not amiss so much as unanticipated." Helena stepped right inside the office to tell her friend what had occurred a few hours earlier.

"So, Miss Archer is here in the clinic?" Mrs Parry's

habitual composure slipped a little, with the knowledge this unfolded under her watch, and no one had bothered to notify her. There was a reason she expected to know who was on the refuge at any given time.

"I believe so. I am going to find her and will return momentarily. You know what it is like in the clinic. I expect things got busy, giving Dr Callard no opportunity to report. I am sure everything is in order," Helena soothed, with a bright smile. Waving her hand, she sped off to the rear of the building, where she found Rose checking a small boy who was lying on one of the beds.

"Rose, my dear what happened?"

Rose spun around on hearing Helena enter the room, hectic colour flaring up her cheeks. "Lady Helena, please forgive my thoughtless behaviour. I did not mean for this to become so... well..."

"Do not fret. I would have done the same thing myself." Helena waved aside her apology. "Now, would you be so kind as to introduce me to this fine young man." Beaming down at Andy, who smiled wanly. During the last hour or so, he had slept a little, but his tumble was a heavy one. He ached all over and was inclined to be querulous.

"Lady Helena Drummond, I would like you to meet Master Andy Fletcher," Rose introduced, while Helena took the child's hand.

"'Tis glad I am to meet you, Andy. You are lucky Rose found you, she has a gift for making people feel better."

"Cor, are you a real lady, and is it because she's a fairy?" Andy whispered, yet to be persuaded Rose wasn't one."

"Yes, I am, and I think that is exactly why?" Helen leant close, and they shared a conspiratorial look.

"I knew it," he giggled. Helena winked, while Rose explained his injuries.

"His father has been asked to collect him on his way home

tonight. Andy must rest for one or two days until we are sure he will not deteriorate without warning and his father cannot miss his shift on the docks. If Mr Fletcher is agreeable, and deems me trustworthy, I would like to offer to sit with Andy on the morrow." She remembered she was a guest of the Drummonds. "That is, if you are not averse."

"I have no problem with your proposal, Rose. You should be more concerned as to whether Mr Fletcher is trustworthy, not the other way around." Helena pondered this for a few seconds. "I do believe I will come along as company for you. Nick or Hugh can drive us." Knowing her husband would want to be sure his wife and their guest were not entering a neighbourhood, or situation, fraught with risk.

Once assured all was in order, Helena left, confirming she would return at the end of the afternoon to introduce herself to Mr Fletcher, and be there to support Rose's suggestion. As promised, she updated Mrs Parry on what had transpired, appeasing that good lady. Then she hurried down the steps to the carriage, asking John to take her to Trentams, where she had a serious discussion with her husband.

he day flew by. Between ministering to Andy, keeping Mark occupied, and assisting Dr Callard with his never-ending queue of patients, Rose did not have a minute to call her own. Andy slept for much of the day, but Rose woke him every hour, a necessity to ensure nothing more sinister was developing.

By late afternoon, the clinic was empty save for Andy. Rose was weaving a riveting tale centred on the fishing boats of Runswick Bay when she heard heavy footfalls along the cobbles. A large man burst through the door, in a towering rage.

"What is the meanin' of this? 'Ow *dare* you keep my son 'ere? 'E don't need no quack, proddin' an' poking' 'im. An' you a slip of a woman. Who do you fink you are?" The man ranted on in this vein for some time.

Andy goggled at his father — for, Rose assumed, this must be he — pressing himself against Rose. Dr Callard was currently occupied elsewhere in the refuge, leaving Rose alone. She was not one to have anyone bawl at her for no reason.

Surely Hugh and Nick had informed him of the accident, and why Andy was here? She could not understand why he was in such a temper. Extricating herself from the child's vice-like grip, she stood, straightened her shoulders, and the moment he took a breath, butted in.

"Sir…"

He ignored her, opening his mouth to continue his tirade.

"**Sir**," she bellowed.

The man was so shocked this delicate-featured woman had shouted at him, he shut up.

Now she had his attention, Rose explained what happened, finishing with, "Andy was unconscious for well over half an hour, sir, and head injuries can be dangerous. I presumed you were already aware of this. Mr Drummond assured me he would call by your place of work on his way to Trentams." She hoped the name of the prestigious shipyard would be enough to persuade the man there was no ill intent.

"My father is a doctor, and I know what I am talking about. Andy has not vomited, but admits to feeling very nauseous, and his head hurts like the dickens. All I ask is you wait until Dr Callard returns. He will answer any questions you might have." Her tones softening as she concluded.

Mr Fletcher thought she had done that adequately herself, impressed with her knowledge. As a coal porter down at the docks, he was used to seeing all manner of injuries and was familiar with certain treatments. Moreover, she called him 'sir', he couldn't remember anyone ever calling him sir.

His anger, building throughout the day — the manifestation of fear for his son, exacerbated by the fact he dared not leave his job to check on him — dissipated with far more rapidity than it had flared.

"Beg pardon, miss, that were unconscionably rude of me."

He removed his grubby cap, twisting it in his fingers. "Will Andy be all right?"

"I believe so, Mr Fletcher, and it is a pleasure to meet you, I am sorry it was under these circumstances." She held out her hand and to his own surprise, Mr Fletcher shook it.

Shortly thereafter, Dr Callard appeared, reiterating everything Rose said, adding he was prepared to let Andy go home if someone would be there to watch over him. Keenly aware many men of Mr Fletcher's ilk often enjoyed a beer or two in the local tavern after a long day's work.

Mr Fletcher scratched his head, perplexed. Tonight, would be no problem. It was tomorrow where the difficulty lay. If he was not at the appointed spot every morning, someone else would be given his job. He couldn't lose the income, but what of Andy?

Rose, foreseeing his dilemma, offered her services. Mr Fletcher stammered a 'no', but she was adamant.

"Mr Fletcher, I am competent enough to care for your son. You need to work, and Andy needs someone to watch over him. I am perfectly capable of looking after a small boy until he no longer requires observing. I can do that either at your home or maybe you could bring him here, to the refuge, on your way to work. Mark may come too if he chooses unless he should be in school?" Lifting an eyebrow at Mark who shuffled uncomfortably — he was hoping to miss school with Andy being hurt.

"He should that, miss. I'd be sore grateful, if you are certain you do not mind." Vacillating.

"It is my pleasure. The three of us are already great friends, and I have no plans that cannot be rescheduled." Blithely ignoring the fact poor Helena might have a variety of entertainments lined up. "My hostess, who will be here shortly has also indicated she might like to accompany me.

The question is, would you prefer to bring the boys here, or shall we come to your home?"

Mr Fletcher had no mind to let anyone see his home. It might just pass muster, but he had his pride. He said it would be more convenient to bring the lads to Sanctuary House.

Dr Callard was in favour of Rose's suggestion, "Moreover, if your boys come here, I will be able to check on Andy periodically," he added.

When the doctor said this, Rose pounced, leaving Mr Fletcher no room for argument. "Good, that settles it. I will be here from six, and I know at least two boys who will be happy to keep your sons occupied, if I happen to be called away."

They had been chatting for several minutes when the door connecting the clinic to the main building opened, and Helena walked in. Mr Fletcher recognised nobility when he saw it and, was bowing to the elegantly beautiful, dark-haired woman who entered the room, before Rose had a chance to introduce them.

"'Tis lovely to meet you, Mr Fletcher, your boys do you credit." Helena, who spent more days mixing with the lower echelons of society than most of her peers, smiled brightly, immediately putting the man at ease.

The four arranged the next couple of days, Mark and Andy listening intently. Andy's head was aching badly again, and he was fractious, prompting them to curtail their discussion agreeing to meet on the morrow at six, as Rose suggested.

Mr Fletcher, with a packet of powder from Dr Callard, to alleviate his son's discomfort, gathered Andy into his huge arms and strode out of the refuge, Mark skipping along behind, his treble tones telling his father all about Rose.

∽

Rose, with Helena's assistance, tidied the clinic. They were putting the last few bits in their appointed cupboards when Nick poked his head around the back door.

"Good afternoon, ladies. Hugh and I wondered whether you might be partial to an ice at Gunther's?"

"How delightful, and the consummate end to a trying day," said Helena beaming at her brother-in-law. "We have two carriages though. Rose and I will meet you there."

Nick's face fell, but he saw the sense in her suggestion. For Rose and him to travel unchaperoned, regardless of the former's insistence it did not matter to her, was unacceptable. Grinning, he tipped his hat and calling an adieu, disappeared.

"Come along, Rose. An ice sounds heavenly."

"Pray give me a few minutes, I must speak with Mrs Parry. This is my first chance to do so."

Helena nodded, saying she would be at the front of the building when Rose was ready. Rose trudged through dim corridors, to the office where Mrs Parry was still buried in papers but paused long enough to wish Rose a good night.

"Thank you for looking after the child today, Rose. Your presence allowed Dr Callard to concentrate on the other patients without worrying he was neglecting the boy."

"It was my pleasure. It was, after all, my fault he was here in the first place, but I did not know where else to take him. I beg your pardon for not coming to apprise you of the details, I admit I forgot in the commotion."

Mrs Parry dismissed her apology, saying she quite understood and looked forward to seeing her the next morning. Rose said her goodbyes and walked to the front entrance, where she found the Drummond carriage waiting.

~

The late afternoon light was hazy after the warm day. People milled about the streets, spilling into the parks, taking advantage of long summer evenings. Cheerful voices, and snatches of laughter mingled with sounds of children playing, and vendors calling the last of their wares.

The carriage trundled along, and Rose breathed it all in, a sensory profusion, but one she savoured. The longer she spent in the city, the less she missed the isolation of Runswick Bay. It was moot, unless a miracle happened, she would be returning home before the year was out.

Following that moment with Nick, Rose was determined to enjoy every minute. If they must part, she would return home with enough memories to last a lifetime. A wickedly delicious plan had begun to form at the back of her mind. It was wanton, brazen in the extreme, and if anyone found out, the consequences would likely be dire, but for Rose, it would be worth it.

Putting it aside for now, she noticed they had arrived at Gunther's. Hugh and Nick were there to assist them down from the coach, each offering an arm, and the four strolled over to the tearoom.

The remainder of the afternoon and evening passed in lively conversation. Nick stayed for dinner, after which he asked whether Rose might like a turn around the garden. Agreeing, she ran upstairs for her wrap, and within minutes the two were in the quiet of the little garden at the side of the house.

Standing shoulder to shoulder, neither spoke, relishing the peace. The sun had fallen beyond the horizon, and above them, the stars were beginning to glitter, winking into existence, as the sky darkened.

Rose released a soft sigh. She was here with Nick and

being so close to him elicited emotions she both welcomed and fought against.

"Rose, I ..." Nick hesitated, unsure how to phrase what he wanted to, what he had to, admit. He tried again, but words failed him. *How did he tell her, she was everything to him, that he loved her beyond measure, but was terrified because their story might not have a happy ending, and to hurt her again cut him to the core?*

As ever, he reckoned without Rose.

"Nick, just say it. I doubt 'tis unexpected. I imagine you are going to tell me whatever it is growing between us, whatever feelings we share, while likely enduring, may yet be ruined because of our different stations in life, the miles which will eventually, inevitably separate us, and your job."

"Our stations in life? Rose Archer do not *ever* suggest we are unequal, that your world, your home is in any way inferior to mine. I am the son of a merchant whose father fell upon luck rather than hard times. 'Tis chance brought me here, into a life less onerous. One step either way and I could be working with Andy's father on the coal barge. Your home may be in a small village, among fishermen and farmers, but it is as rich as mine."

"It doesn't matter though does it. We must part." She tried to sound unperturbed, but unhappiness ringed her tones.

Nick felt his chest contract, he tried to imagine life without her. It was grey, uninteresting, and flat. Worse than the doldrums on the open ocean.

Closing his eyes, he steadied his mind, letting all the noise, and eminently sensible arguments about not taking a wife, flow from his mind. It was his mother's sorrow at the death of their father, which had hardened Nick's heart. He resolved never to be the cause of such grief, and in this he had not wavered.

· · ·

Until Rose.

Out of the blue, a comment Hugh had made when he fell in love with Helena popped into Nick's head. His brother, who had been of similar mind, told him when it came down to it, there was no decision to make; without Helena, he had no life, merely an existence.

The truth of his words echoed in Nick's mind and as though a star exploded, the answer was as bright as day.

CHAPTER 16

*N*ick turned, cupping the elfin face of the woman beside him in his large hands.

Rose could feel the callouses caused by his work on ships, rough against her soft skin, as she stared in his beautiful hazel eyes, hers shadowed by the gloom.

"I love you, Rose."

The words were barely a breath, but she heard them. Holding his gaze, she rested a hand on his chest, feeling the erratic beat of his heart through the satin brocade of his waistcoat.

"Truly?" she entreated. She needed him to repeat it. This was what would keep her warm during the long winter nights when the wind howled around Thistle Cottage. When the waves thundered on the shore. When the snow lay so thick one wondered whether spring would ever break through to end the isolation.

"I love you so much I fear it will break me." Quietly, his tones steadfast, and giving her no chance to reply, bent his mouth to hers. Gently, he teased, his lips moving lazily over hers with sublime tenderness. He let the kiss deepen, gradually demanding more, until their tongues met, the dance tantalisingly familiar. His hands dropped from her face, one to curve around her waist pinning her against him, the other to trace her shape.

Rose simmered under his touch, sensations rippling through her as his hand roamed, prompting her to respond in kind, her fingers searching, trailing over his shirt, until she found a gap. Sneaking her hand under the soft cotton, she revelled in the feel of his skin, warm to her fingertips, causing him to shudder, tiny bumps prickling over his flesh in aroused anticipation.

She tugged the material from his trousers, her hands tormenting him, playing across his back. Sliding around to push up his chest. Delicately, her fingers explored those muscles to which she was first drawn, in a tiny bedroom in a seaside village, miles away and a lifetime ago.

Encouraged, Nick backed them to the wrought iron bench under the plane tree in the middle of the garden, sitting down and tucking Rose on his knee.

His lips left hers, to scatter feather-light kisses down her slender throat and over her shoulder, his fingers twitching at the neckline of her dress, for better access to the soft slope of her breast.

He heard her breathing stutter as his mouth worked its magic and, involuntarily, she arched towards him needing what, she did not know.

"Nick…" desire made her voice languid, her head falling back against his arm as his lips continued to drive her to distraction.

"Oh God, Nick…" never in her life could she have imagined a man who, with barely more than a kiss, could reduce her to a quivering wreck. It was as though her body was becoming liquid. She would not have been the slightest surprised had she slithered off his knee, to dissolve into the grass.

Nick shifted her in his arms, one hand around the back of her head, tangling in her hair, while his other grazed along her cheek. His fingers traced the shell of her ear, along her neck before stroking, unhurriedly, down her body, until he caught the material of her skirts.

Lips back on hers, his hand crept under the layers of froth until able to skim over her legs, gliding inexorably higher until he was so close to her centre, he could feel her heat.

This was madness; his burning passion overruling what was left of his sense. He had to call a halt before they passed the point of no return. As he began to withdraw, his hand was stayed.

Lifting his head, Nick searched her face. Rose held his gaze, her eyes smouldering. Deliberately, she moved his hand back, before dropping her fingers to the fall of his trousers.

Her voice ragged, Rose, recalling her plan, whispered. "I do not know what this is, but I know I want it. I do not care whether this is outside the rules. Here, now, the rules do not apply. I do not care if you cannot give me more than tonight.

"I love you, Nicholas Drummond. I have loved you since you thought I was naught but a fairy, a figment of your fevered imagination. I loved you even when you turned from me, when you told me it could not be. You say you love me, and if this is all you can give, I will gladly take it."

Nick shuddered at her admission. *She loved him. She loved him so much she was prepared to give herself to him without thought of consequence.*

Her unconditional declaration was the most humbling thing he had ever heard, and while he had every intention of bringing her to the peak, he would not take her innocence.

Not tonight, not in a garden, however beautiful. She was no sordid secret, a hidden Rose, a flower consigned to dark corners. She was his Rose, a bloom born to shine, a jewel to be cherished.

"Oh no, my Rose, you are worth so much more than this."

They stared at each other, and time slowed.

The moonrise sent a pale shaft of light glimmering over Rose. Her silvery hair and delicate features compounding the notion she was a fairy, and would vanish forever, leaving naught but the echo of a dream.

Nick sucked a sharp breath.

He brushed his mouth against hers, so light a caress, yet it hinted at a promise, a hope, and a future. His tongue grazed her bottom lip before slipping in to taste her sweetness. Rose welcomed the intrusion, opening to him as their passion intensified.

Nick, consent already given, continued to seek her core, his fingers dragging her to the precipice, at the same time as Rose, eager hands unbuttoning the fall of his trousers, reached their goal.

Her touch was almost Nick's undoing, and he strove to maintain control while Rose came apart around him. His mouth recaptured hers, silencing his name before it flew from her lips in uninhibited euphoria.

Rose floated down from somewhere among the stars, her heart beating wildly, her head in a spin. Nick was holding her close, stroking her hair and speaking, but she couldn't make sense of his words.

"S-say that again," she stammered.

"You are more to me than a quick tumble on a garden

bench, Rose Archer. I told you forever is not for me. I was wrong, you *are* my forever. I hurt you. I pulled away when I should have run towards you, swept you into my arms and never let you go. I believed I was saving you by distancing myself. You saw what happened, you bathed my wounds, you watched over me when I was fevered.

"It could happen again, and to cause you anguish would break my heart, but I cannot stay away. You are the anchor to my ship. Without you I will simply drift away. I do not deserve your forgiveness for my careless disregard of your emotions, but I beg it anyway."

Rose heard the sincerity in his tones, tinged with uncertainty, the dread she may yet reject him. If he only realised it was as impossible to reject him, as it was to forget to breathe.

She reached up, cupping his cheek, her thumb sweeping over the corner of his lip. His words resonated through her mind and she pondered their import. *Was he saying what was expected, or how he truly felt?*

"You must think me a simpleton to assume I do not understand the risks associated with your job. You must realise you are, as am I, as much in danger of death by, say runaway carriage or an accident at the yard or from sickness, as being killed at sea.

"Nick, we should be prepared to take a risk, to face the perils life throws at us, for how else are we able to appreciate its joys." Holding his gaze, she was determined to say the rest.

"That said, I admit your disinterest aggrieved me. To toy with my affections after making it clear we had no hope of a future, was… lamentable. I do not hold with capricious whims. My heart is as fragile as yours. Do not promise me a life you do not want. I love you, I will take what little you can offer, while I am here."

Now was the time to mention the reckless idea she

pondered earlier. "Make me your mistress, then when comes time for me to leave, you are not leg-shackled…"

Nick's jaw dropped, mindful of the significance of her words — the magnitude of which, along with her offer, slammed into him with the force of the west wind. When she came to this last, he placed one finger on her mouth, stemming the flow of words, while twisting his head to kiss her palm, feeling a tremor pulse under his lips.

"Rose, I do not think you understand. I wish to court you, for the world to witness. I was not trying to justify my actions. I was apologising for them. Yes, I long to lose myself in the delights of your body, you bewitch and enchant me, but as husband and wife. I want everyone to know how much I love you. I want you by my side for as many days as the Lord grants us. Capricious my emotions may have been, but they have become steadfast, true and enduring."

He searched her face, tawny eyes on limpid blue. "Miss Archer, my fairy queen, my hidden rose, 'tis time to banish all thoughts of being my mistress from your head, or mayhap revise your suggestion. Will you please do me the greatest honour of being my saviour once again, and agree to marry me?"

Now it was Rose whose jaw fell open. She stuttered helplessly, words tripping over her lips in garbled nonsense, until she clamped her mouth shut. Inhaling a calming breath, and another, then a third, she concentrated on forming a simple response.

Nick watched; his expression wary.

Rose smiled, her fingers sliding down from his cheek, over his waistcoat to grasp his hand, hearing his sharply indrawn breath as she did so, delighted she could affect him thus, with a mere touch.

Letting the moment stretch out, Rose considered his proposal, although her answer was never in doubt. She recalled the first time he looked at her, his eyes riddled with pain, his face grey, and his hair awry.

She remembered every word, every touch, every glance. Even accepting the sea could snatch him away in the blink of an eye was not enough to deter her.

A moment with Nick was worth the risk of a lifetime alone.

"Yes."

Nick heard her softly spoken reply, the answer to his hopes and his dreams. In this moment his heart glowed, and he recognised what was in Hugh's tone when he talked of Helena. Why Jessica was so subdued during the weeks after she first met Duncan.

The chance Rose might decline had sent ice shards along his spine. The silence while she pondered, riven with trepidation. The relief when she said yes — indescribable.

Enclosing her in his embrace, he kissed her, gently, tenderly, his lips a caress.

Rose nestled against him, her arms going up and around his neck, her fingers threading through his unruly locks. The velvety darkness of the night wrapped around them, and they forgot everything else — for a little while — utterly content.

Rose awoke, as usual, with the dawn. The sunlight filtering through her window bathed the room in pale pink and she admired the shadow play on the walls. Her mind winged back to the previous night.

After another heated interlude, during which Nick kissed her into delirium, they decided — discretion being the better part of valour — to return to the drawing room, before Helena dispatched a search party.

"Do you mind if we tell Hugh and Helena?" he asked as they strolled back through the house. "I will write to your father to ask his permission, but I would like to share our news with those closest to me."

Supremely happy, Rose shook her head. "Of course not. I trust they will not be upset. They might see this as precipitous."

"I think Helena believes I have already taken too long," smiled Nick, pausing to drop another kiss on her pale hair.

Holding her hand, they entered the elegant drawing room, to find Helena and Hugh engrossed in an animated discussion about Mr Fletcher and his boys.

That Rose looked rather tousled, her lips a little swollen from being very satisfactorily kissed, was enough for Helena to guess their news. She and Hugh proclaimed their joy when Nick admitted he asked Rose to marry him. The remainder of the evening, short though it was, passed in a haze of good cheer.

Now it was morning, and she had things to do. It was imperative she be at the refuge early. She hurried through her morning ablutions and flew down the stairs, to be met by Mr Saunders who informed her a plate of eggs and toast awaited in the dining room, and the carriage would take her to Sanctuary House as soon as she was ready.

Thanking him, she gobbled the food with more haste than decorum, and was about to rush out of the door when Helena's voice forestalled her.

"Rose, I shall join you forthwith, once I have dealt with the one or two things requiring my attention."

"Thank you, Helena, I should enjoy your company. Thank you for the use of the carriage." Rose beamed at her hostess, then flinging her wrap around her shoulders, and plonking her hat over her bright hair — fled.

Helena smiled, and after greeting Mr Saunders, sat down to enjoy a far more leisurely breakfast.

CHAPTER 17

*R*ose arrived at the refuge five minutes before the hour, hoping Mr Fletcher and the boys had not beaten her to it. The main doors were always open, guarded by retired military men, for under the cover of darkness was often the only time women escaping brutal husbands dared come.

She ran up the steps calling a greeting to Mr Thirlwell and Mr Cooke and hurried through to the clinic. Thankfully it was empty, but she presumed her charges would come in this entrance, rather than the front.

While she waited, Rose ensured everything was prepared for Dr Callard. Clean cloths and bandages, fresh water, sets of bowls and buckets. Satisfied she could do no more, Rose sat down and mused over the momentous changes she was experiencing. Less than three months ago she was merely the daughter of a doctor, in an isolated little village.

Then came the shipwreck and the ensuing chaos. Nick's injuries, tending to his infection, along with the gradual realisation her feelings were far more than concern for a gravely ill gentleman. The awareness his time in Runswick Bay, in her life, was ephemeral, and that once gone, somehow, she would have to pick up the pieces of a heart he did not know he had broken. Now she was in London, and he wanted to marry her.

Rose, while trusting Nick loved her, harboured a niggling doubt they would actually wed. She expected he would wake up to what marriage meant. A lifetime with another by his side. She had no mind to curtail his choice of occupation but imagined he might feel obliged to renounce his sea voyages, especially if children became a consideration.

Rose was moved to ruminate whether he proposed marriage because she had said she would be his mistress. Even though, in her head, it was an answer to her greatest desire, she had shocked herself when she heard the words fall over her lips. Brazen, they may have sounded but she meant every last one. She yearned for Nick to make love to her. His touch sparked a fire only he could douse, and it would be worth being ostracised by her father, the village, everyone.

Moments later, a stampede of feet along the cobbles outside, cut into her reverie, and two small boys burst into the clinic. Andy looked much brighter this morning, although Rose discerned dark shadows under his eyes. Mark whooped with glee when he saw Rose.

"Mornin' miss. 'Ere we are."

Rose smiled at his cheeky grin and stood to greet Mr Fletcher.

"Are you sure you can 'andle them, miss?"

"Of course, Mr Fletcher. I have plenty to keep them occupied. Timmy and Roland will turn up shortly to drag these two into their mischief. How was Andy during the night?"

"'E complained of an 'eadache, but I gave him a dose of them powders and it seemed to 'elp. Neither of us slept well, I am afraid, so he might become crotchety as the day wears on." The boys' father frowned, remained reluctant to leave his boisterous children with so dainty a young woman.

"When he gets here, Dr Callard will wish to examine Andy, and I shall ensure he rests for some of the day." Unthinking, Rose pressed Mr Fletcher's arm. "Andy will be fine, trust me, trust us. Should anything untoward occur, I will send for you."

She smiled up at the burly man, towering over her — taller even than Nick — unaware of how pretty she looked. Mr Fletcher shuffled awkwardly, said goodbye to his sons and hurried away into the morning sunshine.

Rose turned her attention to Andy and Mark, asking whether they had eaten. They shook their heads, and she ushered them along to the kitchens where Sybil Miller, one of the long-time helpers was cooking up a storm.

"Mrs Miller, might I beg a little something tasty for a couple of young lads?" She smiled at the birdlike woman behind the huge counter.

"O' course, me lovelies, sit yourselves, and I'll be over in a jiffy." Rose went to assist Sybil, as Mark and Andy found a chair each and sat, quietly — a most unusual trait.

"Thank you, Mrs Miller. I don't suppose Mr Fletcher had time to get them breakfast before they needed to leave, and I want to make sure Andy has proper meals. He still looks to be in discomfort after his fall yesterday."

Sybil knew all about Andy's tumble. Mark, apprising her of the fact the previous day when he was being shown around the refuge while Andy napped. "He does look a bit peaky," she agreed. "That bruise is nasty too."

Andy's temple, in addition to a sizeable lump, was sporting a bruise of many different hues — from yellow to black and all the colours between.

"It is better there is bruising though," Rose studied the child while Sybil and she chatted. "I think it indicates the damage is less likely to be severe, hopefully confined to the outer layers of skin rather than the skull."

Sybil nodded vaguely, not wise to the subtleties of head injuries. Their conversation moved to other topics as they organised the food and, while Mark and Andy inhaled everything on their plates, other women began to arrive in twos and threes.

Several were residents of the refuge, either because they had nowhere to live currently, or were recuperating from whatever abuse they fled. Andy and Mark quickly became the centre of attention, leaving Rose free to continue helping Sybil.

Helena came soon after, greeting all and sundry in her bright fashion, before gathering the two children, and taking them into one of the classrooms, allowing Rose to assist Dr Callard.

Later in the morning, the good doctor examined Andy, pronouncing himself satisfied the bump on the head was reducing, and unlikely to cause further problems, except perhaps one or two more bad headaches. Rose heaved a sigh of relief; glad it was nothing more serious.

Andy was inclined to grouchiness, but, as small boys are wont to be, was easily distracted with stories. When Timmy and Roland turned up, intent on dragging their new friends into mischief, Andy soon forgot to be cross.

Rose coaxed Andy to rest in the afternoon and, expecting an argument, was pleasantly surprised when he went upstairs to one of the spare bedchambers without fuss. His pallor prompted her to ask Timmy to keep an eye on Mark, while she stayed with Andy. She talked about Runswick Bay until the child fell asleep and was still there when Mr Fletcher arrived a little after four.

. . .

On his arrival, Mr Fletcher, informed of Andy's whereabouts was escorted upstairs by Mrs Forester, one of the staff. For reasons he could not fathom, before entering the room, Mr Fletcher removed his cap, and dragged his fingers through his hair as he greeted the diminutive woman. Cursing the coal dust smearing his cheeks and turning his clothes grey.

"Good afternoon, miss. I 'ope 'e ain't been any trouble." Dipping his head respectfully, he spoke quietly so as not to disturb his sleeping son.

"Hello again, Mr Fletcher. Andy has been the epitome of good behaviour," Rose assured him, indicating a chair, which he sank into gratefully. "Long day?"

He nodded. "Allus is, miss. Mind, 'tis a job and they pay more than a pittance, so I can't complain."

"Hard though, when you have two children." She spoke without thinking, and Mr Fletcher stiffened. *Was the chit questioning his parental abilities?*

Rose, spotting the lowering of his brow, realised her mistake. "My apologies, Mr Fletcher, I was not suggesting you are not a suitable father. I simply suppose all parents worry about their offspring, at one time or another."

"'Tis true. I've 'ad to look after 'em on me own since my Lizzy passed, an' I 'ate leavin' 'em every day, but I has to work. Got no choice. Usually the woman who lives next door watches out for 'em, but yesterday they were up and gone afore I noticed. Funny, that park is a fair walk from 'ome, but they love it. Allus beggin' me to take 'em when I 'ave a free day."

Rose heard an oddly wistful note in his voice. It was apparent he cared deeply for the wife he lost, and their children.

He wasn't typical of many who worked on the docks. The

majority were hard-bitten, surly men, preferring to drink themselves into oblivion at the end of a long day, a brief respite from desperate circumstances, rather than deal with harsh reality by spending time with their long-suffering families.

"Timmy and Roland have befriended them, so both will end up under their wing. Timmy might be quite young, but he is sensible young lad, and won't let harm come to either Andy or Mark," she remarked cheerfully, diverting Mr Fletcher from his introspection.

While they were talking Andy stirred, smiling drowsily at his father.

"Right then my lad, let's get you 'ome. Thank you very much, miss, I reckon we can manage from 'ere on."

Rose agreed, adding if Andy seemed listless or in pain to bring him back. She went in search of Mark, finding him playing some game with Timmy and Roland. Hurrying him out, she affirmed they would meet again soon.

Mr Fletcher and Andy were at the foot of the stairs. As Rose approached, she smiled, causing the tall man to blink; an emotion long suppressed flickering through him. Shaking his head, he thanked her again, gathered up his sons and walked out into the late afternoon.

Unaware of the man's reaction, Rose waved goodbye, before going to tidy the room Andy slept in. When all was set to rights, Rose trudged downstairs to the main entrance, where she saw Helena, who had been teaching all afternoon teaching, waiting for her.

"How is Andy?" Helena asked.

"Tired I think, but he had a good sleep. I expect he will be back to his normal cheeky self by the morrow," Rose replied, with a weary smile.

"Good, I think Timmy and Roland cheered him up today. One would have to be quite unwell to be unaffected by the high spirits of those two." Helena grinned. Calling a goodbye to Mrs Parry, they strolled out into the sunshine.

Rose paused on the top step and breathed in. The air was a little stifled here among all the buildings, but the day was cooling and a breeze beginning to waft through the streets. The golden light of the late afternoon was hazy, making their surrounds seem almost attractive.

"I will miss this when I go home." Rose sighed. Helena glanced at her in puzzlement.

"Will you go home? Now you have accepted Nick's proposal?"

"Oh, I had not thought. I… err… we have not discussed it. Oh… what about Papa?" Suddenly the enormity of the decisions, the changes she must surely have to make, loomed over her. "Goodness me. I suppose we should talk about that." Rose became flustered.

Helena patted her arm. "Do not panic, Rose. Nick will doubtless broach the subject. 'Twas only last evening he asked for your hand, and it will be some time before he hears from your father."

"I do not expect Papa to reject his suit," said Rose, "but I admit, the thought of him being so far away troubles me. He is not aged, but neither is he young, and he misses Mama."

"Mayhap he will consider moving to London, should that be where you and Nick settle."

Rose shook her head. "I would be surprised if he did. His life is centred around the village, and to expect him to leave everything familiar would be selfish."

Helena did not pursue the matter; changing the subject to a ball they would be attending the following evening.

∼

The next week or so rushed by. Caught up in the social whirl of the elite, Rose attended several garden parties and soirees, but the Season was over, and the flurry of balls dwindled — to her relief. She suffered the never-ending social calls Helena encouraged her into with unfailing cheer.

The friends and acquaintances of her hostess seemed genuinely interested to meet the young lady from so far north of the city. One or two Society misses *did* feel moved to whisper behind their fans about what they considered to be her quaint ways, but most were gracious, making Rose more than welcome.

Her days at the refuge, were the most rewarding, even more so when called to tell stories or partake in innumerable games by any or all of the four boys she had come to know.

His heart irrevocably lost, Nick spent as much time with Rose as his schedule allowed, turning up with gratifying frequency. The couple went for walks, sat for long hours in the little garden at the back of Stanton House, and talked about all manner of things.

As promised, Nick wrote to Dr Archer, desperately hoping Rose's father would look upon his request favourably. Until he saw it, in writing, he was wary of planning their future, but the minute he was with Rose, all sense fled, and they enjoyed several conversations around what they expected from marriage.

All in all, life was enjoyable, and for a time, Rose was able to dismiss her insecurities.

CHAPTER 18

*a*fter a summer which had been a wash out, the return of August's habitual heat made London insufferable. Helena was pleased to receive a letter from her sister-in-law Billie, with an invitation to Whiteoaks in the Hampshire countryside, for the duration of the hot weather.

After a brief discussion with Hugh as to whether he would be able to take leave from Trentams, Helena replied by return, confirming they would arrive, all being well, five days hence.

Frantic packing, organising, and sorting ensued, and within three days Hugh, Helena and Rose were heading to Whiteoaks.

Nick would follow, aiming to arrive at the beginning of the following week. Business took precedent over impromptu holidays, and *The Diligence* about to undergo testing to ensure her repairs were sound.

Glum at the thought of being apart even for a few days, Rose remained philosophical. They spent the evening before she left, saying adieu in the most delectable fashion, the memory of which would keep her body tingling until she saw Nick again.

~

The journey to Whiteoaks took two days. While they were rumbling along bumpy roads, Helena explained who would be there. Their hosts, Billie and her husband Giles, who was Helena's brother, of course. Jessica — Nick and Hugh's sister — and Jessica's new husband, Duncan. Theo and Grace, the local doctor and his wife. Helena explained that Theo was also Lady Sophia Beaumont's brother-in-law.

Rose had met Lady Beaumont, patroness of Sanctuary House, during her second week in London, and found her delightful. Taking the time to chat with the newcomer, Lady Beaumont's interest and genuine curiosity about life in the village, as well as the shipwreck, touched and impressed Rose. It seemed news of the catastrophe was in everyone's minds, and to have an eyewitness to both wreck and aftermath was not to be sneezed at.

"Are you sure they included me in the invitation?" Rose queried, faintly. "It sounds like a family reunion."

Helena tutted. "Assuredly, you will be the reason Billie organised this house party. She loves meeting new and interesting people. Moreover, you are both tiny, and she will be glad, for once, not to be the only one who fits into a coat pocket."

Hugh spluttered with mirth at this description. Rose tried to look affronted but the image in her head was too funny, her laughter mingling with that of the others.

The warmth of the afternoon had given way to a mild evening when they rattled up the long gravel driveway to

Whiteoaks. Helena fell quiet as they rounded a slight bend, the first glimpse of the great house coming into view. This was her family's ancestral home, where she lived until her first Season, and it never failed to lift her heart.

Out of the corner of her eye, Rose noticed Hugh take his wife's hand, interlacing their fingers, and experienced a sharp stab of longing for Nick.

Determined not to dwell on his absence, she turned her attention to the expanse of soft red brick in front of her.

Alleviated by creamy quoins at the corners, and a multitude of windows reflecting the changing hues of the sky, Whiteoaks seemed to float. Chimneys scattered across the red tiled roof crowned the building, and Rose felt her mouth fall open in amazement.

"Why it's beautiful," she breathed reverently, leaning forward slightly, as though this would give her a better perspective.

"Thank you," Helena murmured, a gentle smile curving her lips. "I might be a trifle biased, but I agree wholeheartedly.

The carriage trundled to a halt at the foot of a broad flight of stone steps, as a diminutive figure flew through the large wooden doors, and down to the arrivals.

"Helena, Hugh. I am so pleased you are here. It has been an age," blithely ignoring the fact it was barely three months, "and this must be Rose? My dear, I am so excited to meet you."

John dropped the step. Hugh climbed out, helping down his wife and then Rose, both of whom were immediately enveloped in a warm embrace by the whirlwind who, Rose presumed was Lady Willow Trevallier, Countess of Winchester.

An exceedingly tall, dark-haired gentleman followed at a much more sedate pace, greeting Hugh with a handshake, and Helena with a hug. Helena turned to Rose and began formal introductions.

"Giles, Billie, may I introduce Miss Rose Archer?"

"It is an honour to meet you, Miss Archer. We are in your debt." Giles spoke gravely. Billie agreeing with his sentiment, tucked Rose's arm through hers, and giving her no chance to demur, all but dragged her into the lofty entrance hall, ignoring her guest's fiery cheeks.

"Welcome to Whiteoaks," said the countess, spreading her arm in an all-encompassing gesture.

"Your home is remarkable." Swallowing a gasp at the aged beauty of the house, Rose stared around unashamedly, mesmerised by the elegant yet oddly cosy atmosphere. Despite the immense proportions of the interior, Whiteoaks felt warm and inviting, almost snug.

A place where people lived, and laughed, and loved, rather than a showpiece. The rest of the party traipsed behind, chattering about their families, sharing news, and were ushered into the library. A room in which Rose could happily have lived, for the rest of her life.

They stepped over the threshold, and she was held motionless by two things.

Firstly, dominating one wall and flanked by bay windows, two French doors stood open, allowing the evening breeze to waft through, drawing the eye to the view across the immaculately tended gardens and out onto the Great Park.

The second, when she tore her gaze away from the vista, were the books. Dr Archer had lots of books, they were fortunate to own a decent collection at Thistle Cottage, but this — this was beyond anything she could have imagined. Her eyes went wide with astonishment, and she her mouth fell open — again.

"'Tis rather special is it not?" Billie's quiet words as she came up behind her, unknowingly echoing Helena's, caused Rose to turn and smile.

"It is perfection," she whispered. Her hands fluttered out as though reaching to stroke over the leather spines, and she forced them back to her sides.

Billie chuckled. "Please read whatever you like. 'Tis a haven, this room."

"It really is," Rose blushed, aware the others were watching their interchange with amusement.

"It has the same effect on everyone," Helena grinned, as the door opened to admit smartly uniformed man carrying a silver platter, piled with cakes and savoury treats.

"We will be having dinner soon, but I expect you are hungry after your journey. Let us sit, and partake of Sarah's tasty cakes, then mayhap you might like to freshen up and change before the meal. Everything always feels so dusty after a long drive."

"Where's Max?" Helena asked while they munched on the cakes.

"Hopefully, fast asleep. He was fussy last night, and has not slept at all today, until about an hour ago. I know leaving him now will likely disrupt his rest again tonight, but he was worn out, poor baby." Referring to her firstborn son, coming up to six months old. Billie grimaced, making them laugh. "You might laugh now, but it will not be funny when he screams the place down at midnight and you are all trying to sleep."

Giles grinned at his wife's comments. "Regrettably, Billie is correct. Apparently exercising his lungs at the most inopportune moments is my son's latest trick. Our apologies in advance."

The talk turned to baby Max for a few moments, and Rose took the opportunity to observe her host and hostess, more or less covertly.

She was fascinated by how often their eyes met, the secret smiles they shared when they presumed no one noticed, despite it being clear to Rose, everyone did. The way they deferred to each without either feeling patronised or pressured. It was as though they were two halves of a whole, an intriguing connection, and one Rose realised she desired quite ardently.

Escorted up to a charming bedchamber with a view over the Great Park, Rose indulged in a long hot bath. Perfumed soap, an added luxury with which to wash away the grime from her skin and hair, accumulated during the two days' journey along dry dusty roads. A young maid named Lucy arrived to assist. Rose had stammered, she was able to manage without, but Billie wouldn't hear of it.

"I expect 'tis rather nice to be pampered, once in a while." Was her considered response to Rose's protests. So, here she was being duly pampered. Pulling on a dress of the palest turquoise, Rose grudgingly admitted it was easier having Lucy fasten the tiny buttons.

The maid brushed her hair until it shone, twisting it into a simple chignon. A ribbon, in a richer shade than the dress — and procured from where, Rose had no idea — was intertwined through the style, a few strands of hair left to coil down her neck, completing the look.

Finding a pair of suitable slippers, Rose stood to peer at herself in the mirror. Her Papa would be astounded. This elegant young woman staring back at her bore little resemblance to the untidy daughter he had long given up trying to neaten.

Unable to quash her hilarity, Rose gave a wild gurgle, at the same moment as she caught Lucy's eye. The pair burst out laughing, their merriment echoing along the corridors through a door opened by Helena to see whether her charge was ready.

"May I ask what is so amusing, you two chortle like children?" Helena enquired, eyebrows raised in amusement.

"Oh, 'tis only, I look so unlike myself, Papa would scarcely recognise me. He is used to seeing me looking dishevelled, after a long day doing chores or assisting in his clinic. I do not think he could ever imagine I might look so… refined. He will be most grateful you have tamed me."

"I hope we haven't tamed you Rose. I rather like you the way you are." Helena had the oddest impression, to tame Rose would be travesty.

It wasn't that she was unruly or wayward, or anything other than polite and respectful, but there was a whimsical quality beneath her composure, a slight unpredictability, like the restless seas. To calm it would be like squashing her spirit, dulling her sparkle.

Shaking her head to banish such fanciful thoughts, Helena asked whether Rose was ready to go downstairs.

Thanking Lucy, Rose followed Helena and they descended the beautifully carved and warmly carpeted stairway, across the polished hall to the library. The great French doors stood open still, and Rose asked whether it was acceptable to take a short stroll.

"Of course, you must treat Whiteoaks as your home while you are here…"

"I couldn't possibly, 'tis a grand estate," Rose interjected.

"Oh pooh, yes you can. A grand estate it may be but 'tis also a home. One well-loved for generations, and part of the reason for this, is because people are relaxed and comfortable here. Not expected to behave with caution, as though walking on thin ice," Helena assured as they crossed the threshold out into the gardens.

～

The next few days were full of fun and cheer. Rose met Nick's sister, Jessica along with her very new husband, Duncan. A veteran of the recent wars, Duncan initially appeared a taciturn gentleman. Later Rose was to discover he had suffered greatly during the conflict, the loss of his lower left arm being the least of it.

Jessica — in what Rose was coming to recognise as inimitable Drummond fashion — had refused to allow Duncan's demons to scare her away, drawing him out of his shell. Taciturnity turned out to be reticence and, once introduced to Rose, his demeanour became open and friendly.

Helena had shared a little of Duncan's history with Rose, adding he considered himself unmarriageable; preferring not to burden someone he cared about with his darkness.

She heard echoes of Nick's reasoning in Duncan's story. No, they were not the same per se, but both eschewed the idea of marriage for fear of bringing pain to their loved ones. Rose wondered whether Jessica might be amenable to talking with her. Nick was her brother and surely it would be beneficial to share her concerns with someone who understood.

She also met Theo and Grace, another couple whose love glowed like an aura around them. In an era where so many marriages were arranged purely to enhance status, power, political alliances, or monetary gain, that each of the four couples present married for love, was astonishing, and an anomaly Rose hoped she might soon become part of.

CHAPTER 19

*L*ast minute disasters notwithstanding, Nick was due to arrive at Whiteoaks by Monday evening, or as late as Tuesday, depending on the trials. Jessica — not all that astutely — sensed an anxiety in Rose and thus, on the Sunday afternoon, asked whether she might enjoy a walk over to Oak Stanton for luncheon at her home the following day.

Rose accepted with pleasure and, to Jessica's amusement, was pacing the courtyard at the rear of the house, when Duncan and she drew up, shortly before nine.

"Good morning, Rose, isn't it a splendid day?" Jessica called as the carriage rounded the corner of the outbuildings. Duncan was in charge of estate carpentry, his days constantly busy with repairs and such like. He was also a gifted carver, shaping wood into creatures so lifelike one expected them to jump off the shelf and dash into the wild blue yonder.

Duncan grinned a greeting at Rose as he hopped out to assist Jessica down, bending to kiss her upturned face. Rose glanced away, offering them a modicum of privacy, although neither seemed in the slightest embarrassed by so overt a display of affection.

"I shall walk back with Rose this afternoon, and we can ride home together," Jessica said as she waved a goodbye, the two women falling into step along the gravel driveway. Duncan waved back and headed to the workshops.

"What a glorious morning for a walk," she continued, and giving Rose no chance to feel shy, launched into a bright conversation about London, and what Rose had seen so far.

The walk to Oak Stanton took about half an hour. They didn't hurry, enjoying the fresh air and comfortable chatter. When they reached the little village, Jessica became a guide, explaining who lived where and what each of the few shops sold. She pointed out The Gables — home of Grace and Theo — the church, and the alehouse, commenting about the latter,

"It can be rowdy sometimes, but they do serve a scrumptious pie."

The pair turned down a leafy lane, the dappled light sending intricate patterns across the ground. Jessica pushed through a gate nestled in a low hedge and led Rose up a path bordered with newly planted lavender. The door was opened before they reached it, and a large lolloping creature of indeterminate breed bounded out to meet Jessica, its body winding around her legs in quivering ecstasy.

"Trixie, I've barely been gone an hour," she chuckled, crouching to ruffle the dog's fur, while Trixie made little whining noises in response, pushing her head under Jessica's chin. Rose giggled, the sight totally unexpected, yet fitting.

"This is Trixie," Jessica introduced the dog to Rose, the former immediately demanding attention, the latter obliging with aplomb. "I found her trapped in thorns over on Whiteoaks estate, just before Christmas. It was the day I met

Duncan." Her gaze took on a distant quality, memories of the snowy morning never far from her mind.

"It was a fortuitous day, although I don't think either of us realised it at the time," she smiled, wryly.

Rose mused whether she dared ask her hostess to elaborate. She had no mind to seem inquisitive, but something told her it would help quell her own misgivings.

Ushering Rose through the cool house, they paused while Jessica stuck her head into what Rose presumed to be the kitchen to ask whether they might have a cup of coffee, before continuing out into a sunny garden at the centre of which stood an enormous copper beech tree. A smartly attired young man followed them, draping a colourful rug on the grass under the tree.

"I love sitting here. 'Tis cool and shady, and so relaxing. Both Duncan and I have busy work lives, and 'tis a pleasant spot to spend a little time together at the end of the day, away from everyone else." Jessica explained she acted as district assistant for Theo, making home visits. She examined and, where necessary, re-dressed wounds, checked on those who were sick, ensuring all was as it should be with the doctor's growing list of patients.

Rose listened, asking questions here and there. A doctor's daughter, she appreciated better than most how much a local community relied on the person dispensing care, and how often patients needed someone to chat with, to alleviate the loneliness, rather than actual medicine.

The two became engrossed in conversation and the morning flew by. Over luncheon, taken in the garden, picnic style, Jessica broached a question, the answer to which she was desperate to know.

"Rose, I hope you do not think me impertinent, but it seems you are on tenterhooks for the arrival of my brother.

Might I be so bold as to ask whether your affection for Nick is sincere?"

Rose stared at Jessica over the rim of her teacup. With fingers that suddenly trembled, she placed it back in its saucer and folded her hands tightly in her lap.

"I'm not... errr... until... Nick has... and I do..." Rose stopped abruptly, aware her words, as ever, were garbled. When the topic of conversation revolved around Nick, she seemed to lose the ability to speak with any intelligibility, and it was irksome.

She rubbed her forehead distractedly. She wanted to confide in Jessica, but worried Nick's sister would think she was trying to force him into something he was not ready for. *Goodness, this falling in love business was like walking through sinking sand.*

Jessica watched the confusion of emotions play across Rose's elfin face and sought to soothe her.

"I have no mind to upset you, but I know my brother and I do not wish him to cause you undue anxiety."

Rose's head shot up at this. "Y-you th-think *he* is toying w-with *me*?" she blurted out, her chest aching at the notion that after all this, after all his fine promises, she was right — he didn't really want to marry her. "I b-beg your pardon, th-that was not wh-what I was going to say," she stammered, her cheeks glowing pink.

"Why don't you tell me from the beginning. From the night the ship was wrecked?" Jessica's gentle request and encouraging smile, snuck in under her reserve, and words spilled out of Rose almost too quickly.

Jessica was able to piece it together, recognising the other woman's dilemma. It was similar to the one she had suffered, before Duncan could be persuaded, he was worthy of her love.

While they talked, Jessica shared a little of her romance

with her husband. How he too rejected the idea of love and marriage, determined not to impose his demons on someone for whom he cared.

"It was clear, almost from the moment we met, what we had was more than a fleeting *tendre*, but because he was blockheaded enough to think me incapable of coping when he suffers a dark spell, we came to blows frequently. It took time and dogged patience to convince him of the error of his ways, and I am endlessly glad I refused to let his nonsense dictate my actions." Jessica's voice was warm, her love for Duncan, unmistakeable.

Rose reached out and pressed her hand. "I too am glad, for the love you two share is a rare gift."

"Not so rare, I think. I am witness to the strength of your affection in the tone of your voice and the glow in your eyes. The way you talk about my brother is how I talk about Duncan, how Helena and Hugh talk about each other; the Elliotts and the Winchesters are the same."

Rose started to speak, then stopped. She could not bring herself to tell Nick's sister what troubled her, but Jessica was a canny soul, and read Rose's expression with little difficulty.

"You fear Nick will change his mind?" she asked gently.

Rose nodded slowly. "He told me he would never subject someone he cared about to the worry of him not returning, and in light of this might yet decide his offer was imprudent. Words spoken in the heat of the moment without due consideration."

Her voice dropped on a pensive sigh. "I'm not sure he comprehends, to stop loving him is impossible. Even if he decides marriage is not for him, 'tis too late, I love him, I will always love him. Married or no, near him or no."

Jessica grasped one of Rose's hands and leant forward. "Rose, trust me when I say, Nick would not offer for you if he was not sincere. He told you marriage was not part of his future, and we Drummonds are not easily swayed, just ask Duncan," she grinned wickedly. "What my brother feels for you must be a powerful emotion, for you have turned his nonsensical ideas on their ridiculous heads."

Long forgotten memories filtered into her mind.

"Of the three of us, I believe Nick was most affected by Papa's death. He was in his last year at school when it happened, and Hugh had to bring him home. It wasn't as though Papa was lost at sea. He died from a sudden fever.

"Maybe what triggered Nick's determination never to place anyone else in such an untenable situation, was because of the time it took between Papa's death, and Nick hearing the news. It was two days before Hugh reached Nick's school, and once told, he had to face the journey home, knowing he would never see Papa alive again.

"To remain unaware of a loved one's death for days, and if at sea, months. To go about your days as usual without knowing the most distressing news was about to destroy your happiness, became something he could not contemplate."

Rose pondered Jessica's words. "I understand, but he must realise it makes no difference whether he is at Trentams, or at sea, or walking along the street two minutes after saying goodbye? The sorrow will be the same regardless.

"We have to take a gamble, we need to trust our hearts will not shatter, otherwise we cannot live. I would rather enjoy one brief moment with him, to have that memory to keep me warm, than be protected from the risk of being crushed by grief and miss what is so precious.

"My grief would crush me whether we are together or not. I might crumple, I would certainly be devastated, it would take me an age to recover, but I will not dissolve, and I would not be without that one moment for the world."

Rose sucked in a ragged breath. The sheer depth of her

feelings for Nick threatened to overwhelm her, and she had no mind to cry in front of Jessica, she was stronger than that. Steadying herself, she became aware Jessica's expression had taken on a curious expectancy, a secret smile hovered on her lips.

Rose frowned. *What was so amusing?*

A sound prompted her to twist around on the rug.

It was Nick.

He was here, in Jessica's garden.

Rose blinked, certain she was imagining him. That she so desperately needed him to be here, to tell her he loved her, to promise he would not snatch away what was within their grasp, she had manifested him out of thin air.

How long had he been there? Dammit, had he heard all that?

Unable to move, not even a finger, she opened her mouth, but nothing came out, not a single word. Jessica murmured something about needing to check with one of her staff, and hurried away, her grin becoming a bright beam.

His business at Trentams completed, the initial trials on *The Diligence* undertaken successfully, Nick headed to Whiteoaks using the fastest mode of transport available to him — horseback.

Setting off as soon as it was light the previous morning, he had ridden steadily, throughout the day, and long into the night, stopping only when essential. Hermes, his powerful stallion, ate up the miles easily but Nick had no mind to exhaust the creature by pushing him to his limits, despite his urgency to see Rose.

Breaking his journey at one of the coaching inns, Nick

slept long enough that Hermes would be fed, watered, and rested, before he was in the saddle again. A journey, which usually took at least two days by carriage, was swallowed up in a little more than half the time.

Upon his arrival at Whiteoaks, Billie, after greeting him with her customary hug, informed him Rose was visiting with Jessica. After a quick freshen up, Nick hastened to Briar Cottage. Welcomed by Miles, the Barrington's butler who explained the ladies were in the garden, Nick was ushered through to the rear of the house.

He hesitated before stepping back into the afternoon sunshine, taking the opportunity to admire his betrothed and his sister, unseen.

Their two heads were close together while they talked, Jessica's flaxen locks, dark compared with the silvery blonde swathe, no longer confined to its tidy style, spilling over Rose's shoulders. Rose was speaking, and her words pierced his heart.

Nick loved her. Of that there was no doubt. Nonetheless, and despite his attempt to banish it, at the periphery of his mind like a warning, a persistent dread lurked. The one which, until latterly, had prevented him from considering marriage.

He had believed, by distancing himself, by not allowing anyone to get too close, he was protecting them, saving them. As he listened, it hit him with the same implacable force as the mast, which had tossed him into the sea scant months ago — the only person he was protecting was himself.

He came out into the sunshine, the movement catching Jessica's attention. Holding his sister's gaze, Nick inclined his head towards Rose. Jessica, in quick understanding, began to smile. He took another step, and at the sound of his footfall on the flagstones, Rose turned.

CHAPTER 20

"*R*ose?" Nick stared at her, something indefinable shimmering in his gaze.

"Nick...?" Her whispered plea almost lost on the breeze, as she scrambled to her feet, brushing down her skirts. She swayed slightly and blinked again. *Was he really here, or had she fallen asleep and this was a dream? No, no, surely, she would not be so rude as to fall asleep when visiting someone?*

He came closer. "Did you mean everything you just said?" Nick's quiet question, answering her silent one.

"There would be no point saying it otherwise. I did not expect my audience to be more than one." Her tone was cool, a hint of pride in her voice. Her chin came up, and there was a slight narrowing of her eyes. *He had better not ridicule her.*

He spread his hands and shrugged, diffidently. "My apologies, I thought to surprise you. I miss—"

The uncharacteristic hesitancy in his voice and his faltering expression, propelled Rose forward. Nick had come for her, *for her*! Arriving hours earlier than expected, and not waiting at Whiteoaks, he had made the effort to seek her out. Her heart swelled. Lifting her skirts, Rose ran across the garden, straight into his arms, uncaring how indecorous it was.

"You did that, and I missed you too," she murmured, brushing her lips to his, sensing he needed assurance as much as she did. They were the same in this, both confused — bewildered at the welter of new emotions and sensations, falling in love engendered.

Nick had done a complete about-turn, from refusing to contemplate marriage to declaring he could not live without her as his wife. She in turn, never wanted to be someone's chattel, to be deemed a possession, her life reduced to another's whims.

With Nick, to be his partner in marriage, to be granted a say, to be listened to and considered, to be cherished and adored, was all she wanted from now until her last breath.

Nick wrapped his arms around her, revelling in the way her hands splayed over his back as she moulded herself against his lanky, yet muscular frame, and the way her silken hair entangled itself under his fingers as he cupped her nape. Rose tilted her head, her eyes, bluer than the summer sky with just a hint of violet, sparkled up at him.

"I love you, Rose Archer."

"I love you, Nicholas Drummond, now please be so good as to kiss me."

He obliged.

Time slid by, their kiss deepened, the inevitable fire smouldered. Before their ardour got the better of them, Nick lifted his head, kissing the tip of her nose and then her forehead, holding her close, his heart thundering like a racehorse at full gallop.

Rose trembled with the force of her emotions, but underneath the passion, it seemed to her, in that moment, with that kiss, their relationship underwent a subtle trans-formation.

What began as a tentative connection, a fragile affinity, had reshaped and reformed, into an unshakeable bond.

Her insecurities fell away.

Nick rested his chin on her hair, his fingers absently stroking up and down her spine, which did little for her composure.

"I received word from your father."

Rose jerked backwards, "What did he say?" Unsure she wanted to know. She believed her father wanted her to wed, but mayhap was not so pleased with the probability of her living so far away. "No, do not spoil this moment, his answer will not change between now and tomorrow." An impish grin twitching at her lips.

"He approved my suit and said he will write to you. He also mentioned he might travel to London before the year is out."

The information startled Rose. "Coming to London? Did he say why?

"I think he wishes to reassure himself, Trentams is a legit-imate company and this whole thing is not a ruse in order to whisk you away and sell you to the nearest slave trader." He waggled his eyebrows and leered in a most salacious fashion, making Rose giggle.

"'Tis a shame ..." she started to say.

"You want to be sold into slavery?" His astonished inter-ruption turned her giggle into outright laughter.

"No, silly, the part about being whisked away. That sounds perfect." Her wistful tones, eliciting another searing kiss.

"Soon, my love." Nick gave into temptation. His hands roamed over her, searching and teasing, and a soft moan flew over her lips. "God, Rose, I cannot stop touching you. When you are near, my hands have a mind of their own, and refuse to behave. 'Tis only the proximity of my sister, and her staff, not to mention your innocence, preventing me from taking you right here in the garden."

"If you continue with your seduction, I guarantee I will be unable to summon up a single argument to counter that suggestion. Mayhap we should curb our... err ... enthusiasm? I do not expect it will burn out in the next few hours. Let us go and find Jessica, 'tis impolite to be kissing in her garden, ignoring her generous hospitality." Rose moved out of his embrace but tucked her arm through his, needing the contact.

The significance of her words not lost on him; Nick contented himself with a light squeeze of her fingers while they made their way through the cottage to the cosy parlour.

They found Jessica, apparently engrossed in writing a letter, although if one looked closely there were scarcely more than three words on the paper. She glanced up when they came in, an intuitive smile playing across her lips.

"Thank you, Jess. Your consideration is appreciated." Nick greeted his sister with a warm hug. For several moments the three chatted about his journey, and the status of *The Diligence*.

Jessica was well aware of what had just transpired. "You are certain you are restored to full health?" She ran keen eyes over her brother.

"I am. I was treated by a skilled doctor, and his assistant was most attentive," Nick replied, his gaze swinging to Rose, as he dropped a wink.

"I imagine he was an ornery patient?" This to Rose.

"Your brother did have a tendency to be fractious," Rose agreed. "He refused to listen to reason, and 'twas only by resorting to threats were we able to persuade him that rest was the most expeditious way to recuperate."

Her mouth twitched in recollection of their squabbles over whether he should or should not visit the wreck. "He believed himself perfectly capable of rowing out to check the ship, despite not being able to stand upright or, for that matter, speak with any coherence."

"Telltale." Nick murmured, grinning as Rose's cheeks reddened, his mock jibe a reminder of the day her father operated.

"Merely stating facts," Rose countered archly, and proceeded to give Jessica an overview of his injuries. This quickly developed into a serious discussion, both women studying him intently, until Nick, uncomfortable being the centre of such pointed scrutiny, suggested it was time to return to Whiteoaks.

Jessica chuckled, and asked whether they minded her joining them. "I could sit here and wait for Duncan to come home but I enjoy the walk, and I get to see what he's been working on," she explained.

With Hermes plodding alongside, relieved at the sedate pace, and occasionally nipping at Nick's hair, the three sauntered slowly back to Whiteoaks, engaged in animated conversation about all manner of subjects. When they approached the workshops, Jessica stopped, and drew Rose into a quick hug, as Will came out of the stables to take Hermes.

"Don't let him walk all over you," she whispered, while Nick was distracted. "'Tis your independent spirit, and a nature not quite tamed which caught his attention." Releasing Rose, she waved goodbye to Nick and headed for the workshops, calling a 'Hello' as she reached the door.

"What were you two muttering about?" Nick asked.

"Naught to interest you," Rose contended.

"Mayhap I should be the judge of that."

"Mayhap one day I might let you," she teased, with a grin. "I presume Billie is aware of your early arrival?"

"Of course, she was the one who informed me of your whereabouts." They walked in through the back door — as everyone did at Whiteoaks, convenience taking precedent over formalities — to be met by Thomas who informed them the others were partaking of refreshments in the library.

Giles, Billie, Hugh, and Helena glanced up when the couple entered, smiles wreathing their faces

"Nick!" Helena's delighted cry echoed around the room. "You are early, the journey must have been untroubled.

"It was, thank you, Helena. The road was quiet, and Hermes was glad to have his head."

"He arrived early enough to visit with Jessica," Billie threw in slyly, earning a grin from her husband, and a raised eyebrow from Hugh.

"How fortuitous," Hugh remarked, a muffled snort to his right prompting a confused glance at his wife. "What? What have I missed?"

Rose blushed becomingly and sat in one of the leather wing-backed chairs, making no comment at all, concentrating fiercely on a slice of cake. Nick, collecting a cup of coffee as he passed the table, went to perch on one of the window ledges.

Helena leant across to murmur in Hugh's ear. Her husband chuckled, but wisely refrained from further comment. The moment passed, and the company relaxed, Giles setting everyone at ease by posing a question about the following day's entertainment.

Five couples gathered for an afternoon at The Gables, Theo and Grace Elliot's beautiful home. Rose was ecstatic to discover Grace owned chickens and goats, dragging Nick into the large field at the back of the property to coo over them. Nick was not quite as enamoured but suffered the indignity of having goats jump on him, because the sound of Rose laughing was worth a ruined pair of trousers.

Not far away, several horses grazed under the shade of the trees. Their soft nickering as they nuzzled each other, the high-pitched bleating of the goats, combined with the buzzing of bees and chirping of birds, created a kind of chorus. The quintessential refrain of country life, the whole scene... picturesque.

"'Tis so peaceful," Rose sighed, resting against Nick, after they stood up, brushing dust off their clothes from the attentions of the goats. "A most welcoming and friendly village," the yearning in her voice, had Nick turning her in his arms.

"Do you miss Runswick Bay?" he asked, searching her face

"Oddly enough, no, but there is an irresistible mellowness to this place, which draws you in. It begins the moment you step foot in the district and holds you captive. I really don't want to leave." She smiled, sliding her left hand up Nick's unbuttoned waistcoat, over his jaw line and into his hair, bringing his head down until their foreheads touched.

"Hark at my being fanciful. Mayhap it was the glass of sherry I drank prior to luncheon. I feel quite slumberous."

Before her head talked her out of it, Rose pressed herself to Nick, fitting herself to his shape. Her right hand inched around his back, seeking under his shirt.

The day was warm, the men had been persuaded to shed cravats and jackets. They were among friends, and a little informality was acceptable on occasion.

Rose exploited this informality, her left hand dropping

from Nick's neck to join its partner stroking over his heated flesh. She leant into him, inhaling his scent. A hint of soap, freshly laundered linen and just a whiff of whisky. Intoxicating to her senses, and dearly familiar. Her fingers grazed a tortuous path over his skin, wrenching a guttural groan from somewhere deep inside him.

"You would tease me?" he growled. She nodded, a roughish smile curving her lips. "Well now you must pay." He was about to kiss her when she wriggled free and, hoisting her skirts, sprinted across the grass.

Nick got such a shock at the abrupt switch, he stood motionless for precious seconds trying to work out what just happened. With a muffled roar, he shot off after Rose, long legs reaching her in less than twenty strides.

Catching her around the waist, he spun her around, pinning her against him.

"You might try to run but 'tis futile, you will never escape."

"Pah," giggled Rose struggling in his iron grip, "how do you imagine you will stop me?"

"Like this…" and he crushed his mouth to hers.

Willingly, Rose surrendered.

CHAPTER 21

They found the others in the cool of the drawing room. Jessica — curled up on the floor next to Duncan, her hands idly playing with the silken ears of Trixie, the dog currently trying to get onto her lap — was deep in conversation with Theo about some patient they were concerned about.

Duncan and Giles were engrossed in a discussion with Hugh concerning investment in trade to the Americas.

Billie, Helena, and Grace were playing with baby Max, who was placidly blowing bubbles.

Nick was hailed to balance the argument the men were having regarding which goods were less perishable. Rose joined Theo and Jessica, her thirst for knowledge piqued when she overheard a comment about traditional remedies.

The afternoon passed in relaxed fashion, the company's banter light and friendly when something Helena said tweaked at the back of Nick's mind.

"Jess? What was the name of your elocution teacher?"

Slightly baffled by the turn of the conversation, but game to see where it led, Jessica twisted her position on the floor, the better to look at her brother. "Miss Erica Allard, why? What has the old dragon done now?"

"Dragon?" exclaimed Billie. Sensing a good story, she spun in her seat, grinning at the expression on Jessica's face.

"Yes. Dragon. That vile woman must suck whole lemons for her supper. Her face is invariably pinched, and her nostrils are permanently flared as though there is a bad smell under her nose." Jessica's lovely face scrunched up in a fierce scowl.

Hugh chuckled, "I remember her. She was not enamoured of your knowledge, and occasional use, of maritime terminology. Now I think about it, anything business related abhorred her. She considered it unseemly, to the extent she penned a scathing letter informing me it was vulgar for young ladies to speak in such a manner."

"It was nothing to do with her what I did or did not learn. She was not my schoolteacher," Jess groused.

Duncan rumbled out a laugh, his hand resting on his wife's shoulder as he spoke, "What did you do? Start singing sea shanties? Curse like a sailor?"

"No, dear me no. I was never anything other than polite. Unfortunately, one day, fed up with her gross ignorance of anything related to ships and shipping, I chose to inform the vile old witch, the correct terminology for the left and right of the boat was port and starboard. I admit, I may have sounded vexed, but her reaction far exceeded my remarks." Jess raised her hands in exasperation.

"Jess," interposed Nick, "you should not speak ill of the dead."

"Dead?" Her eyes widened in shock.

"Yes. I read it in the paper before leaving London. One Miss E Allard, murdered in a most heinous attack, for refusing to hand over her sovereign purse."

Jess stared at her brother, knowing she ought to feel chastened but all she felt was the most regrettable urge to giggle. Nick watched as she pressed her lips together, mirth brimming in her eyes. A strangled gurgle escaped.

"Are you quite well, love?" Duncan queried solicitously bending to check his wife. Mildly concerned about her reddening cheeks. "I suppose the news is somewhat upsetting."

Jessica shook her head. "Mmmmm..." was all she managed.

"Jess!" The warning note in Hugh's voice should have been enough, but it was too late.

Jessica doubled over, laughter spilling out until she had tears in her eyes. Her merriment, however unseemly, was infectious, the others joining in by degrees, the room ringing with unbridled hilarity.

Jocularity once more back under control, they resumed their various conversations, before Nick's question had so completely diverted them. During a pause in their discussion about balms and ointments, Rose glanced at Jess.

"Would you mind if I asked, what are elocution lessons?" Quietly spoken, unwilling to seem uneducated.

Jess grinned, "'Tis the art of speaking properly."

"But your diction is so eloquent." Rose frowned.

"Thank you, maybe now, but until I was about ten and five, I tended to be lazy with my pronunciation. Mama decided it was a worthwhile exercise to engage Miss Allard twice a week. Oh, they were tortuous afternoons."

Jessica contorted her face into the most appalling grimace, and rattled off the list of Miss Allard's rules, in a sing-song voice, rather like a ditty, making those in hearing range laugh again.

Rose squirmed uncomfortably in her seat. She was aware

her Yorkshire accent was unrefined, and one more mark against her suitability as a wife for Nick.

She pondered this, and Nick turned, in time to see a shadow flit across her fairy-like features. Her eyes darkening from blue to violet. Excusing himself, he made his way over to where she was fidgeting.

"Rose?"

She lifted her gaze.

"What's wrong?

Standing, she moved to the fireplace, away from inquisitive ears. "Nick," she rubbed her forehead, "is my... would it be better if... I worry that..." her words trailed off. *Dash it all, she sounded like a feeble milksop. Nick, would my standing among your friends be enhanced if I spoke correctly? Rose, you are pitiful.* Mimicking a child's petulant whine in her silent self-mockery.

"Rose, what is it love?" Uncaring that they were in a room full of people, Nick took her hand, threading their fingers together. The rub of his thumb over her palm, soothing.

"Am I... is the way I speak... should I attend elocution lessons?" The words came out in a rush.

Nick gaped at her. "Why would you want to do that?" Completely perplexed.

"Is not my accent also vulgar? Mayhap not the most appropriate for..."

Nick did not allow her to finish. "Rose Archer, please do not belittle yourself. Your voice, your accent is what saved me when at my most vulnerable. Your soft lilt and gentle tones warmed me when I could not sleep for pain. It is not something you should hide or erase, it is part of you, and for me one of the most important. Without the sound of your voice, calling me back from the brink, refusing to let me give up, I might easily have let go."

He held her gaze, hazel on blue, until she smiled. In a bold move, he leant close, brushing his lips against the curve of her ear, his cheek grazing hers.

"I want to listen to that beautiful accent when you greet me, when you plead with me to possess you, when we lie tangled together. My name the last thing on your lips before you tumble into sleep."

Rose blushed as pink as the roses climbing the wall at one side of the garden. "Well, good sir, your silver-tongue convinces me. Mayhap elocution is not as essential as I imagined." She squeezed the fingers still entwined in hers.

Sharing an ardent look, in place of the kiss they both desired, their quiet exchange — perhaps fortuitously — was rudely interrupted by an ear-splitting bellow from Max who had decided he needed feeding immediately, and that was not soon enough.

His red face, pumping fists, and disgruntled wails prompted Billie to whisk away her squalling son, to a quiet corner of the house to assuage his hunger.

The distraction was the cue for the group to think about returning to their respective homes. The gathering had been convivial, but Theo, with an eye to his wife who was increasing, knew she needed to rest and would not while their friends were present.

By the time Billie had satisfied her son, carriages were waiting and, in dribs and drabs, goodbyes were said, the couples going their separate ways.

"Might you be amenable to a stroll back to Whiteoaks?" Nick ventured as Rose and he walked through the wicket at the end of the Elliott's garden.

"I think that would be lovely, as long as no one thinks we are breaking any rules." Rose smiled, glad of the chance to be alone with Nick.

Nick turned to Hugh. "Rose and I would like a few moments to ourselves, and wondered whether you would consider our walking back to Whiteoaks a breach of etiquette?"

Hugh shrugged, and glanced at Helena who considered their question.

"I do not imagine anything untoward will occur between here and there," she smiled, ignoring a smothered snort from Jessica, who knew *exactly* how diverted one might become in a quiet corner of the estate. "We shall see you back at the house." Allowing Hugh to assist her up into one of the carriages.

Billie and Giles appeared with the pile of paraphernalia they needed whenever they left the house with Max in tow.

Reiterating their thanks to Theo and Grace for welcoming them into their home, Rose and Nick waved to the others as they trundled by, horses and carriage wheels kicking up clouds of dust. Soon it was quiet. The only sound the hum of bees and trill of birds. The late afternoon haze softened the surrounding scenery as the couple sauntered slowly back towards the great house.

Her arm tucked under Nick's, Rose was content to walk without chatting. It was enough they were together; conversation unnecessary. They covered the distance quickly, too quickly, and Nick deemed it essential to prolong their promenade, by stopping every so often to exchange a lingering kiss.

A delay Rose had no complaint about whatsoever.

August slid by in a blaze of glory, each day bright and sunny, and although overly hot, England basked in its warmth. To date, the year had been miserable weatherise, a few short weeks of soaring temperatures a worthy compensation.

Hugh and Nick returned to London halfway through the

month. Business in the shipping trade never stood still, and there was much to which they were required to attend.

Rose missed Nick, but while at Whiteoaks they had sought each other's company as frequently as politeness decreed, cherishing private moments, snatched here and there.

Comfortable with her hosts, and grateful for their attentiveness, Rose did chafe a little at the endless round of entertainment.

When she thought no one noticed, she disappeared for long walks through the Great Park. Her caution was wasted; it was rare anyone avoided the many eyes and ears of the Whiteoaks staff.

Billie sympathised with her guest's need to be alone and made no mention of it. Occasionally, one of the other ladies asked whether they might join Rose, especially Jessica, who casually remarked there was naught more beneficial than a brisk walk just after dawn, when the day was at its coolest.

From habit, Duncan started work at first light, and Jessica had assured Rose it was no hardship to accompany him to Whiteoaks. Thus, the two young women, who were becoming fast friends, arranged to take a constitutional every morning, weather permitting.

With Trixie bounding along at their side, Jessica and Rose vanished for hours, arriving back at the big house with cheeks flushed from exertion and fresh air.

As the month moved on, Jessica discerned this bright young woman was everything she could hope for in a sister-in-law. She was endlessly happy her brother had finally seen sense and fallen in love.

∾

Too soon their sojourn in the country drew to a close. In truth, although Rose had enjoyed herself immensely, she needed to be occupied. It was lovely to relax, to allow others to provide for your every need, but she was used to hard work. Her days were normally full, from dawn until dusk, but now time was beginning to weigh heavily on her hands.

Moreover, she missed Nick, alternating between incredulity and frustration that, despite knowing him for so brief a time, being apart made her heart ache. This, so feminine a notion, galling.

She had survived nearly one and twenty years without him, a mere month should be borne easily. That said when they began the tedious process of packing, excitement, prompted by the knowledge she would see him before the week was out, began to bubble.

Whiteoaks, never particularly quiet — the sounds of a busy estate continually wafting around the main house — became a hub of noise. Staff bustled around preparing their guests for the journey back to the city.

Trunks appeared, clothes were cleaned, pressed, and folded, lavender sprigs placed carefully between the thin sheets of paper separating each garment to keep them fresh. Carriage and horses were readied.

It was time to go.

Rose, with Jessica's help, and Duncan's expertise, had procured a small token of her gratitude for Billie and Giles. The couple had made her very welcome, treating her as though family, and she appreciated their kindness.

Penning a short note thanking her host and hostess, she left it, along with the gift — a wooden bowl carved out of the palest wood, in the shape of an oak leaf — in her bedchamber to be found after her departure.

The day of their departure dawned. Waving madly as the carriage trundled down the long driveway, Helena and Rose called out good wishes and thank yous in the most unrefined manner, although neither appeared in the slightest remorseful.

Helena watched as Whiteoaks disappeared from view, her expression pensive. She loved her childhood home, and it was always a wrench to leave. She was a philosophical soul, and before long, her cheery smile was back, and the two women fell to gossiping about what they might have missed while away.

~

They arrived back in London as the afternoon was waning, the glow of the candles in Stanton House an inviting sight. The front door to number 16 Bedford Street was flung open, Hugh and Nick tumbling out with little regard for poor Mr Saunders, whom they almost knocked flying in their haste to greet their womenfolk.

Hugh whisked Helena out of the carriage before she had chance to place one foot on the step, spinning her around and kissing her right there in the street.

Rose swallowed a giggle at Helena's shocked squawk, allowing Nick to hand her down in a much more demure manner. Totally ruined when he leant in and brushed his lips to her forehead, whispering,

"I missed you, my Rose. 'Tis all I can do not to steal you away into the shadows."

Rose smiled up at him, inordinately pleased at his welcome. "I missed you too," she replied quietly, while they were being ushered inside, Mr Saunders instructing the footmen to organise the luggage.

Tired though both Helena and she were after two long days of travel, the smell of a hot meal overrode all other desires. Following a quick wash to freshen up, they joined the men in the dining room.

While they ate, chatter flowing back and forth, Rose realised this family, this house, nay home, was vitally important to her. She felt as though she belonged, and not solely because of Nick. The camaraderie between them, more indicative of a connection stretching back years, rather than the scant months they had known each other.

Musing over how that was possible, Rose concluded the Drummonds were a naturally inclusive, open, and affectionate couple, who did not judge and were respectful of all.

While at Whiteoaks, Rose was privy to stories from Giles and Helena's childhood, and admired their father's ethos in ensuring his offspring empathised with people from every station in life. The more she knew of these people, the less she wanted to say goodbye.

She hoped she would never have to.

CHAPTER 22

*L*istening to Hugh and Nick's conversation, it transpired there was some trouble brewing at Trentams, well not at Trentams per se, more it affected one of their staff.

Kennet Alexson, a reformed pirate and Lynette's beau, had been run to ground by his former crew. Seemingly they desired his presence on the ship he fled a year ago, and Kennet was concerned, in their determination to fulfil this desire, they posed a threat to the shipyard, its employees and most importantly, Lynette.

Mr Alexson had apprised Hugh of the risk, immediately he became aware of it, and although they increased their vigilance, the yard had not received an overt approach.

Rose had met Mr Alexson several weeks past. He was one of the tallest men she had ever seen, towering over Hugh and Nick, even Archie — who resembled a house. The man wore a patch over one eye, a faint scar either side, the only evidence of the damage beneath. He exuded power, and seemed a grim man until he smiled, which was infrequently and usually when with Lynette.

Rose understood his demeanour. Life at sea was harsh. Now, just as Mr Alexson was about to embark on a new, less perilous chapter, with a woman he clearly adored, it looked as though all efforts to sever his past had been fruitless.

Mindful of the near tragedy, which occurred the previous year at Trentams, Hugh was not prepared to take any chances with his wife's well-being. He informed Helena she was not to travel without the protection of one of their footmen or grooms.

"I doubt they will think to come after my family, but I will not ignore the potential, however small. This applies you also, Rose. Your father would never forgive me should anything untoward befall you while under my guardianship."

Rose acknowledged Hugh's concern with a smile and a nod. "Thank you for your solicitude, Hugh. You may rest assured, I shall do nothing to impede my safety. I do not know London enough to wander at will."

Helena asked a few more pertinent questions, but as Hugh and Nick knew only what they had already shared, there was little to add. "The main thing is to let either Nick or me know if you fear you are being watched or followed. As I say, I do not imagine us to be in danger, but these men are unscrupulous and could use us to force Ken's hand."

When Nick and Rose took the air in the tiny garden, Nick reiterated Hugh's warning.

"Please be observant of your surroundings. If anything were to happen to you…" he did not finish his sentence.

Placing a finger on his lips, Rose murmured, "Hush my love, I will take every care. I cannot foresee a circumstance where either you or your brother, or any number of the staff from here or the refuge would not guard me. Do not fret for me, 'tis you I am worried about. If these men want Mr Alex-son, surely it will be Trentams they target?"

Tilting her head to one side, trying to read his face. "Do try to avoid unnecessary bloodshed, although the sight of your bare chest…"

Her cheeks fiery red, Rose clamped a hand over her mouth, completely forgetting in whose presence she was. To admit she had studied his naked torso was wanton in the extreme; such things normally confined to the marriage bed. She heard a laugh rumble through Nick's chest.

"Oh, my love you have no idea what your words do to a man." Drawing her close he scattered kisses over her hot face. His mouth sought hers and the inevitable passion flared.

A ragged moan was torn from Rose, Nick's hands roving over her petite frame. This heat, this ardour continued to astonish her, but there was also an underlying tenderness. An exquisite gentleness, engendering a trust, and a faith that all he wanted was her happiness. It was as liberating as it was sobering. She wound her arms around his neck and pulled his face close to hers.

"Tell me," she all but purred.

"Tell you what?" His beautiful hazel eyes twinkling in the half-light.

"What my words do to you." Her mischievous smile, an invitation.

So, he did.

After a month in the country, life in London quickly resumed its regular routine. The three days Rose spent at Sanctuary House became four. The changing season brought with it a plethora of new maladies, not helped by an abrupt change in the weather which reverted to being cold, blustery, and wet.

A long list of complaints from numerous patients kept Dr Callard and Rose busy from the moment the clinic opened until they closed the doors, often hours later than usual.

The lurking threat at the shipyard seemed stalled, although they remained on high alert at all times. Mr Alexson was convinced something was afoot, a notion supported by Lucas Withers, friend of the Drummonds and a man whose occupation was shrouded in mystery.

That said, if not for the constant presence of either Nick, Hugh or one for the Drummonds' grooms, Rose might have forgotten it all together.

September became October, and Rose received a letter from her father. Dr Archer congratulated his daughter on her betrothal, mentioning he hoped to arrive in the city in about a month, should that prove acceptable. Excited to see him, Rose spoke to Hugh and Helena, saying she would find lodgings, because it was an imposition to stay on at Stanton House.

"You will do no such thing," Helena expostulated. "You and your Papa are like family to us, and he will either stay here with us or at Drummond House. Goodness me, we have rooms a plenty." Helena tutted, while Hugh added his agreement.

Rose raised her hands in supplication. "'Tis only, you have been so generous, and I do not wish to outstay my welcome."

"Psht," Helena huffed, biting back a less than polite excla-mation. "I will write to your father forthwith, and invite him," she continued in a tone that brooked no argument. "That should ensure he does not feel as though he is foisting himself upon our hospitality. Imposing indeed..." Helena continued to mutter under her breath about saving Nick's life and repaying a debt.

"Helena, please. In truth I will be glad to stay here, this house has come to feel like home to me. It's just... I... because..." Rose trailed off, biting her lip.

Glancing across at her guest, Helena grinned suddenly, and bouncing out of her chair, hurried around the table to hug Rose. "Good, we shall say no more about where you and the good doctor will stay. You are both important to Hugh and me, not to mention Mother Drummond, who will be pleased to make the acquaintance of the man who saved her son's life."

Saying she would write that day, and begging Rose to provide her home address, Helena swept out, leaving Rose rather breathless.

"If you think *she* is a force to be reckoned with, it's a good job you have never had Billie on your case," Hugh spoke, his deep voice brimming with amusement at this interlude. "'Tis time I was not here." Folding his napkin and placing it alongside his plate, Hugh stood, sketched a bow, and strode from the room to ready himself for the day.

Smiling to herself, Rose hugged the letter from her father. He had trained in London and she wanted him to take her to all his old haunts, while she showed him the parks, the museum and the art gallery. Oh, and the bookshops, he would lose himself in the bookshops.

Thus, Rose had much to be happy about. Her betrothal to a man she loved more than life itself, a visit from her Papa, and her days full of the most rewarding work.

The state of contentment was not to last. One cool afternoon, the threat to Mr Alexson materialised. Lynette was kidnapped, prompting all at Trentams, along with Lucas

Withers and his men to raise a search. By the time the danger was subdued, a series of blunders had set in motion a most unfortunate chain of events, which would almost cost Rose her life, if not her sanity.

～

The first Rose became aware something was amiss, was the afternoon a burly man arrived at the clinic at Sanctuary House, virtually carried in by Mr Edgeworth and Mr Buckle, two of the guards. Dishevelled, dusty, bloodied, and barely conscious, initially Dr Callard presumed the man drunk; roughed up in a bar fight. On the heels of Mr Buckle, Roland ran in shouting it was Ned from Trentams.

"How on earth do you know that, Roland?" queried Rose over her shoulder as she began to wash the filth from poor Ned's swollen face.

"'Me an' Timmy knows 'im. 'E's one of our mates," Roland replied, saying he had spotted Ned struggling up the steps into Sanctuary House, and called for the two guards. "Don't know wot 'e's doin' here mind, 'e should be at the yard this time on a Wednesd'y …" he left that dangling, frowning in puzzlement. Neither could the others offer any explanation.

Leaving the reasons why for now, Rose and Dr Callard began the task of cleaning Ned's wounds. Cutting away his shirt, which was ripped anyway, they surveyed the damage.

He had taken a severe beating, angry red marks already starting to bruise. His face looked as though it had been stomped on, and his knuckles were scuffed and raw.

Hovering on the edge of unconsciousness, Ned hissed when the cool water, liberally mixed with vinegar and salt, touched his sore flesh, which along with the pungent aroma brought him back to his senses.

"Mrs Collins," he muttered, through split lips.

"What about Mrs Collins?" Rose asked.

"They took her, couldn't stop them."

She could see Ned's every breath was an effort, every word a husked croak. Grimacing, when Rose massaged ointment over his chest to soothe and hopefully alleviate the worst of the bruising, Ned was unable to prevent a groan.

"I'm sorry Ned, but this will help. Truly," Rose smiled at his disbelieving expression, and kept talking, distracting him from what the doctor was doing to treat the lacerations to his face.

"What do you mean they took her?"

Ned told them, in short bursts. He was escorting Mrs Collins to the refuge for her afternoon shift when a gang of thugs set upon them.

"I think they were Mr Alexson's pirates," he elaborated. "I landed a few punches but there were too many, and the last thing I 'eard were Mrs Collins ticking them off for 'urtin' me."

Rose bit down on a grin. She had come to know Lynette quite well over the last few months and understood her to be a woman who did not suffer fools gladly.

"I need to go after 'em." Ned tried to get up from the chair they had lowered him into, wincing when his aching ribs protested.

"Sit down, you great lummox," Rose admonished, tutting. "Lot of use you will be if you do not allow us to fix you up. We can send a runner to apprise Trentams what's happened... please, Ned, sit down," when Ned tried, once again to stand.

"Come on, you must see you are of no use in this state, and 'tis unfair if Mr Drummond has to worry about you in addition to Mrs Collins." Her words persuaded the man to resume his seat.

He suffered their ministrations with barely restrained

impatience, but his face was grey with pain, one eye so swollen he could not see out of it. Added to this a probable broken nose, at least three cracked ribs and split lips, Ned reluctantly admitted he felt rather worse for wear.

"She were under my protection," he grumbled, while Dr Callard bandaged his ribs in the hopes of restricting his movement for a day or so until they began to heal.

"I do not see what more you could have done, bar getting yourself killed," retorted Rose, in no-nonsense tones. "We need to let Trentams know with all haste." As she said this, another stranger barrelled through the door, Mrs Parry in a bit of a fluster, close behind.

"Ned, bloody 'ell!" The newcomer gawked in shock at Ned.

Rose started to explain what seemed to have happened.

"Yes, we know," the man interrupted, "Young Timmy turned up at the yard. 'E saw what 'appened and followed 'em. Mister Drummond is organisin' to rescue Mrs Collins."

Mrs Parry took this in without batting an eyelid. Sanctuary House was used to the most bizarre of incidents, this was merely another in a very long line. The clinic was now full of people, making it difficult for the doctor and Rose to work.

Taking over, she dispatched the man, whose name was Bert, back to the shipyard to confirm Ned was safe. Roland was sent to the kitchen to request a hot drink for Ned. The two guards, persuaded Ned was not going to attack either Dr Callard or Rose, returned to their posts.

This left three, and blessed peace reigned. Before long, Rose and the doctor, satisfied they had done all they could, assisted Ned through to the big dining room, where a hot meal, and a welcome cup of tea awaited, courtesy of Sybil Miller.

Roland had blurted out a half tale, and Sybil, friendly with

Lynette, was worried. Rose could do little to assuage her anxiety, except confirm those at Trentams knew.

"It is fortuitous Timmy saw the brawl unfold. His quick thinking may well have saved the day. Rose said. "Helena is quite correct. These lads are worth their weight in gold!"

CHAPTER 23

There was naught anyone at Sanctuary House could do except wait. Roland ran off to the shipyard at some point during the afternoon, returning to tell anyone who would listen, there was a plan in place, and they hoped to bring the pirates to justice before the day was out.

Rose, worried about Lynette, found herself unable to concentrate, and decided a walk might prove beneficial. In the confusion, she forgot Hugh's instruction to take an escort and, even if she had, would have presumed the threat no longer applied.

The pirates had their prize, she was of no importance. Slinging a warm wrap around her shoulders, she slipped out of the back door and, intending to be gone less than ten minutes, never thought to leave a note, or tell anyone where she was going. For some reason, there were no sentries guarding the rear entrance at that particular moment.

Not a single person saw her leave.

. . .

Lost in thought, Rose strolled along narrow streets, the darkening light of the autumn afternoon, throwing everything into shades of grey. She was fascinated by the difference in the buildings here compared with the district where the Drummonds lived.

Houses tightly packed together, several families occupying each one and, although for the most part looked clean enough, were shoddily constructed, giving them an air of decay.

The odour of overcrowding, poverty, unwashed bodies, and stale beer permeated everything. To Rose, it was as though the inhabitants had given up. They could see no respite from the hand fate tossed them, so why bother?

Saddened that so beautiful a city allowed such degradation of humanity to continue right on the doorstep of the refined suburbs, her appreciation of what Sanctuary House achieved increased a hundred-fold.

Deep in contemplation she bit off a yell of surprise when a small hand slipped into hers. Glancing down, she saw it was Andy Fletcher.

"Andy, what are you doing here?" Astonished, Rose crouched until she was eye level with the child.

"We live just around the corner," he grinned cheekily. "Come on, I'll show you."

"Oh, I'm not sure your father would want me to visit without an invitation. Is there a park we could go to instead?" She tried to divert him, but Andy guffawed.

"A park? 'Ere? Don't make me larf" He dragged her along the street, and down two more until he stopped outside a shabby doorway. Pushing it open, he tugged her hand. "Come on Miss Rose, Mark's 'ere too."

Rose peered into the gloom, her eyes quickly adjusting, and she made out the interior. Everything they owned was here, on this one level. Mark was sitting at a well-scrubbed table, his swinging feet banging the chair legs, the tip of his tongue just sticking out, in concentration.

Rose spied a book, open in front of him, one grubby finger running across the pages, presumably under the words he was reading. A smile twitched at her mouth. Helena was constantly trying to get the four boys interested in stories, but they preferred games to books. It seemed she was successful, after all.

Opposite the door, at the far side of the room, a cot was built into an alcove, another slightly larger bed tucked into the corner, a wicker chair by its head. To her left, a small kitchen, complete with stove, shelf, and sink. On her right, three threadbare armchairs were grouped around a grate, where a fire was laid but not lit.

The room was chilly but not unbearably so. Rose guessed that to have the fire burning all day was too costly.

Mark glanced up, his eyes widening when he saw Rose in the doorway.

"Andy," he hissed, "Da will be mad if he knows you brought Miss Rose 'ere."

"Do not fret, Mark, I will be gone before your father returns from work. Andy did not expect to see me so close to your home and was excited to show me where you live. 'Tis delightful."

Mark flushed and closed his book. "I can make a cup o' coffee," he said proudly. "Da showed me 'ow."

"I should like that above all things," Rose replied sinking a curtsy, which made both boys giggle. Without commenting, she offered to help the child, and between them, they procured a reasonably hot drink, which almost resembled coffee.

It was obvious to Rose, Mr Fletcher maintained a clean and tidy home, despite the lack of space and the comforts, even she in as isolated a village as Runswick Bay was used to.

Taking one of the seats by the fire, Rose listened to the two boys while they prattled on brightly about what they had been doing. In return she told them about her holiday at Whiteoaks and what had happened to Mrs Collins.

They knew and liked the latter, and as with Sybil, were always under her feet in the kitchens begging for any scraps of food, when she prepared the meals. Not wanting to scare the children, Rose played down the peril of the situation without detracting from the seriousness of it.

"This is why you must always tell someone where you are going," she concluded, blithely ignoring the fact she walked out of the refuge without so much as a by your leave.

Mindful of the time, realising she had been out far longer than intended, Rose stood. Saying goodbye to Andy and Mark, she was pulling her wrap back around her shoulders, when the door flew open and Mr Fletcher came in.

Taking in the scene at a glance, his brows drew together and the smile on his mouth turned down.

"What is the meaning of this?" he growled. "You bleedin' busy-body! Come to check on me 'ave yer? Come to make sure me boys are not starvin'? Well get out, an' don't bother coming back. We're fine, we don't need yer 'elp."

Mark tried to intervene, but his father waved him away.

"Be quiet, Mark."

Rose paled, then flushed red, mortified he assumed she was interfering.

"Mr Fletcher, please I had no id—"

"Get out!" he roared.

Rather than yell back, as she had the first they met, this time Rose fled, unwilling to make the situation worse by trying to argue.

Unfortunately, she could not remember the route Andy took to their home, and all the streets looked the same. Assuming she would eventually come upon the refuge she just ran in what seemed like the right direction. It was nearly dark.

The streets were unfamiliar and the further she went the more lost she became. Slowing her steps, she scanned her surrounds, searching for anything she might recognise. Panic coiled through her. Too late she recalled Helena's words when they were at the coaching inn, on their journey to London.

'London is not like Runswick Bay. There are many who do not treat ladies properly and if by chance we become separated while out, please do not try to make your own way home. Stay where you are, and I will find you. I know the city, and it is easy to take a wrong turn, becoming lost in the maze of streets, where unscrupulous people lurk.'

Bloody hell.

∽

Back at Sanctuary House, Dr Callard was bewildered. *Where on earth was Rose?* She was here moments ago and now it was as though she vanished into thin air. He poked his head outside and scanned the alley. No sign of her. He called for Roland.

"Have you seen Miss Rose?" He quizzed the boy when he appeared in the doorway.

"Not since she left the dining room after you had your meal. Mebbe she went 'ome?"

"Unlikely, for she would be staying for the afternoon clinic." The doctor replied.

"I'll go see if she's in one of t'other rooms." Roland scooted off, tearing through the refuge, yelling for Miss Rose, bringing exasperated complaints down on his head for disturbing the quiet in the process. He did not appear in the slightest repentant as he ran up and down the corridors. No one had seen Rose. Returning to the clinic Roland updated Dr Callard, then said he would have a quick look around outside.

After a fruitless search, the lad informed the doctor she was nowhere to be found, at which point the latter, given recent events, became more than a little perturbed.

It seemed as though Rose had completely disappeared.

The minute Rose fled the Fletcher's house, Andy and Mark swarmed all over their father, crying that Miss Rose had not come to check up on them, that it was Andy who found her walking through the neighbouring streets, and brought her here for a hot drink.

"Was only bein' polite, Da. It's cold outside and she's a nice lady. She took care of me." Andy's lip trembled and his voice wobbled, as he squeezed back tears. "You told us allus to be polite."

Realising his mistake, Mr Fletcher swung Andy up into his arms. "I'm sorry, son," he muttered, "I thought..." he didn't voice his fear Rose might think him incapable of caring for his children.

He knew it was unfair to leave them alone for hours on end, but of late they spent their days at the refuge. Under the friendship of Timmy and Roland, his sons had begun to show an interest in learning. He often came home to find Mark buried in a book, painstakingly forming the words that told the story therein.

Shaking his head, and horrified he caused Miss Archer to run, here where she could so easily become lost, he gathered the two boys, and set out to look for her.

Halfway to the refuge, the three came upon Timmy, who was coming back from Trentams. The lad regaled them with the tale of Lynette's kidnapping, gratified by their avid faces during the telling.

"Have you seen Miss Rose?" Mr Fletcher asked when he could get a word in edgeways.

"Why, she missin' too?" Timmy's jaw fell open. Two women disappearing in one day! This was becoming a real adventure.

"Yes, but I do not think she was kidnapped, just got lost on her way back to the refuge. We need to see whether any of the men here might help look for her."

Rushing up the steps, Timmy was about to yell for Mrs Parry, when that good lady met him at the front door.

"Yes, Timmy, thank you, I already know. Dr Callard informed me Miss Rose has vanished. A meeting is required I think." Ruffling his tow hair, while greeting Mr Fletcher, and ushering them all into her office, where the doctor was already waiting. Mrs Parry asked them each to tell what they knew and between them they built up a better picture.

"So, it seems Miss Rose went for a walk, met up with Andy, went back to your home, Mr Fletcher, then left in a hurry, presumably without knowing how to get back here? Do I have that right?" Nods all around.

"Heavens, the woman could be in all sorts of trouble. Before we panic, I think we need to organise a proper search. Timmy, please go and ask all the guards to come here, and then I have another job for you."

Timmy dashed off to do as he was bidden. Dr Callard, Mr Fletcher, and Mrs Parry continued to discuss the likely routes Rose might have taken, but it was pure conjecture.

The districts surrounding the refuge resembled rabbit warrens. Streets and alleyways twisting and turning, too easy for anyone unfamiliar with them to be lost forever. Not to mention the danger from those who lurked among them.

"Tis my fault, Mrs Parry," Mr Fletcher admitted. "I was

angry with her, suspected she was meddlin' and raised my voice to her."

Mrs Parry peered at him over her spectacles, causing him to flush bright red, hearing how childish he sounded.

"My apologies, I never intended this to 'appen."

"I don't suppose you did, Mr Fletcher, but why you might imagine Miss Rose would ever interfere with the way you care for your boys is beyond me. Naught we can do about that now, let us hope we find her quickly, so you are able to apologise." She held his sheepish gaze until he inclined his head. "Then I'll say no more, I expect you will berate yourself enough."

Turning her head when Timmy reappeared with several men traipsing in behind him. Most of those who acted as guards or wardens were retired soldiers, astute in what was required in a search and, within minutes of hearing what Mrs Parry had to say, were hurrying down the steps and into the gloom.

Needing to attend to any patients at the clinic, Dr Callard excused himself, while Timmy and Roland took a message to Helena. Regardless of whether they found Rose quickly, Mrs Parry decided to inform Helena now. Rose was her guest and friend, she needed to be told immediately.

Now all they could do was wait.

CHAPTER 24

*H*opelessly lost, Rose was trudging disconsolately along a dark street, desperately hoping she would recognise something, anything, enabling her to retrace her steps to the refuge, or Trentams or Stanton House.

Anxiety that her absence must have been noticed — and doubtless reported — combined with a growing certainty she would never find her way home, was slowly reducing her to a state of utter panic.

Why on earth did she decide to go for a walk? *You thoughtless girl,* she castigated herself. Being a practical-minded young woman, she conceded there was no point giving into fear. Best thing was to keep walking, and pray she reached the outskirts of this district in short order.

Unbeknownst to Rose, many of the streets were not straight, they ran in peculiar curves, meeting, then separating with and from others. It might appear you were heading in one direction but was entirely possible you were either going in a completely different one, or worse, doubling back on yourself.

The other problem was the sun had set, and the moon was yet to rise, leaving Rose unable to use either a guide; the early evening in that curious gloom before it is totally dark.

Hunching into her wrap, the temperatures plummeting, Rose strove to keep going. Venturing along a street which looked promising, she swallowed a squawk when a figure loomed up in front of her.

"Lost are yer?" a nasal voice with a broad cockney twang enquired.

"Not lost so much, as slightly off course," Rose replied in what she hoped was a confident manner. "Would you be so kind as to tell me in which direction I should go, to find Sanctuary House?" Presuming everyone hereabouts knew about the refuge.

"It would be my pleasure, follow me."

"Oh, thank you Sir, I am most grateful." All too trustingly, Rose fell into step alongside the man, nerves prompting her to talk about anything that came into her head.

Bearing the ostentatious name of Obadiah Matthews, the man who had spotted Rose walking in circles, listened to her garrulous chatter, quickly identifying her as being from much further afield than London, her accent clearly northern.

Now what was such a pretty young woman doing in this hellhole?

To Obadiah, she was like a gift from God. He was on the lookout for fresh meat, and she fell right into his lap, so to speak. *Well it would be better if she fell into others' laps — face first —* an evil grin curving his thin lips.

She couldn't be an innocent, not walking these streets, but she had the look of one who was. That would please his regulars. Some of his girls were a bit long in the tooth, with a tendency to plumpness, and his customers would pay handsomely for one such as this chit.

"What is your name?" He interrupted her monologue.

"I beg your pardon, sir, 'tis Rose." She smiled, and even in the darkness, Obadiah could see she had a good set of teeth. One more thing in her favour.

Hooking his arm in invitation, he encouraged, "Come, my pretty blossom, Obadiah will soon see you warm and comfortable."

Rose hesitated, suddenly unsure. Unease prickled at the edge of her mind, but she had no real alternative. If she refused his offer, where would she go? He seemed polite, if not a tad brash. His attire was clean and tidy, and he was wearing shoes. Ignoring her instinct, currently screaming at her to run, Rose slipped her arm through his, and followed his lead.

Not all that far away, the wardens were returning to Sanctuary House in dribs and drabs, each reporting their lack of success in finding Miss Rose. Helena arrived with Barnaby and John; outwardly calm, inwardly wishing Hugh was with her.

At present, her husband, along with most of the Trentams staff as well as Lucas Withers and his men, were hopefully, in the process of rescuing Lynette, and capturing a gang of pirates. Informing them of this latest catastrophe would have to wait.

It was a long night.

Shortly after midnight, a messenger arrived to tell the waiting group, the pirates were all dead but, tragically, it seemed Lynette had also lost her life in the melee. His audience was horrified. Lynette had just begun to live again, after years of being abused by her husband… the man who set fire to the refuge a little over a year before.

Moreover, Lynette was recently betrothed to Kennet Alexson, the man for whom the brigands searched. That she was killed in such iniquitous circumstances, devastated those listening, and for a while, everything else paled into insignificance.

The messenger, Frank — one of Withers' men — was pressed into partaking of a hot drink. When he stood to leave, and with no other information forthcoming about Rose, Helena made a decision and asked whether he would be so kind as to wait a few more moments.

"Are you going back to Trentams, Frank?" He nodded, "I need to send a missive to Mr Drummond. Please will you take it for me?"

"Of course, Lady 'Elena." Tipping his head, Frank resumed his seat, and his conversation with Mr Fletcher, while Helena hurried away to the office to pen a brief note to her husband, outlining what they believed happened with regard to Rose.

Returning to the dining room, where everyone had gravitated — it being large with plenty of chairs — she handed Frank the note, mentioning almost as an aside that it concerned Miss Rose.

"Something else awry, Lady 'Elena?" Frank queried; abruptly aware this impromptu gathering might not be because of the pirates.

"I am afraid so, Frank. Miss Rose is missing."

Frank's jaw dropped. "Why did yer not say so earlier, m'lady? We need ter find 'er."

"I realise that, Frank. We have been looking for her, while similarly important matters occupied you all. You cannot be in two places at once," she replied bracingly. "Regrettably, she has not returned, and now we have another person for whom to search."

Frank shook his leonine head and, tucking the note into his pocket, dashed out into the darkness.

Hours ticked by and they heard nothing, unaware when Frank reached Trentams, he was informed Mr Drummond and Lucas were at the site of the brawl, supervising the clean-up. Frank headed that way, only to be told, Mr Drummond and Archie had repaired to Withers' office.

By the time he trudged up the stairs to the quiet suite of rooms in a nondescript backstreet, Frank was exhausted, and dawn had broken.

Knocking, he was admitted by Lucas, whereupon he handed the note to Hugh. Frank remarked it seemed Miss Rose had vanished. No one had seen anything of her since the previous afternoon.

A series of curses echoed around the room, while the four men pondered this latest news. They were tired beyond measure but knew Rose's likely fate if found wandering lost and alone.

Sleep would have to wait.

Frank was instructed to go home and get some rest, to which he retorted. "Rest is for babies, there's a lady missing."

Knowing it was pointless to argue, Withers hurriedly completed the report, which would be handed to the magistrate later in the day, then the four made their weary way to the refuge.

Helena met them as they climbed the front steps. Worried at the delay in hearing from Hugh, she was about to go to the shipyard. "Hugh, oh thank goodness." She flung herself at her husband who held her close, kissing her forehead. "Oh, what a terrible night you have all suffered, and now this."

"Fret not, love. We shall find Rose. Ken has Lynette, and I

will try to check on him later today. I think he needs to be left alone with his grief for a little while."

Helena nodded her understanding, and hugged Hugh tightly, before releasing him to greet Archie and Lucas.

"Where's Nick?" she asked.

"I presume he went home," Hugh replied.

"He needs to know, this is Rose. He would never forgive us if we did not tell him. Heavens, her father is due in three days' time. I pray we find her before then."

"I am sure we will, now come, let us hear what happened." The little group walked back into the refuge as the weak winter sun began to creep over the horizon.

Rose had been missing for more than twelve hours.

Rose woke to a veritable cacophony of sound and it took her a few moments to work out where she was. Glancing around the unfamiliar room, memory flooded in.

Oh, this was bad, this was very, very bad.

It did not take her long, the previous night, to realise the man she trusted would escort her safely back to Sanctuary House, had absolutely no intention of doing so.

After screaming for help, to no discernible effect, and unable to extricate herself from his death-like grip, Rose found herself shoved through a shadowy doorway almost hidden down a dark alley.

Too late, she noticed the shingle announcing they were about to enter 'Obadiah's Cavern'.

Wriggling, she once again tried to flee, but he caught her, slamming her against the wall. One hand under her chin, he lifted her clear off the ground.

"Don't even think about it, my pretty. Sanctuary 'Ouse my arse. Yer don't need them do-gooders. Much more fun working for me. You do as yer told and yer'll be fine. Step out of line an' yer'll rue the day yer were born. Do you understand?"

He squeezed her throat until she saw spots, terror making her nod jerkily. He let go, and she crumpled to the floor, coughing, and wheezing.

Oh Papa, she thought, trying not to be sick, *I wish I had never left Runswick Bay.*

"Florrie!" Obadiah yelled, and after a few moments, a buxom woman appeared at the top of the rickety stairs. "New one fer yer. Thinks she's a lady, very lah di dah she is. We'll use that and sell 'er as such, that'll give 'em a treat. Find 'er a room, and make sure she's ready fer tomorrer night."

Rose wasn't given time to ponder what this meant as Florrie thumped down the stairs, and grabbed her wrist, dragging her up behind her ample body.

"Please, please, let me go," Rose pleaded. "I just took a wrong turn. Helena will be looking for me. Oh God, where am I?"

"Obadiah's place." As though that answered everything. "Can't let yer go, more'n my life's worth. You'll just 'ave to grin and bear it."

"Grin and bear what?" The horror of where she was, beginning to nudge at the back of her consciousness.

"'Is customers. Mind 'e's right, you are a pretty one and no mistake. Them wot come 'ere will be pleased to 'ave you."

"Have me? Please, what are you saying?"

"Why this is a brothel, my lovely. You will be a popular addition to 'is menu."

Rose swayed on her feet. Everything Obadiah said, dropped into place. She moaned, and her stomach rebelled. "Sick…" she muttered.

Florrie pushed her into a room at the stop of the stairs, grabbing a bowl from the floor. "'Ere, use this."

The stench of urine hit Rose, causing her to vomit again, and again, until she was dry retching. Desperate to steady her breathing, and settle her fractious insides, she sank to the floor, a cloud of dust rising around her. *This place was a hovel. It was filthy, and she was expected to... let a man...* she could not finish that thought.

Nick, oh Nick, I'm so sorry, I love you, but now we will never get to share that love, to experience the intimacy which was so tantalising close. By the time you find me, if you ever do find me, it will be too late. I will be tainted, debauched by men who care nothing for who I am. I did not expect this to be my fate, or our goodbye.

Heart cracking, sobs rose in her throat. Rose forced them back. She refused to give in to feminine tears or allow anyone the satisfaction of knowing they were going to break her. There must be a way to escape. As this idea ran through her head, Florrie's words cut in.

"Don't think about trying to run, he'll kill yer soon as look at yer. As far as 'e's concerned you're 'is property now to do with as 'e pleases. To live or die is in your 'ands. Do right by 'im, and 'e'll feed and clothe yer. Upset 'im and you'll regret it for the rest of yer life, short as it will be."

Shuddering, Rose straightened her shoulders, and lifted her head, pride coming to the fore.

Florrie saw this and nodded. "You'll do."

Left to sleep in a dingy room, which stank of unwashed bodies and other things, which did not bear contemplating, Rose huddled on the bed, trying to come up with a way of escape.

The window was barred, and despite her small stature,

she would not be able to squeeze through the gap. The door was thick, and heavy, and Florrie had locked it from the outside. It was a prison, from which, Rose could see no way of fleeing.

Finally, she fell asleep from sheer exhaustion. Even the fear of what she was about to be subject to could not keep her awake.

At least in dreams she was free.

CHAPTER 25

Dragging herself off the bed, Rose opened the shutters, and scanned the room to see whether there was a bowl in which to wash. A chamber pot stood under a little wooden table, but oddly, she had no desire to relieve herself. Her stomach ached, and her head was thumping. She felt sticky and dirty, the dust from the floor, and the mud from the street clinging to her skin and gown.

A key turned, and Florrie stood there, hands on hips.

"Come with me." The older women led the way through to a room with several basins. "'Ere's where we wash. Make sure you wash properly before and after each client, they don't want to smell another man on you."

"I am expected to… have… more than one man a night?" Rose croaked, her stomach roiling again.

"O' course, it's by the hour 'ere, my lovely." She ran experienced eyes over Rose's tiny frame. "I'll find yer a nice gown, and we'll get that one cleaned. It's fair decent. If Obadiah is selling you as a lady, that'll help the illusion."

"Florrie, I am not a lady, I never said I was a lady, but I do know one. I am her guest and doubtless, she will have organised a search party for me by now. If you want to avoid the weight of the law hammering down on this place, you would be wise to let me leave. I promise to say nothing of what transpired here. Moreover, however hard I tried, I could not find this place again."

She gazed at Florrie her glorious eyes shadowed, terror lurking in their forget-me-not depths.

Florrie hesitated. In truth, this chit did look quite refined. Her skin was lightly tanned but clear and glowing — she was the picture of health. Her nails were not torn or dirty. Her hair was glossy, and so pale it was like moonlight. *Hell's teeth Florrie*, she chastised herself, *you're goin' soft*. Firming her resolve, she shook her head.

"Don't even think abaht it. I were like you once. I 'ad a nice job in an 'ouse up past Covent Garden. Fell on 'ard times they did, 'ad to let me go, and I couldn't get another position. I was starvin', sleepin' under a bridge when Obadiah found me one night, and brought me 'ere. I won't lie ter yer, it's awful. I 'ate servicing these men.

"Most are crude, rough and, if you upset 'em, can be downright dangerous. But I got nuthin' else, nowhere to go. 'Ere, I 'ave a bed, a place to wash up, and food in me belly. Keep your 'ead down, in more ways than one," she gave Rose a sly smile, "make all the right noises, at the right time, and yer'll be fine."

Rose went as pale as her hair. "If this is supposed to make me feel better about being dragged in here against my will. About lulling me into a false sense of security. I think you might need a lesson in prevarication," she bit out.

A wry smile curved Florrie's lips. "By you 'ave some fire. The gents love that. A bit o' spirit is very seductive. Play on it."

"I have no intention of being seductive, or fiery, or alluring, or anything. If they want me, they will just have to take me, but I will not lead them on, or entice them in any way. I have never…" she clamped her mouth shut. Rose could not admit to being innocent. Florrie would not believe her anyway.

Florrie crowed with laughter. "Oh, me dear, you are a gem. Obadiah will like watching them break you."

"Watch? Obadiah watches?" A whole new wave of horror swept through Rose, and she gagged, clinging to the basin to stop from fainting, or vomiting again.

"O' course. He needs to know you're satisfying 'is clients. You'll be a popular draw, new and seemingly untouched.'

"I *am* untouched," Rose murmured under her breath, eyes closing to banish the images Florrie's words engendered.

"A virgin? Go on with you."

Rose lifted her face back to Florrie's, and the woman gasped.

The truth was clear in the young woman's haunted eyes, and for the first time in more years than she cared to count, Florrie wavered. Unbidden, memories of what Obadiah did the last time she thwarted him reared up, and she shook her head. "Well, that's as may be, naught we can do abaht it now. You're 'ere and that's that." Looking away, uncomfortable under that devastated blue gaze.

Rose sagged. Her last hope, appealing to Florrie's better nature, wasted. Straightening her shoulders, she sucked in a calming breath, all expression fading from her face.

"Right," she said hardening her heart, "you might as well tell me what I am supposed to do?"

Her first lesson in becoming a successful whore began.

Nick burst into Sanctuary House, looking as though he had been yanked through a hedge backwards. The news Rose had vanished was the last thing he expected to be woken by after a night of seemingly unending horror. Upon entering the dining room, he was astonished at the crowd already gathered; unaware they had been there all night.

"Helena," his eyes sought those of his sister-in-law but what he saw in them filled him with dread. "Where is she?" His words barely more than a whisper.

"I'm sorry, Nick we do not know. She went for a walk last afternoon and after a slight altercation with Mr Fletcher, no one has seen her."

Nick's eyes swung to the tall man, propping up the wall. "Altercation? Care to elaborate?" he growled. Mr Fletcher explained his part in this debacle, and it was all Nick could do not to let his fists fly. Only the knowledge this would delay even longer held him back. "You thought my Rose a meddler?" he ground out, glaring at the taller man. "If there was time, I would teach you more manners. After all she did for you and young Andy."

Mr Fletcher opened his palms in an apologetic gesture. "Believe me, the minute she ran, I knew my accusation to be erroneous. I wish I could retract them, sadly, I cannot. Now we need to find her. If you want to thump me after that, fair enough."

Nick was about to shoot back a sharp retort when he saw the distress in the older man's face. He was hurting too.

"No, 'tis me who should apologise. This is not the time to argue right and wrong. 'Tis a time to come together to find her." He shut his eyes, an image of Rose grinning up at him, her head tilted to one side filling his mind. He could not lose her. "Can any of you give me a report?"

Several people began to speak at once. Nick held up his hand. "One at a time, please. Mr Buckle?" Indicating one of the sentries. The army veteran spoke slowly, but succinctly, his detailed update enough for Nick.

"So, you have been going out in groups, checking an area then coming back to report, then the next group goes out to cover the adjoining area? Is that correct?" Nods all around. "Is anyone still out?"

"One group of three, oh and I think Timmy was with them. Hopefully, they will bring news," Helena confirmed, trying to sound positive.

Nick paced up and down the room, throwing out theories, all of which had been addressed. Shortly thereafter, those searching returned despondent. Nothing. Not a sign, not a hint, not even the slightest whisper could they find regarding Rose.

Outside, the day was beginning, sounds of people going about their business filtered through the open windows. If there was any trace of Rose, it would likely be lost under the city's bustle. To Nick, sending out endless search parties was futile. The locals would clam up, if a group of ex-military men started asking questions. Most steered clear of anyone in authority,

"Might I suggest, instead of sending out search parties, have one or two people on a rotation basis, casually wander the local neighbourhoods. Without drawing attention, listen to conversations in the streets, tearooms, and taverns.

"A fresh face, a person as distinctive in appearance as Rose, and whose accent labels her as being from beyond the confines of London would be fodder for gossip? A word here or there might give us a lead. Timmy and Roland know these districts well, maybe they have a few friends who might help for a little coin," he proposed.

Timmy and Roland grinned their assent. Not to be left out, Andy and Mark jumped up and down, waving their hands in the air.

"We'll help, we'll help," they chorused, "and 'cos we're small, we can sneak into places you lot can't. Adults often talk in front o' youngsters finkin' we're not listenin'," Mark added, importantly.

Helena was about to decline their suggestion as being too risky when Mr Fletcher interjected.

"If you promise me to go with either Timmy or Roland, I think that is a good plan." He turned to Helena. "Lady Helena, trust me. My boys will not place themselves in danger. They are used to these neighbourhoods and can slip in and out unseen. Timmy and Roland are also streetwise, their faces familiar to most around here. People would not think to curb chit-chat in their presence, they're just lads who run errands."

Helena could see the sense in his argument, and to ignore what might prove pivotal was unthinkable. She gathered the four boys to her and spoke seriously. "Mr Fletcher believes you to be artful, and cautious. To find Rose is vital, but you must not, I repeat not, put yourselves in harm's way. Do I make myself clear?"

Four tousled heads nodded.

"If you come across information, which might lead to her whereabouts, come back here and tell an adult. Do not try to find her on your own." She grinned at the wide-eyed expressions of the boys standing at her knees. "You are too important to me and I will be most upset if anything were to happen to you."

"We promise."

"Trust us m'lady."

"We'll be careful"

"I'll keep an eye on 'em."

All four spoke at once, and this last was Timmy, self-appointed leader of any lad who came to Sanctuary House, in whatever capacity. Smart as a whip, and fiercely loyal to Helena, he would ensure the safety of the others.

There was little else anyone could do. Nick refused to

leave, but suggested Helena and Hugh go home, both had appointments to which they must attend. Helena was coazed into accompanying her husband home. In truth, she was almost asleep on her feet, and Hugh would not allow his wife to overdo things.

The refuge resumed its habitual veneer of organised chaos, and to outward appearances it was business as usual. None would guess the feverish efforts behind the scenes to locate, a diminutive visitor, who in so short a time had become as family to them.

~

Surprisingly, given her circumstances, the day flew by for Rose. Whether it was mounting terror for what the night would bring, or the fact Florrie did not leave her to herself for a single moment, Rose did not know.

According to Florrie, it was not unheard of to service several clients every night, and thus the girls slept through the day, their lives nocturnal. Rose met some of them who were kind in their way; probably glad someone else was there to spread the load, so to speak.

Each girl had her own 'theme,' whether that be a style of dress, or a sexual favour exclusive to her. Rose would be known as the Spirit of the North. Her silvery hair and petite frame, easily conjuring up the illusion she was descended from fairy-folk. Florrie was given instructions that Rose was to wear nothing but a chemise.

Obadiah liked offering his customers the opportunity to inspect the goods before they paid for them.

As evening drew close, Obadiah unlocked the door to Rose's room and came in. He stood with folded arms, studying her. Trying not to squirm under his lewd scrutiny, she held his gaze defiantly.

"I am of a mind to have an auction," he stated, baldly.

"And this would be of interest to me because...?" she demanded; glad her voice was steady.

"You are the prize." He leered, taking a step forward and running one finger down her front, between her breasts and down towards her abdomen. Rose lurched backwards, his touch sickening. Obadiah grabbed her wrist and pulled her against him, his whisky-laden breath, noxious.

"Do not flinch from me, or any man," he hissed, his lips grazing her ear. "You are alive only because you are useful. Any of my clients complain, I will slit your throat and drop your body in the Thames."

Rose could not prevent the whimper, which slid over her lips.

"That's better, moan for me, my pretty flower." Obadiah's free hand stroked over her throat, his thumb applying pressure — the threat clear.

Rose closed her eyes, forcing everything from her mind. "Rest assured, I will not disappoint you." Praying this would be the case, because she suspected she would probably be sick over the first man who requested her services. *What choice did she have anyway?*

She thought of Nick, and his gentle caress, his sublime lips, and his tender hands. The full impact of her predicament struck her, and she was unable to stop a tear from trickling down her cheek. This was now her life. She would never be free of this odious man, and those desperate to defile her body. All she had left of Nick were memories. Those, she would hold on to, no matter what.

These clients of Obadiah might steal her body, but they would *not* steal her mind.

"You have an hour, wear this." He flung a garment onto her bed, turned on his heel and strode out, locking the door behind him.

Rose picked it up and held it in front of her. It was made from such fine material you could see right through, leaving absolutely nothing to the imagination. Once again, her stomach fought; the meal she had eaten not so long ago, bubbling up.

Swallowing, Rose took several deep breaths to control the nausea, and knowing the alternative could be much worse, prepared for the night ahead.

CHAPTER 26

*F*lorrie came to take her downstairs into the main room of the brothel. Rose had seen it earlier, a large, spacious but squalid salon in the harsh light of a winter's day. Cheap furniture, a polished wooden floor, slightly sticky underfoot — which, Rose persuaded herself, was the result of many spilled drinks, and several candelabra scattered about.

Five doors led to dim corridors and curtained alcoves where each client was serviced. If a customer paid for more than an hour, the girls were encouraged to take them upstairs, their bedchambers being less functional than these lower rooms.

By night, the salon took on a different aspect. The glow from the candles made it almost welcoming. The chairs now covered in brightly coloured sheets, the floor freshly scrubbed, and at one end, a makeshift bar set up to serve drinks. It was approaching eight o'clock, the noise of chatter and raucous laughter spilling out when Florrie opened the door.

Rose gulped and tried to pull away.

Florrie had expected as much and tightened her grip. "Come on, girl. Once you've done it the first time it gets easier."

"He said he's going to auction me off."

Florrie peered at her in the gloom. "Well, aren't you the lucky one?"

"Don't know how that's lucky?" Rose grumbled.

"You will be sold to the one with the most coin, usually a gent. Some of them do have peculiar predilections, but they don't hurt you. Well, not often, they just require a little extra for their money."

"Like what?" Rose rejoined, tugging backwards. She wanted to know before stepping into her nightmare.

"Some like to tie you up. Some like to use things other than their... err..." with a mind to Rose's supposed innocence, Florrie went with "...male member. Then there's them as likes to go up yer back passage."

Rose went white. The world around her receded. The sound from the room, so clear a moment ago, became muffled. Florrie was speaking but it came from a long way away.

"Control yourself, woman," she spat. "There'll be no faintin'." She shook Rose, who staggered, desperately striving to regain her composure. "Stand up, let me look at yer." Florrie regarded her dispassionately and nodded. "You'll do. Now come on, 'ead up."

Florrie opened the door.

The sight that greeted Rose was like a ghastly parody of the first ball she attended with Helena. Men dressed in outfits more suited to an audience with the king than a bawdy house, lounged about the room.

The quality of their attire suggested to Rose, this place

must be closer to the West End than she believed. Surely, no one who could afford such clothing, ventured deep into the Rookeries — unless they wanted to hide their licentiousness. She suppressed a shiver

The girls, in various stages of undress, swanned about, carrying drinks, or leant provocatively over a gentlemanly shoulder, breasts all but exposed. Glancing around, Rose saw some of the girls were virtually naked, men taking advantage of what they offered right there in full view of everyone. Her eyelids swept down, blocking the scene for a moment, and she heard Obadiah's nasal tang.

"Gentlemen and… gentlemen…"

Laughter rippled through the room. This was obviously a time-honoured greeting.

"Good evening one and all, welcome to my humble abode. Tonight, we have a special blossom among us. Rose, come here please."

Raising her eyes to him in shock, Rose met his gimlet gaze. He jerked his head, and, despite legs, which felt as though they were sinking into mud, Rose forced herself to move across the room.

Terrified she would trip over, and bring Obadiah's wrath upon her, Rose walked with regal bearing, her head held high, her graceful movements eliciting a collective sigh from an audience fallen speechless.

Prior to coming downstairs, Florrie had arrived in her room to make sure Rose was presentable. The older woman brushed her hair until it glistened opting to leave it loose, in a silken swathe, which kissed her waist.

The chemise hid nothing, her slender frame clearly visible through the cobweb-thin material. The candlelight flickered over her elfin like features. To a man, those observing felt a rush of blood to their loins.

"May I present Rose, my Spirit of the North. Descended

from the fae, she will take you to an enchanted land, and weave her magic, leaving you breathless, and spellbound."

There was a clamour as men started demanding her services. Obadiah gave them their head for a few moments but just as the hubbub reached fever pitch, he raised one hand.

The silence was immediate.

Rose clenched her fists, nails biting into her palms. The thought of all these men using her without conscience — overwhelming.

"My Spirit of the North should be savoured, thus only the most worthy will have the chance to taste her delights." He licked his lips and there was a roar of appreciation from the crowd.

"Beginning tonight, and for the next five days, I will let you admire her, touch her — I understand the importance of inspecting the goods before you buy..." he dropped a slow wink, the men whistled, and the girls giggled. Rose stood, motionless, her face devoid of all expression. "...but no more. Anyone who does not adhere to this will be banned from the Cavern for life. I do not care a fig for your status. In here, those rules do not apply, mine do."

Glaring around the room, Obadiah waited until each man acquiesced to his directive. "I will repeat this every night for five nights, and on the fifth night the highest bidder will win Rose, to enjoy her pleasures until dawn."

To remain unmoved by Obadiah's announcement was the hardest thing Rose had ever done. It wouldn't just be an hour; it would be a *whole night*? Her insides turned to jelly. She heard it was painful, the first time, and that was with someone who cared about you, who was sensitive to your needs — well, she always hoped that would be the case.

Now she would be given up as a sacrifice to the man with the most money whether he was a tender lover, or a raging bull. Determined none would see her fear, Rose somehow maintained her poise.

Obadiah took her hand and paraded her around the room, stopping to allow men to fondle her, anywhere they liked. She suffered them stroking her cheeks and running their fingers through her hair — tugging it not so gently, palming her breasts, gripping her waist — hands digging into her skin. They made her bend over and groped her legs. One man even dragged his finger against her centre. It was all she could do not to scream.

She did not speak and did not make eye contact. The more they touched her, the more she withdrew into herself. This was not her. This was an outer shell. They would never reach her heart. One customer called her the ice queen, another overheard him and quipped he would make her melt.

At the end of an interminable two hours, Obadiah led her from the room, where Florrie waited.

"Take her to her chamber. She is ready," he instructed. Turning to Rose, he grabbed her chin and squeezed hard. "A little less ice, my girl, or you'll be sorry." Slapping her cheek just enough to smart. "If you do not cooperate, I will hand you over to one of my private clients. His penchant for knives and ropes will have you begging for one of them." Tossing his head towards the salon. "Go on, get a good night's sleep, tomorrer you will be on show all night."

Florrie jostled Rose up the stairs, and into her bedchamber. Never had such squalor looked so inviting. Florrie locked the door and clumped down the stairs. Sounds of men taking their pleasure reverberated around the building, echoing off the walls, but Rose shut them out. She was finally alone.

~

The next five days unfolded in a pattern, both for those looking for Rose, and Rose herself.

Every night, Rose was paraded around the salon, her price increasing with rapidity. She was poked, prodded, and manhandled, with little care for her sensitivities. After all, to them she was naught but a whore, not entitled to the luxury of feelings.

Men of every status, who could afford to, or were of a certain propensity, came from far and wide to see this fairy princess who graced Obadiah's Cavern. Most believed the tales of an ethereal elfin beauty exaggerated, until they saw her.

Rose remained stubbornly silent, refusing to look at any of those bidding on her — her reserve merely adding to her allure.

News of the auction spread, but since there was a long-standing ban on keeping a brothel, precise locations of bawdy houses remained vague. Patrons took care not to reveal their whereabouts.

Moreover, the trade was not touted as such, relying on an owner being canny enough to circumvent the law, advertising his, or her, establishment as a bar or gaming hell — the 'serving wenches,' an unexpected bonus.

At the same time, the Drummonds, Lucas Withers and his men, along with many of the staff at Trentams and Sanctuary House were desperately trying to find Rose. It was as though she had never existed.

Nick was tortured by thoughts of what she might be suffering, wishing he had listened to his heart instead of his head, for by now they would likely be married, and she would be safe.

His common sense *did* tell him her disappearance was an unfortunate accident and would probably have happened whether they were wed or not, but he still blamed himself.

Two days after Rose vanished, Dr Archer arrived. His initial reaction was one of rage that these bloody city folk could not protect his daughter. He entrusted her to their care, and they broke their word. After haranguing all three Drummonds at length, he stopped abruptly and sank into a chair, head in his hands.

"Please, please forgive me. I know 'tis not your fault Rose is missing. She is a headstrong woman and has always been thus. Should an idea pop into her head, she would act on it immediately, without any thought to the consequences."

"We believe naught was amiss, until she fell afoul of Mr Fletcher, who thought her interfering in the lives of his two sons. His temper, and demand she leave, saw her fleeing from his home in an area with which she was unfamiliar. Someone must have seen her, found her wandering and taken her in." Hugh did not elaborate on this knowing full well where women, lost and alone, ended up. The problem was discovering which one she had been taken to.

"We have numerous people working around the clock, trying to find her." Unwilling to compound Dr Archer's distress, Hugh couldn't be equivocal where the man's daughter was concerned. He added, delicately. "There have no report of bodies matching Rose's description, so we must assume she is alive."

"Of course, she is alive," interposed Nick harshly, running a hand through his shaggy hair. He was gaunt, and pale, and had barely slept since receiving the news. The moment he shut his eyes, a pair of frantic bluebell coloured eyes, pleaded for rescue.

His Rose — alone, scared, and hidden.

He had to find her.

~

Almost a week since she had stepped out of Sanctuary House to stretch her legs, and partake of a brief constitutional, Rose woke at midday. Tonight, was the night she would lose her innocence. If she was honest, it was lost the moment Obadiah intercepted her, but tonight it would be physical.

There was no recovering from this, it could not be reversed. Should she ever escape this hellhole, or by chance, someone recognised, and rescued her, she was already ruined.

No one wanted someone else's cast offs, especially as she would now be considered a prostitute — socially far below anyone in the Drummond's genteel circle. She would be sullied.

Rose clung to the belief that *if* she was ever freed, her Papa would take her in, for otherwise she might as well stay here. Her dream of a life with Nick smashed into tiny pieces and flung to the four winds.

Two attempts at flight had left her so terrified of Obadiah, Rose understood why Florrie assured her death would be preferable. The first time she was caught trying to sneak out, she was warned in terms, which left her in no doubt if she tried again her punishment would be severe. Rose was determined to escape, but her bid was always destined to fail. The Cavern was like a fortress — bars and locks everywhere. Not prepared to give up, she tried again and was caught again.

Obadiah roared his anger, grabbing Rose by the hair, and hauling her up to her bedchamber. Screams for help, flying fists, and scratching nails were ignored or batted away, as though merely an irritating insect.

Taking care not to mark her anywhere his clients would see, Obadiah made his... disappointment, clear. It was an easy matter for a man of his strength and size, to gag, and then tie Rose to her bed. Using a knife, he slashed at the thin chemise, Rose was expected to wear during the day.

The flimsy material fell away, exposing her to his greedy gaze. Her skin prickled in abject horror, made worse when he pressed the needle-sharp point of the blade against that most secret part of her. The sting of the knife sliding back and forth was enough to bend her to his will.

Not satisfied, Obadiah lay next to her on the bed. Raised up on one elbow, he dragged the blade across her abdomen, drawing lazy circles around her breasts jabbing at their dusky peaks with the tip.

Her terrified eyes never leaving his, Rose refused to utter a sound, and was quite sure she didn't breathe. The knowledge he would carry through with his tacit threat, enough to banish any thought of escape.

"Remember, my pretty blossom," he bent close to her ear, the blade at her throat. "I could take you now. You cannot stop me, but if you are as innocent as you claim, it will spoil the prize. Consider yourself lucky."

He smiled grimly, before removing the bindings, and the gag. Standing, he stared at her shivering body on the grubby cover, until she thought she might scream all over again.

"Do not forget." Was all he said and left the room, locking it securely behind him — Rose, a quivering mess.

Lucky? Lucky! Sucking in several lungs full of air, praying for the dizziness to fade, Rose tried to bank down the foreboding beginning to take hold.

Florrie, entering the room moments later, shook her head in an 'I told you so' fashion, and informed Rose it was either the shredded chemise or nothing for the rest of the day, at Obadiah's instruction. An example to any girl who might deem it a worthwhile exercise to copy her.

Rose succumbed to her fate, behaving in the manner expected of an obedient whore.

Throughout the week, the other girls took gleeful delight in explaining what Rose should do, when with a client. How to pleasure a man, how to make him quake at her touch, how to avoid getting with child — the list was endless. Most of their suggestions revolted Rose, but she had no choice. If the man who won the auction was not satisfied, she would bear the brunt of Obadiah's temper and, with first-hand experience of what *that* entailed, she had no desire for it to be repeated.

In the relative privacy of her room preparing for the debacle to come, their pearls of wisdom, while dispensed with good intentions, only increased her despair. Sitting in front of the cracked mirror, Rose brushed her freshly washed hair, staring at her fragmented reflection. Her face was leached of all colour, giving her a ghostly cast, prompting her to pinch her cheeks, trying to force some pink into them with little effect.

Florrie unlocked the door and threw a gaudy gown onto the bed. "'Ere, Obadiah wants yer to wear that. It'll give the winner something to play with. Lots o' layers to be undone or cut away."

If possible, Rose blanched even more, tremors running through her. Taking a steadying breath, she shut her eyes, as always summoning up an image of Nick. She feared she was losing the picture, that he was already fading from her mind, that she was so determined nothing would touch her soul, everything else was slipping away.

Deliberately, and ignoring the jolt of pain piercing her heart, she recalled each of his features. His dark blond hair, always a little unruly. His beautiful hazel eyes, twinkling whenever they fell upon her. His large yet gentle hands, long slender fingers, which could transport her to the heavens, and his lips. Oh, his lips! That slow sweet smile, the caress of his mouth on hers, the way their tongues danced, tasting each other.

Blinking back treacherous tears, Rose heaved a long sad sigh and let him go.

CHAPTER 27

*E*arlier that same afternoon, Roland and Mark tumbled into Sanctuary House yelling for anyone who might be within hearing range. Mrs Parry and Nick, who had yet to leave, poked their heads out of the main office.

"What is it boys?" Mrs Parry quizzed, smiling at the two lads who were jumping up and down in excitement.

"We think we've found 'er, we think we've found 'er!" they shrieked in unison.

Nick grabbed Mark's hands and made him stand still. Crouching until they were eye to eye, he asked, "Rose? Please tell me you mean Rose?"

"Course, I mean Rose. You can buy her, she's for sale." Totally unaware of the significance of his statement.

Nick was so shocked he sat on the floor with a bump.

"What do you mean she's for sale?' he asked faintly, sure he had misheard the child.

"She's being auctioned off," Roland interjected, his tones flat. Nick and Mrs Parry hustled the two boys into the office and shut the door.

"Start from the beginning please, Roland," Mrs Parry instructed. Sitting on the chair, his legs swinging, Roland explained Mark and he were on their way back to the refuge when they overheard two men talking about a fairy for sale.

Intrigued Roland had crept as close as he dared, and while pretending to tie his shoelaces, listened into their conversation.

"From what they was sayin' there's been an auction runnin' for five days, and tonight she is sold to the highest bidder." Roland, while only ten and two knew exactly what this implied, and spoke quietly, his tones respectful.

"Do you know where this auction is being held?" asked Nick holding his breath. They needed to get her out now, tonight would be too late.

"Obadiah's Cavern, it's down an alley off Neal St, in Seven Dials."

Nick gaped at Roland. This was barely two miles away. *Rose had been there all this time, and no one had seen her?* It beggared belief.

"We cannot tarry, if they are going to sell her..." Nick shook his head trying to rid it of the image now forming. Her eyes, those beautiful blue eyes, never far from his thoughts, floated into his mind — tear-filled and desperate.

We will rescue her, but we cannot go in without a plan." Mrs Parry's practical tones broke through his urgency. "Roland, please go to Trentams with all haste, and tell Mr Hugh what you told us, asking him to attend Sanctuary House at his earliest convenience. Where is Timmy? Do you know?"

Roland shook his head "Dunno, Mrs P. Probably begging a bun from Mrs Miller."

Mark, please go and see whether Timmy is in the building, and if he is, ask him to come here as quickly as he can."

Mrs Parry smiled at Mark who grinned back, and bounced off, happily.

Nick, knowing Helena was at home with Dr Archer, organised an errand boy to take a note to Stanton House, apprising them of the new information, and dispatched another to Lucas Withers.

Within the hour all were gathered, a sense of renewed purpose pervading the room. Lucas, once up to date, decided Nick should go to the cavern, and bid on Rose, ignoring Nick's spluttered protest.

"Come on man, use your brain. We cannot turn up, and demand she be handed over. We need to think the way they do. Whatever the offer is, double it, throw coin about as though you are rolling in it, largesse is always good distraction. Flirt a bit with the other girls, play the game. Once you receive your prize, walk her to freedom and safety, through the front door. We will be waiting. Should anyone stand in your way, we shall arrest them. The threat of Newgate, or even Bedlam, is usually enough to make people like Obadiah see sense."

For a plan, it seemed rather simple, but Nick conceded they were usually the easiest to accomplish. In one of the rooms on the top floor of the refuge some garishly flamboyant clothing were unearthed, which fitted him. He looked like a fop, but it suited the character he was about to play. Someone produced an elaborately handled cane, and another an eyeglass. A large and inordinately ugly ring was procured.

Nick's guise was complete.

"I feel like an idiot," he muttered, catching Helena's twitching lips, while the remainder of the gathering surveyed him.

"Who cares what you look like? This is for Rose," reminded Hugh.

"Bring my daughter home safely, and I will gladly bless

your marriage," Dr Archer said, the strain of the last few days etched on his haggard face.

"I fear marriage may be the last thing she will wish to consider after this," Nick replied sadly. "I suspect she has not been treated well and will likely find the touch of another man... abhorrent."

"Let us hope whatever dark place she has been to, might hold a little light. Rose is made from sterner stuff than you give her credit."

Nick acknowledged the doctor's optimism, with a grim smile. "One step at a time, Dr Archer. Let me bring her home, and then we shall see."

One last check and, hefting a large pouch of coin, Nick left the refuge, taking a hackney through the darkening streets. Lucas Withers and his men followed at a reasonable distance; they knew where Nick was headed, no need to rush.

~

In Obadiah's cavern, preparations were complete. The salon was decked out as though a festival was about to take place. Colourful swatches of material were looped over shuttered windows.

Candles in ornate holders burned on every surface. Chairs brushed clean. The floor swept. Glasses polished, and drinks ready.

For Obadiah, this would be a profitable night. Everything had to be perfect.

Rose was dressing in the gown Obadiah had demanded she wear. Layer upon layer of triangles, fashioned from gossamer fine material in shades of gold, silver, and the palest pink —

it flowed around her as she moved, giving the impression she was floating.

I suppose he thinks this enhances the image I'm a fairy, she grimaced into the mirror. *Oh, that I was, I would turn him into a toad.*

Dreading what lay before her, for the first time in her life, Rose longed for a glass of spirits to numb her senses.

She was ready. This was it. She could delay no longer. Rubbing her feet in an attempt to get them warm, she fought for calm. Shoes were forbidden in Obadiah's salon; the wearing of them might prompt a girl to flee.

Rose was under no illusion how that would end. Moreover, at this time of the year, bare feet on dirty, dank, and frigid pavements was not an inviting prospect — another, subtle yet invisible, manacle imposed.

To Rose, feet chilled to numbness, was a small price to pay if freedom was attainable. It was being caught that prevented her risking it. *Although,* she mused, remembering Florrie's warning, *maybe death* was *preferable.*

Florrie unlocked her door and came in, as always without invitation.

Standing, Rose waited for her judgement.

"You'll do nicely." Florrie paused, adding in gentle tones. "Tonight, is the night, Rose. You cannot stop this 'appening. Some gent will win the auction, and you must make this a night 'e will never forget. Do not do anything stupid. Obadiah will kill you without compunction, if 'e thinks you might try to outwit him. Any innocence you are clinging to will be taken this evening. Accept it." Her voice became flat and unyielding.

Rose bowed her head, swallowed her panic, then lifted her face and locked eyes with Florrie.

"Lead on."

. . .

A hush descended over the salon when Rose entered. Her white face and silvery hair, the perfect complement to the shimmering gown in which she was bedecked. Terror clawed at her throat, when she noticed how many avaricious eyes undressed her while she walked among them, and even had she tried, she could not utter a word.

Nick, sitting in the shadows at the back of the room, momentarily lost the ability to breathe. Here she was, his beloved Rose, albeit hidden under an inscrutable façade. As he studied her, she scanned the room.

Despite being feet from her, he discerned a hint of anger in her gaze, not quite crushed by her fear. Her proud bearing, testament to her strength of character. It was all he could do to remain in his seat, behaving in the insolently nonchalant manner he had assumed on his arrival.

Obadiah addressed the room. "My esteemed guests, this is the final night for the auction. My Spirit of the North is awaiting her fairy king. The man she will pleasure until dawn breaks the spell of the night. Last bids please…"

The price for Rose was already high, and Nick was stunned to hear the figures being thrown at Obadiah. His heart broke for Rose. She stood motionless, only the chaotic pulse fluttering at her throat indicated her distress.

Nick waited until the bids died down. He spoke almost absently, naming an amount. It was double the highest sum offered.

The room fell silent. All eyes turned to him.

"I beg your pardon, sir. May I ask that you repeat your bid?" Excitement laced Obadiah's tones. *This was turning out to be far more lucrative than he could have imagined. A fool and his money.*

Nick stood, and strolled forwards. He tweaked the hair of one or two of the girls, patted one of them on her ample rump, stroked the cheek of another — the epitome of a rake.

The girls sighed and fluttered their lashes. If this extremely fashionable, and extraordinarily handsome, gentleman didn't win Rose, they would be more than happy to serve his every need. Sexually and otherwise.

At the sound of his voice, Rose stiffened, and tried to appear unconcerned. She blinked, and narrowed her eyes, certain she was imagining things.

How could he be here? Was she so desperate for him to find her she had conjured him up out of the winter's mist?

He came closer, and stood directly in front of her, apparently inspecting what was on offer. He trailed a finger down her face, along her throat and over her décolletage.

She raised her eyes to his, a previously inconceivable hope stirring in their cerulean depths.

"She seems comely, I believe she would be a most suitable f..." Nick stopped, and grinned around the room dropping a lascivious wink, "...bed fellow. I do enjoy a bit of magic."

The crowd roared with laughter.

"Do you have the price?" Obadiah demanded. Nick tossed the pouch up and down in his palm, the coins rattling, then tipped them onto the closest table, the pile glinted in the candlelight.

Seeing what was deemed to be her worth, reduced to a heap of shiny discs on a shoddy table, drew a sibilant hiss from Rose. Regardless that her purchaser, nay her saviour was Nick, and aware Obadiah would likely punish her later for her reaction, she couldn't help it.

Obadiah growled. "Do not even think about it, my little blossom. This man has paid good coin."

Facing the room, he announced Nick to be the highest bidder, and in a moment of aberrant benevolence, offered any who wanted to indulge their fantasies, a free hour with the girl of their choice.

Cheers erupted and, as it all seemed to be in good fun, a few of the men clapped Nick on the back congratulating him on his prize.

Rose remained as through frozen. She did not dare react to Nick's presence, praying with everything in her, it was a ruse to steal her away. Nor did she believe her rescue imminent, not entirely convinced she wasn't dreaming. Her heart hammered in her chest, until she thought it might burst clear through. *Please let this be real.*

Obadiah counted the coin, his face one enormous leer, as he dropped each one back into the pouch, pocketing it with villainous glee.

"She's all yours, good sir. Rose, take him upstairs, I do not want to see either of you outside that chamber until the morning." He smirked at Nick. "Remember..." he leant so close to Rose, her eyes watered from the alcohol on his breath, "...I will be watching and listening. Make his fee worth it."

Rose swallowed, her fingers itching to scratch the bloody man's eyes out, but she merely inclined her head. "As you wish."

She turned to Nick, who had heard everything Obadiah muttered, his disgust at this excuse of a human being, reaching monumental proportions. He had to get Rose out now.

"Sir, if you please?" She held out her arm in invitation, and he could see the tremors rippling through her hand. With outward indifference, Nick hooked his arm around hers, but when his fingers came to rest on her hand, he applied a subtle pressure, rewarded by a flicker of her eyelids.

She led him out of the salon, and was heading towards

the stairs, when Nick steered her to the front door. Still not sure this was happening, and with Obadiah's warning ringing in her head, Rose spun around.

"What are you doing? He'll kill me." Alarm in her voice.

"No, he won't. Come, my beautiful Rose, I do believe 'tis time we took our leave."

She stared at him, unmoving. *It wasn't a dream.*

"Rose, please let me be your knight in shining armour. There are others waiting outside for my signal, who will... deal with Obadiah Matthews.

"You are really here?" Standing on tiptoe, Rose stretched up to touch his face, to prove he would not dissolve into imagination. Slender fingers, icy cold, stroked his jaw line, and he closed his eyes at the sensation so light a touch evoked.

The terror of the last few days swirled around them, and unable to help himself, Nick risked pressing his lips to her forehead.

"I am really here, and you are safe."

At his assurance, a change came over Rose.

"One moment." She took two steps, then retraced them grasping Nick's hand. "Please come with me, I fear if I look away, when I turn back you will be gone."

Nick smiled gently and, kissing the back of her hand, followed her lead. Rose marched into the salon, where all manner of depravity seemed to be unfolding.

Nick gaped at the sight, praising God and every other deity, Roland and Mark were fortuitous enough to overhear an indiscreet conversation.

This was what Rose would be expected to do. A red haze suffused his vision, as anger more terrible than anything he had ever experienced flared. Before he could do anything, he was halted by furious voice.

"Obadiah Matthews! Look at me. **Look at me**!" For so

petite a person, Rose commanded the attention of the whole room.

All eyes swung to where she stood in front of Obadiah. To be fair, the man was forbidding. His height and bulk, enough of a threat to most, but he no longer held any sway over Rose.

He had lied and cheated, pawed her, paraded her, and sold her. It was time to smash the fetters by which she had been so cruelly bound.

"You conniving, scheming, underhanded scoundrel. All I wanted was a kindness. To be shown the way back to Sanctuary House..." a few mutterings began at this. The chit *wasn't* a lady-bird disguised as a virginal fairy queen after all? And wasn't that the refuge under the protection of some well-respected members of the *ton*?

A handful of the patrons slunk away, guiltily aghast at what they were very nearly a party to. Tipping a light-skirt from Obadiah's stable was one thing, but to de-flower an unwilling innocent. Oh no, no, no, no. That was never part of the agreement. Willing whores were all they wanted.

Others remained, relishing the spectacle.

"You stole me, threatened me, and thought nothing of selling me to one of your reprehensible customers. I would like to see how you would handle it, should our positions be reversed. I hope you rot in hell, you *foul* bastard."

With that, wholly unladylike-like curse, and uncaring her feet were bare, Rose aimed a well-timed kick to Obadiah's groin.

An agonised groan wrested from his throat. In slow motion, he tipped forward, and Rose bunched her hand into a fist, bringing it back ready to punch him in the face. Her hand was stayed, and Nick murmured.

"Allow me." He delivered a solid uppercut, and Obadiah dropped like a stone.

Rose swiped her hands together in an easily recognisable gesture. Recalling his expression when he hefted the bag of coin... her *price*... she seized the opportunity to rifle in Obadiah's copious jacket pocket.

Snatching the pouch, she turned to Nick.

"Please, take me home."

Swinging Rose into his arms, Nick strode out of the salon and along the corridor. Shouldering open the heavy wooden front door, and into the chill night, letting the door slam on Florrie's mournful wails.

"He's all yours," Nick called when they exited the Cavern. Several men peeled out of the shadows, slipping silently into the brothel.

Still unable to credit he was holding her, and she was finally safe, Rose laid her head against his shoulder. Breathing him in, she shut her eyes.

The rhythm of his stride was soporific and before they reached the carriage secreted around the corner, Rose was asleep.

CHAPTER 28

*N*othing woke Rose, not Nick's climbing into the coach, nor its rocking as they rattled through the mean streets to Sanctuary House. Settling her onto his lap, Nick pulled the carriage rug around her slim frame, and with one hand massaged her feet, which were blue with cold.

She murmured his name in her sleep, snuggling closer, unconsciously sliding her arms around his waist. Laying his cheek on her shining hair, he talked to her all the while, hoping his voice provided comfort and security.

It wasn't long before they rolled to a halt outside the imposing double doors. Someone must have been keeping watch for, as he climbed out, there was flurry of activity. Several people rushed down the steps, led by Drs Archer and Callard.

"Rose, Rose, my dear. Good God, she is frozen, quickly we must get her indoors, and warmed up." Dr Archer fussed over his daughter, who did not stir. Refusing to relinquish her, Nick nodded towards the entrance. Helena, grasping what he meant, ushered everyone back inside.

Nick followed Helena and the two doctors upstairs to one

of the private chambers, where he was persuaded, to place Rose on a bed covered with layers of thick comforters between which someone had thought to tuck a warming pan.

When Nick stepped away, Rose groaned. Her eyes fluttered open, seeking and finding his. She jerked upright, reaching for him, his name a stuttered gasp.

"Don't leave me," she entreated. "Please, Nick, don't leave me."

He sank onto the bed, and uncaring how inappropriate it was, drew her close. Now was not the time to be worried about the rules.

"Your Papa is here, my dearest love, 'tis only fair he be with you. I promise to stay close by, should he, and Helena, permit it."

Swivelling in Nick's embrace, Rose swung her head around the room, spying her father at the other side of the bed, his face haggard.

She blinked. *Papa? Here? No, he couldn't be. She* had *to be dreaming.* "P-papa?" She croaked, incredulously. "Oh Papa, I am so sorry," and with that Rose burst into wretched sobs.

The past few days coalesced into a storm of weeping, enough tears spilling out to float an ark. Dr Archer moved to the bedside, and enveloped his daughter in his arms, rocking her as he did when she was a babe.

Nick was torn. He wanted to comfort Rose, but knew father and daughter needed this time together. Hesitating, his decision was made for him, when Helena took his arm.

"Come, Nick. Let us find a hot drink, and I do believe Mrs Parry might have a bottle of brandy at the back of the dresser in her office, purely for medicinal purposes, of course." A cheeky twinkle in her eye, Helena encouraged Nick to leave the bedchamber. "You can return in a little while. Do not fret."

· · ·

They walked into the dining room to be met by a crowd of expectant faces. All knew Rose was safely back in their fold, but they wanted more details. Sybil Miller, along with Archie, had stayed on this evening, and brought over a tray with hot drinks for Nick, as well as for the men under Lucas Withers' command who 'dealt with' Obadiah, after Nick had carried out Rose.

Savouring the rich brew, Nick pondered his words. "I cannot tell you what Rose endured, although from the little I witnessed, I do not imagine it was pleasant. Suffice it to say, while she appears in reasonable health, she is... reserved and, in my humble opinion, holding herself under rigid self-control. Her father is tending to her, and I trust he will be able to confirm she has suffered no physical damage. We can only pray, now Rose is safe and surrounded by those who love and care for her, the horror will begin to fade."

A few questions were thrown out about the brothel, which Nick left Lucas Withers to answer. Closing it down or even escorting the customers from the premises was not in their purview, their only concern — Obadiah Matthews. Lucas had made it abundantly clear to the proprietor, should there ever be even a whisper of a hint that Obadiah was anywhere near Miss Rose Archer, he would be the one wishing he had never been born.

Lucas also took pains to remind him of the law regarding brothels and suggested... politely, Obadiah might consider treating his girls with a little more respect, should he deem regular visits by interested parties an imposition.

Needless to state, Obadiah was persuaded. Lucas and his entourage left him and his customers to their evening, satisfied they had instilled the fear of God into that most reprehensible specimen of humanity.

A feeling of elation pervaded the room; this last week had been traumatic on so many levels. First the attack on Ken and Lynette — the latter, who to the stunned disbelief of all, survived the grievous wound inflicted on her by the pirates. Followed by the disappearance of, and subsequent search for, Rose.

Against the odds, both incidents had resulted in favourable outcomes, and while healing was necessary and would likely be protracted, senseless tragedy had been averted in each case.

It was close to midnight, and all sitting around the room had supported Nick throughout his vigil. Fatigued from long hours of waiting, and glad to know Rose was back amongst them, the company slowly dispersed. Time enough for further review, if required, in the days to come.

Nick thanked everyone for their encouragement and succour during the preceding days, shaking hands and being hugged by all and sundry as they left. People who he barely knew a week ago had become, if not friends, certainly close acquaintances.

Mr Fletcher, two sleepy boys trailing at his side, said, "Mr Drummond, you will never know how glad I am Miss Rose has been found. Forgive me, I …" He shuffled, awkwardly, unable to finish his sentence.

It was clear to Mr Fletcher, the man in front of him loved Rose, and that she returned his affection. The flicker of emotion, first sparked months ago when she smiled at him in almost exactly the same spot where he now stood, died a little, then steadied. She was not destined for him, but their acquaintance had proved he was ready to let go of his wife, should he be lucky enough to meet another.

Nick, recognising the pain of loss in Mr Fletcher's

expression, and feeling benevolent now Rose was safe, grasped his hand and shook it firmly.

"There is nothing to forgive, Fletcher. It was not your fault." His lips twitching wryly when Mr Fletcher arched a sceptical brow. "Yes, maybe you could have reacted with less... err... vehemence, but I understand your motives. I am sure Rose will reiterate my sentiment when she feels up to visitors." The sincerity in Nick's voice convinced Mr Fletcher as little else would.

"Thank you for your magnanimity. I am not sure I could be so charitable, were our positions reversed." Inclining his head, Mr Fletcher lifted Andy into his arms, and took Mark's hand, hurrying down the steps. The three immediately swallowed up by the darkness.

As the stragglers disappeared into the frigid night, Nick headed towards the stairs to check on Rose.

Hugh arrested his steps. "'Tis time we returned home also, Nick. Naught we can do here. Rose will doubtless appreciate some undisturbed rest, and probably the presence of you and her father. The rest of us will be surplus to requirements for a while. Please send a message if you need anything."

Helena gave Nick a warm hug. "I am pleased she is found and seemingly unharmed, at least physically. I know I need not remind you but, be patient. It will likely take some time for her to feel comfortable with people again. Remember how she cared for you when you were injured? Now 'tis your turn."

She smiled and squeezed his hand, while Hugh was trying to usher her towards the door. "I will visit with your mother in the morning and tell her the good news. I am coming Hugh, tsk." She grimaced over her shoulder at Nick, who smiled his first real smile since the afternoon Rose disappeared.

"Thank you," he mouthed, as Hugh — grinning at Helena's admonishments about rushing her away, and not in the slightest repentant — finally got his wife through the door.

Nick stood for a moment in the quiet of the great entrance hall. The smell of freshly polished wood, and the sharp night air wafting through the doors, cleared his dulling senses. Exhausted beyond rational thought, he was also supremely content.

His Rose was safe.

Bounding up the stairs two at a time, he slowed his steps when he approached the bedchamber wherein Rose lay. Knocking quietly, he was admitted by Dr Archer. Rose was awake, her tear-stained face eliciting a pinched sensation in his chest. Upon Nick's arrival, Dr Archer said he would be back shortly and, in tacit approval, left the couple alone.

Nick walked over to the bed and sat on the chair the doctor had vacated. He stared at Rose, searching her face, imprinting her delicate features in his mind. The gnawing dread at how close he had come to losing her, continued to lurk. Unwilling to cause her further distress, he made no attempt to touch her, but let his hand rest on the heavy covers.

Rose stretched out to stroked over his poor scuffed knuckles, before lifting his hand and entwining their fingers together.

Nick held her gaze. Her eyes, glittering with unshed tears, called to mind a lake rippling in a summer breeze and he felt himself leaning towards her. He could happily drown in those eyes. As this thought passed through his mind, he became aware Rose was pulling him, and he raised a quizzical brow.

"Hold me?" A whispered plea.

"Are you sure? I do not wish to…" he faltered, concerned it was too soon, that it might cause her to relive her ordeal.

"Nick," she chided softly, "I am not broken. Bruised and a little battered, but you should know, the only thing that kept me sane was the thought of you. Your hands, your smile and your kisses.

"Even when I presumed, I would never see you again, 'twas imagining your face helped me put one foot in front of the other. When I was…" she hesitated, "…on display, I did not see the customers leering at me, undressing me with their eyes, testing what was offered," she shuddered, and he flinched. "I saw only you." Needing to clarify, she blurted out, "Nick… I… they didn't…" to find the words got stuck. She couldn't say it after all, it was too raw.

"My darling, while I would, of course, prefer you had not been subject to such base proclivities, nothing will ever change my love for you. Even had I been too late to stop what Obadiah intended for you, it would not, it *could* not, diminish how I feel.

"If anything, the love I bear has deepened, become more enduring. Your fortitude in an intolerable situation should astonish me yet with you, my Rose, I have come to expect nothing less. I am only sorry it took us so long to find you."

Rose studied his face, noticing lines not there before, a hard edge overtaking what remained of his carefree boyishness. "Nick, I hope you can forgive me for causing such distress."

Reaching up, she cupped his face with her free hand, her thumb smoothing new creases at the corner of his eye.

"It was my own fault. I do not deserve to be rescued, but I

am endlessly glad you did. Had I not been so incautious, none of this would have happened."

"That is as maybe, but never say you are undeserving. Mr Fletcher did not need to shout at you. Obadiah Matthews had no call to snatch you up, and lock you away, serving you up to be debauched."

His words harsher than he intended, but it was better to clear the air now. He did not want Rose to think he would reject or deny her, whatever she was subject to during those awful days. "None of this was your fault."

She did not look convinced, so he took a gamble.

"Rose Archer, I love you, and will do so until the Lord takes me. I want to spend the rest of my life demonstrating that in as many ways as possible." He smiled, his rare and tender smile he reserved especially for her.

Grazing the tips of his fingers over her throat and around her nape, tangling his hand through her glimmering hair, he brought her face close until their noses brushed.

Rose closed her eyes; dark lashes a smutty curve on pallid cheeks.

He waited, hoping she would grant him permission.

In that moment, Rose felt the spark smoulder, her body recognising the other half of her soul; relief sweeping through her at the knowledge she was not repulsed by Nick's silent petition.

Lifting her lids, faces so close their lashes meshed, she discerned apprehension in his gaze, and the icy tentacles strangling her heart began to melt.

Deliberately placing both hands on his chest, Rose delighted in both the erratic thud pulsing under her fingers, and the sharp intake of breath she heard hiss across his lips.

Leaning closer, she slid her arms up, winding them

around his neck, shaping herself to him as best she could, a slow burn coursing through her veins.

"Rose…" Nick sighed against her mouth — capitulation inevitable.

"Kiss me," she murmured.

Tenderly, and with the most sublime sweetness, Nick captured her lips with his, taking care not to rush, holding at bay the fire already spiralling along his body at even so gentle an embrace

Rose responded, her love for Nick drowning out the clamour in her head, while his love for her doused the last vestiges of terror, which continued to prowl at the periphery of her senses.

Rose had no idea how long they kissed, but forever would not have been long enough. Every moment their lips touched brought her back, a little more, from the brink of despair.

Each stroke of his fingers obscured repellent memories, replacing them with far more pleasurable ones. Rose was not naive enough to presume it would be so simple a task, that a kiss could banish the nightmare, but it was a wonderful start.

CHAPTER 29

*T*he sound of heavy footsteps prompted them to break apart, both breathing heavily, cheeks flushed. Nick smiled, ruefully, tucking a lock of silvery hair off her face, before dropping a kiss on her nose.

"I love you Rose Archer, never forget that. Through thick and thin, through high and low, I will always love you. If these last few days have done anything, they proved I cannot abide my life without you in it. You are my reason for breathing, my light, and without you by my side, my heart is not whole."

The door opened before Rose could reply, but she squeezed his fingers and held his gaze, her eyes telling him what he needed to hear. He returned the squeeze and grinned at Dr Archer's quizzical expression.

"I trust you two have used the time alone advantageously?" Dry humour laced his tones. "Now my daughter, I do believe 'tis time you rested." Placing the tray he was carrying on the little table beside the bed, he handed her a steaming cup from it.

"I have brewed this tincture, which should give you an

undisturbed sleep, while I..." his glance flicked to Nick, who started to speak, "...and young Drummond here, will watch over you." Smiling, when Nick relaxed nodding in gratitude. "Come Rose, please drink this down."

Reluctantly, knowing how disgusting her father's remedies tasted, Rose swallowed everything in the cup, grimacing at the noxious flavour. Shuddering, she handed the cup back.

"That was vile, Papa. You should be cosseting, not poisoning, me." She gave him a mock frown.

Joseph twinkled at his daughter. "Rest my child, time enough to berate me on the morrow. Now, before you nod off, would you like to divest yourself of this monstrosity?" Motioning to her dress.

Rose looked down. *How could she have forgotten she still wore that despicable gown?* A trickle of panic threaded through her, and as unwanted images reared up in her mind, she yanked at the neckline. Nick's attempt to mitigate her horror, ruined, when it flooded back with a vengeance.

"Please, please get this off me." Hysteria mounting, Rose dragged at the delicate gown, the sound of ripping material echoing though the room.

"Calm down, pet. 'Tis just a dress." Her father tried to placate.

"It's not *just* a dress, Papa." She stared at her father, aghast. "Obadiah was selling me in this dress. To wear it was to surrender myself. To accept his ownership of me. To succumb to whatever he dictated. My only alternative, probably death." Her voice dropped, becoming bleak.

"Had Nick not found me tonight, I would have been lost. Subsumed within the abominable spectacle Obadiah created. I was lucky. No man was allowed to sample the goods before they bought, but I was already falling, disappearing into a horror from which there would be no respite."

The enormity of what she had scarcely eluded, caused her

breath to catch, as tears spilled over once more. Deep sobs wracked her slight frame, her misery, palpable. Without thinking, Nick drew Rose close, rocking her, words of love and devotion tumbling over his lips, his cheek cushioned on her hair.

Dr Archer watched, noting with poignancy how his daughter responded to Nick's ministrations. Her fingers crept around his waist, fisting his jacket, her head nuzzled into his neck, unconsciously finding her comfort, as her sobs slowly became hiccups.

The knowledge this subtle shift was inevitable, in no way lessened the ache that his daughter now belonged to another; alleviated, marginally, by Nick's obvious love for her. Few were lucky to experience such enduring affection.

Rose sniffled, using the handkerchief Nick gave her to wipe her tears and blow her nose. Her eyes sought her father's, and she smiled, albeit wearily. Then realising in whose arms she lay, started to sit up, only to fall back against him — the tincture whisking her into oblivion.

Ensuring she was indeed asleep, Nick propped Rose carefully against the pillows, turning away, as Dr Archer undressed his daughter. Once it was removed, Nick took the dress and, balling up the hated garment, headed off to drop it in the fire at the back of the kitchens. Hurrying down a corridor he nearly ran into Mrs Parry and Dr Callard.

"Oh, my apologies. I assumed everyone else had gone home." Halting his headlong dash.

"How is she?" Mrs Parry asked, pressing her hand on his arm.

"Exhausted, distraught, overwrought, heartsore," Nick shrugged. "Along with many other emotions I suspect. She is finally asleep. Dr Archer concocted some foul-smelling and, judging by Rose's face, equally foul-tasting drink to give her an untroubled slumber. I am going to toss this onto the fire if you have no objection. I doubt anyone is so desperate for clothing they need something made from this." His lip curling at what the dress represented.

Mrs Parry smiled her understanding. "No objection at all," she pointed, "along there to your left, the kitchen fire is alight. Be careful not to burn yourself. I was coming to tell you, Mrs Miller left some food on the bench by the hatch. While I doubt Rose would be inclined to partake at the moment, she might be coaxed into a mouthful when she wakes. You all need to eat."

"I shall speak with Dr Archer," interposed Dr Callard. "I have some experience in the trauma Rose may experience in the aftermath, and the sooner we are watchful for the signs, the better." Nodding, mostly to himself, the doctor strode towards the staircase, calling a soft goodnight to the other two.

"I will be in my office. Do not hesitate to ask if there is anything you require."

"Mrs Parry, you should go and seek your bed. We can manage here, and you barely left these past days," Nick begged the kindly soul.

"'Tis of no matter, Nicholas," Mrs Parry was one of very few people who called him by his full name, and he rather appreciated it. "The night is almost over. I shall stay until Mrs Forester arrives. There is always plenty to keep me occupied, and I am wide awake."

She patted Nick on the arm, a habit, which although made him feel like a child, instead of a grown man of six and twenty, was also curiously comforting.

Grinning, he thanked her, and they went their separate ways. Nick found the kitchen, where he dropped the gown onto the smouldering embers, watching as the flames sputtered and coiled around the material.

It seemed to shrink and melt, and in the blink of an eye was reduced to ashes. His mouth curved with grim satisfaction. He waited until the blaze died down, then checking the fire screen was secure, turned his back and left the room, gathering up the platter of food on his way past.

Upstairs, the two doctors were engrossed in an almost inaudible discussion regarding manifestation of shock. Nick acknowledged them before resuming his seat at the bedside, and disregarding convention, slipped his hand underneath Rose's, caressing her fingers gently.

Despite the lateness of the hour, Nick was not tired, or maybe he was beyond sleep, unable to quiet his turbulent thoughts. The events of the evening continued to race through his head, like horses at full gallop, banishing any chance of rest.

Contemplating the diminutive woman lying so still and pale in the narrow bed, ruminating at how one, tiny, seemingly insignificant twist of providence delivered her back into his arms, Nick embraced his destiny.

Yes, he loved Rose. Yes, he had vowed their love was forever, and yes, he had proposed but, prior to this week, he had not truly appreciated precisely what that meant. The bone chilling dread she was lost to him was something he never wished to face again. Added to this had come the realisation that without Rose by his side, he would only be half-alive, existing rather than living.

Kennet Alexson's expression, scant days ago when he believed Lynette killed, reared up in Nick's mind. He recognised the man's pain. It was as though his heart had been torn from his chest, while it still beat.

For years, Nick had believed himself incapable of caring, of loving another to the exclusion of everyone else. Neither did he want the responsibility of such emotion — for that way unhappiness lay. His mother's sorrow at the loss of her husband, along with the awareness his job could be perilous, had only served to cement his decision.

Until Rose.

The hours ticked by. Rose, plagued by night terrors, shattered the peace several times with tormented cries and garbled mutterings, which oddly, furnished the two men watching over her with a more comprehensive picture of what took place during those five days. Also apparent, was that her despair in the belief she had no escape, was nothing compared with the deadly loathing Rose bore for the man who had destroyed her innocence.

Even in the throes of anguish, Rose seemed aware of Nick's presence, reaching for him blindly, and only settling when he held her close, his voice soothing her. Dr Archer was, once again warmed. Rose had found a man who would never deliberately hurt her and would probably give his life to protect her. Any last qualms about losing his daughter to another, one whose home was far from Runswick Bay and everything familiar, fell away.

The grey dawn crept in, the darkness lifting by almost imperceptible degrees. To the relief of the pair watching over her, Rose settled into a deeper, more healthful rest. Unable to keep his exhaustion at bay, Nick, without relinquishing her hand, adjusted his position until his head and most of his upper body was on the bed. In an instant he too was fast asleep.

Smiling a little sadly the doctor stood, and despite it

being unheard of to leave an unmarried woman alone with a man, even though betrothed, quietly left the room, making his way to the adjoining bedchamber Mrs Parry set aside for him.

For a little while, Sanctuary House was silent.

The regular hustle and bustle of a typical day at the refuge was in full swing, long before Rose awoke the next day. The weak winter sun streamed in through unshuttered windows, soft rays falling across her face.

Blinking, Rose glanced round, momentarily confused by her surroundings. The room was unrecognisable. It was much more spacious than her little attic room at home, larger than the one she had been allocated at Obadiah's, but smaller than her bedchamber at Stanton House.

Brow creasing, unease snaked through her, and she pushed herself up on her elbows. She suppressed a shocked squeak when she spied Nick, half-reclining in what was undoubtedly a very uncomfortable position, alongside her.

A smile warmed her lips, and she took a moment to study his beloved features. Black-brown lashes fanning out above his cheekbones were not enough to disguise the bluish shadows under his eyes. Tousled hair flopped across his forehead, and curled around the collar of his crumpled shirt, his charcoal grey jacket long since divested and dumped onto a chair in the far corner of the room. His cravat was untied, and hung limply around his neck, the deep red silk like a rivulet of blood splashed over the white of his shirt.

Unable to help herself, Rose grazed two fingers along his stubble-darkened jaw line. Pale under his tan, Nick looked as tired as she felt.

Carefully twisting the other way, Rose spied a glass of

water on the table next to the bed. Gratefully, she swallowed the contents, cool water sliding over her parched lips and raw throat. Frowning, she tried to recall why her throat was sore, but couldn't. It was too hard to concentrate anyway, and she presumed someone would enlighten her soon enough.

Her hand catching soft fabric, Rose looked down to see she was wearing an old nightgown, which definitely wasn't hers. No matter, anything was more tolerable than that revolting dress.

Sighing, in part with gratitude and in part with fatigue, she snuggled under the covers. Lying on her side, and resting on one elbow, she slipped her hand into Nick's, gently rubbing her thumb over his.

Deeply in slumber, Nick became aware of a light touch. The image of an elfin-like woman — hair so fair it might be spun from moonlight, and eyes of forget-me-not blue — drifted into his dream. Her lilting voice called to him, her smile coaxing him awake. Slowly he climbed through the weighty layers of sleep.

The picture began to dissolve. *No, he found her. He rescued her. Surely it was not all just a dream?* Fighting the lassitude, he jolted upright, his muscles screaming from hours of lying in so awkward a position. Eyes tracking left to right searching for Rose, the sun was in his eyes, he couldn't see her.

"Rose…" his voice was hoarse.

"Hush, my love, I am here." Her soft reply reassured. Nick shuddered, relief pouring through him. "I did not mean to wake you. You looked so peaceful, but I needed to hold your hand."

"I thought… I feared…"

"'Twas naught but a dream. Mayhap we were sharing them, for when I awoke, I was worried I had imagined my rescue. That my knight in shining armour was a fantasy, yet here you are, a little rumpled but still my knight."

She cupped his cheek, then slid her hand around his nape, bringing his head to hers. "Kiss me, Nick. Prove to me you are real."

So, he did.

CHAPTER 30

*L*ater that day, Helena and Hugh arrived to convey Rose home to Stanton House, where she was welcomed with great joy by the whole household, much to her embarrassment and, if she was honest — delight.

Nick accompanied them, and at Helena's insistence stayed. In truth, he did not want to be far from Rose. In fact, and accepting he was being irrational, if she never strayed beyond his sight again, he would be a happy man.

While Rose recuperated, Dr Archer encouraged her to talk about her ordeal, believing if she did not it would fester, and she would find it impossible to heal.

In the days that followed, Rose shared some of what happened with her father, Nick, and her hosts. but because most of what Obadiah expected, nay forced upon her, was not a usual topic of conversation in genteel surroundings, she refrained from telling them the whole truth. It was too raw, too crude.

Moreover, once the relief at being rescued faded, Rose remained self-recriminatory, despite everyone's insistence she was not to blame. If she had not left the refuge that afternoon, or told someone where she was going, or taken an escort — even had that been Timmy or Roland — none of it would have happened.

No one, not even her father was able to sway her opinion. The episode plagued her wakeful hours, and when she did fall asleep, stalked her dreams, recurrent nightmares disturbing her rest.

Her appetite, already diminished during her captivity, was now almost non-existent, and it wasn't long before Rose became waif-like. The bright blue of her eyes, huge in her pale face, lacked lustre, taking on a bruised look, and she forgot how to smile.

The hours of darkness were the hardest, for that was when she had been at her most vulnerable. Nick, seemingly attuned to her distress, found her wandering the quiet halls, or shivering in the moonlit garden, or reading in the library. Desperate for even an hour of sleep, but unable to settle.

Disregarding propriety, Nick persuaded Rose to sit with him on the chaise, or in one of the huge wing back chairs by the fire, whereupon he read out loud from one of the many books lining the walls, his voice quickly lulling her to sleep. There in the quiet of the library, cuddled against her beloved, was the only place her rest was undisturbed.

Pondering the likelihood of Rose becoming embittered, a shell of her former effervescent self, Helena had a brainwave.

Theo and Grace Elliot were in London with Beatrice, their very new baby daughter, for a short visit with Theo's family. Helena was certain her friend would prove the perfect solution to their problem.

Prior to meeting Theo, Grace had suffered what her husband described as something akin to battle trauma, resulting from sustained maltreatment by a man who had since, and to everyone's relief, died. Helena asked Grace whether she might have a little time to chat with Rose, guessing she was probably the only person who had any inkling of the tumult clouding Rose's normally eminently sensible, and practical brain.

Grace declared herself pleased to help in any way. Theo's mother lived relatively close by and was more than happy to watch over Beatrice, thus, whenever Grace had a spare hour, she called on Rose. The two quickly became close friends, perhaps perceiving a kindred spirit. Grace revealed some of what she had borne at the hands of a maniacal duke, conceding certain sights, sounds, and even smells, still had the power to provoke a panic attack, although rarely now.

One afternoon, maybe a week after Rose was found, and in the middle of a conversation about how to cope with the aftermath, Rose blew out a hefty sigh, admitting her over-riding emotion was one of guilt.

"Why?" Grace, not particularly surprised, pressed — sensing a breakthrough.

"They looked for me for five days and nights. All those people set aside everything important to them to search for me. *Me*, who by rights should know better than to wander the streets of London alone. Helena cautioned me, before ever we arrived, not to be gullible enough to assume it was a safe city, regardless of how benign it appears to an outsider. She was right, and I stupidly forgot her warning, placing everyone else at risk. Nick might have been..." she closed her eyes and forced that thought out of her mind. He had not been hurt, but...

"Rose, just because you decided to take a stroll in the fresh air, does not give anyone the right to steal you away, Surely Nick, your father, Helena, everyone has assured you of this."

Rose nodded, cheeks flaring red. Everyone vowed she was not to blame, but it continued to gnaw at her. "They have..."

"So why do you not believe them?" Grace interrupted

"I fear they are being kind. That beneath their assurances they are angry at my reckless disregard for my own safety, and subsequently theirs. That their smiles and kind words hide the truth." Rose bent her head, several strands of shining hair unwinding from her neat chignon falling across her face, hiding her humiliation.

"And what is the truth?" Grace leant forward and slid a gentle finger under Rose's chin, tilting her face so she could read her bewildered expression.

"That I am naught but an ignorant country bumpkin, unsuited to the sophisticated life of a Londoner. An upstart, who should pack up and go home." Azure eyes glistening with unshed tears.

Rose knew her argument was pathetic and, in her heart of hearts, untrue, but her naïveté, the child-like innocence, so much a part of her, had been savagely stripped away, and she felt adrift. Everything she trusted; the goodness of her fellow man, the honesty — integral to everyday life in her tiny village — unceremoniously extinguished.

Grace sat back, contemplating the younger woman. "Rose, everything you are feeling is a natural reaction to your experiences. I was the same. It was not until Theo cared enough to draw me out of the empty void I had fallen into, that I begin to trust it was not I who should be shouldering the guilt, but he who inflicted it upon me.

"For two years, everyone I knew, shunned me. I never spoke to my parents again. My life contracted to my home and the few staff my father had allocated me. *Of course*, we feel guilty, for why else would such a punishment be meted out?"

Rose searched her friend's face, reading the truth in her words. A tiny measure of hope beginning to form.

Grace smiled. "It was not easy. I shut down, locked away all my emotions and, had circumstances not been so fortuitous, would likely remain thus. Theo saved me. His patience and love soothed my soul and warmed my heart. I was already halfway in love with him before I braved sharing my story, certain he would turn away from me too, but he did not, and I thank the Lord every day that he came into my life.

"Please do not allow Obadiah Matthews to have the same effect upon you, because even though you are rescued, he holds you captive. Not only do you need to accept you cannot change what he did to you, but also that *he* is the cause of your suffering, not you.

"You had no choice. *He* was the one who abused the situation, not you. Imagine how gleeful he would be, knowing he remained at the forefront of your thoughts? Do not give him that power."

Grace poured another cup of tea for them both, giving Rose a moment to consider her words.

"How do I banish him, Grace? Every time I close my eyes, his face, his rapacious leer fills my mind. His callous laughter mocking my pleas to be released, echoes in my head. I have tried everything, to no avail. I feel as though I am drowning." She could not mask the despair in her tones.

"Have you spoken of this with your father, with Dr Callard, with Nick?"

"How can I? What father wants to hear how his daughter was manhandled by men whose only thought was to use her body for hours on end before casting her aside, ready for the next customer? It would be too painful. Nick is my betrothed, if I tell him... them..." Rose couldn't say it. The fear — if she revealed the whole truth about those days at the Cavern, regardless of Nick's declaration, of her father's compassion — they would spurn her.

"You expect they would reject you, treat you with contempt?"

Rose inclined her head, pale cheeks once again awash with hectic colour.

"Rose Archer, have you so little faith in the love these people bear for you, you believe they would scorn you, now, when at your most vulnerable? Your Papa witnessed the horrors of war and how it affected those who fought it. Nick is not some lily-livered milksop, quick to abandon you without compunction.

"They are *not* Obadiah Matthews. These are the people who cared enough to hunt for you, to comb the streets unwaveringly. To follow every lead, even if it seemed improbable. Goodness, gracious me, Rose, you give them no credit."

Grace was deliberately trenchant. She needed Rose to get angry, to resist the melancholy threatening to overwhelm her. She wanted her to understand, that to hide what she had endured in a bid to protect those she loved, was futile, and would only serve to hurt herself.

Unbidden, Grace recalled Rose telling them about Nick's wounds, and the concern they might prove fatal.

"Remember when Nick was injured? You said he hovered at death's door, that the poison might be too deep to be eradicated. You did not know him, yet you stayed with him night and day, tending to his wounds, talking to him, and keeping the fever at bay.

"'Tis the same for him now, only the fever, the poison, is in your mind. Let him tend to you. I have observed him when near you, however hard he tries, he cannot conceal his anxiety, and his love for you is so strong as to be almost tangible.

"Come now, Rose, Nick is no guileless boy. He works with sailors, and moreover, bawdy establishments are rife in the neighbourhood surrounding Trentams. He knows what happens in brothels even if 'tis somewhere he has never frequented." Grace could see her words were having an effect.

Rose was silent for several moments. "I never thought about it from their perspective, only that I do not wish to cause them further anguish. The dread it would become common knowledge, subjecting Papa and Nick, not to mention Helena and Hugh, to scurrilous gossip by those who take glee from humiliating or decrying others."

She tapped her chin, contemplating everything Grace had said. Like the abrupt end to a summer squall, the tempest in her head calmed. The waters would likely be ruffled for a while, but the storm quieted, the clouds cleared, and her heart lifted.

Rose was quiet for so long, Grace worried whether she had misread the girl. Her blunt approach having the opposite effect. She was about to speak, when Rose smiled and took her friend's hand.

"Thank you, Grace. Thank you for taking the time to listen, and to push through barriers I did not realised I had erected. I am more grateful than you will ever know. I need to talk with Nick and Papa. You are correct. 'Tis time I stopped concealing the truth and, for once, allow my heart to rule my head."

"I am honoured to have been of help. Sometimes, talking with one who has suffered in a similar way is beneficial. Each understands the other's agony, whether it be of the body or the mind."

Almost as an afterthought, Grace continued, "Jess is a good person to talk to, another sympathetic ear. Duncan considered himself maimed beyond reprieve yet look at them now. If you ever require a greater perspective, might I suggest you visit Dr Napier's wards at St Bart's. The patients there are a shining example of refusing to allow catastrophe to define you."

She patted Rose's knee, before standing to take her leave. "I do believe my work here is done, and we return to Oak Stanton the day after tomorrow. I wish to be home before the winter forces us to remain in London."

"May I write, if I have more questions?" Rose asked shyly.

"Of course. Perhaps you might consider writing a journal every day. A place to note down how you feel, whether you feel happy or sad and if 'tis the latter, why. It is a way of monitoring your progress and seeing patterns emerge which may not be obvious.

"Most importantly, please do not keep it all inside. Your Papa is correct, it *will* fester. You only have to look at what it has already done to you. Today is the turning point, you have faced it honestly, and from here on, I think your healing will be expeditious."

Grace drew Rose into a warm hug and kissed her cheek. "I hope we meet again soon."

Walking from the room, Grace turned back once with a farewell smile. Calling to Helena that she was leaving, she spent a few moments chatting with her friend, while waiting for Saunders to bring her cloak, and the coach to be driven around to the front of the house.

Rose watched through the window, as the carriage rolled away, contemplating all they had discussed.

She needed to see Nick.

EPILOGUE

*W*hen Nick arrived home, it was early evening and already dark, the short winter days waning by mid-afternoon. After Grace left, Rose spoke with her father, a man acutely aware his daughter was holding something back.

His occupation aside, Joseph Archer was used to reading the slightest twitch, nuance, or expression. How someone stood from a chair, or walked, or spoke, or turned their head.

Most folk he dealt with bore a healthy dislike for doctors, and understated their symptoms rather than the opposite, impelling him to rely on instinct, in conjunction with what little they grudgingly told him, in order to reach a diagnosis.

Rose found it challenging in the extreme, to vocalise the interlude, but she persevered and eventually it was done.

Appalled at what she had faced, and astounded she believed she was protecting him by withholding the whole story, Joseph sent a prayer of thanks that Helena had the foresight to invite Grace. Rose was returning to him, little by little, and he hoped now she had unburdened this last, and hardest piece, she had no more need to hide.

. . .

As had become his habit while staying at Stanton House, before going to his bedchamber to change, Nick sought out Rose.

He found her sitting in the parlour talking quietly with her father, Hugh, and Helena. Her gaze flew to his when he came through the door, a smile curving her lips, and Nick registered two things.

Firstly, she seemed lighter of spirit than she had been since he carried her from the Cavern and, secondly, her eyes sparkled. He sucked in a breath, and halted his steps, knowing if he took one more, he would haul her into his arms and kiss her senseless.

Rose stood, and uncaring where she was, and in whose company, closed the gap between them.

"Welcome home, Nick. I missed you today." Standing on tiptoe, she stretched up and brushed her lips to his. Nick gulped, and the other three began a heated debate on some political machinations, ignoring Nick and Rose completely.

"I missed you too," he replied, gruffly.

"Might you spare me a few moments before dinner?" Catching his fingers in hers, the deliciously familiar frisson beginning its irresistible glissade up her arm. "There is something I must tell you."

"Dinner will be served at seven," Helena threw over her shoulder, indicating their discussion was perhaps not quite so... preoccupying.

Ignoring his sister-in-law's comment, Nick raked his eyes over Rose's face, reading uncertainty in the cerulean depths of her gaze. "Of course. Give me a few moments to freshen up. Mayhap we could meet in the music room?"

"That would be lovely." She grinned. He dropped a kiss on her forehead and dashed out, thundering up the stairs. Rose excused herself, sauntering after him. Picking up a candelabrum from one of the polished wooden cabinets scattered around the hall, she continued on to the music room, situated at the rear of the first floor, overlooking the mews.

The drapes were tied back neatly and, not anticipating its use, the fire was laid but unlit. Shivering a little, Rose placed the candelabrum on the table near the piano, rubbing her hands up and down her arms wishing she had a wrap.

Mayhap to meet here was not such good idea, although she mused, *it certainly stops the brain becoming addled.* Leaning against the window frame, she stared out into the night, corralling her thoughts into some semblance of order.

A light tread along the hall and the door swung open.

Nick hesitated on the threshold as Rose turned. Silhouetted by the moon just peeking over the rooflines, she was bathed in its ethereal glow and, as ever, Nick could not dismiss the notion Rose was part fae.

They stared at each other in the gloom, the flicker from the candles creating wild shapes across the walls. Rose felt her heart thrumming; *dear lord how she loved him.*

"I…" she paused, running her tongue over suddenly dry lips.

Nick groaned and in three strides, was by her side, sweeping her to his tall frame.

"We can talk shortly, first I need to say hello." One arm around her, fingers splaying over her waist, his other hand tangled through her lustrous hair. Slowly, deliberately, he bent his head, and kissed her.

Leisurely and with infinite tenderness he moved his lips over hers, rejoicing in her soft whimper as she opened to him, his tongue tasting the velvety sweetness, the merest hint of cherry and wine. Utterly intoxicating. The kiss deepened, as passion swirled and pulsed around them.

Moulding herself against him, Rose became aware of how much he wanted her, eliciting an immediate response, heat pooling in her core. She tugged at his shirt, hearing his breath catch when her fingers danced over his warm flesh.

Encouraged, Nick slid his hand from her waist, to trail enticingly up and down her spine, fighting a reckless urge to undo the multitude of tiny buttons, and caress her satiny skin.

"Nick, please…"

Lifting his head, his breathing quickening, Nick stared down at Rose, her eyes, dark in the shadows, reflecting the smouldering desire he knew must be in his.

"What, Rose? What do you want?" A quiet petition, his tones while part-tentative, and part-challenging, held a tinge of hope. Hope she might surrender to him, little knowing she already had.

"You, please, I want you. Bring me back to life," Rose stuttered, as his fingers teased across her throat.

Nick smiled, one of his rare smiles and wove his magic, drawing her to the brink of ecstasy, with his fingers and his lips, only the determination to wait until they were wed, preventing him from making her completely his.

The evening slid by, and piece-by-piece, kiss-by-kiss, Nick reanimated her soul, revived her heart, and restored her body.

. . .

They had yet to talk, Rose needed to divulge the last of her tale, but all at once, it seemed inconsequential. Their love would withstand any onslaught.

What had threatened to tear them apart made them stronger. As when a ray of sunshine cleaves the ominous darkness of a tempest, their future together was, finally, clearly illuminated.

A little more than a year later

Nicholas Drummond walked through the gate, letting it swing closed behind him with a loud clang. The front door was wrenched open and a veritable whirlwind flew out, into his waiting arms.

"You're home early," his delighted wife cheered, tilting her face for his kiss, which he bestowed with satisfactory ardour. Uncaring how improper it was, Nick lifted Rose until she hooked her legs around his waist, carrying her indoors, where he kissed her into a dizzy spiral.

"How was your day?" she gasped, when he deigned to relinquish her lips.

"Very productive. The Indiaman is complete, ready to begin sea trials next week." The couple chatted about their respective days, while heading up to their bedchamber.

Closing the door, Nick walked across into the dressing room where he filled the large bowl on the table set up for the purpose, with warm water, and prepared to wash off the dust and grime. The unavoidable result of working in a shipyard.

Rose followed him and, curling up on one of the chairs, watched as he stripped down, admiring the powerful muscles rippling along his taut frame. Her fingers itching to trace them.

Expecting Nick to be involved in the trials, Rose took pains to mask her trepidation, the storm eighteen months previously never far from her mind. It was part of his job, and she knew he loved it, overseeing the sea-trials of three of the last five ships completed by Trentams since her arrival in London.

She did not ask whether this would be the fourth. Instead she unfolded herself from the chair and sashayed across the room. Coming to stand behind him, her hands circled his hips before gliding all the way up to his chest.

Nick turned, fitting Rose to him. He pressed his lips to her forehead and her cheek, before recapturing her mouth to resume the heart-stopping kiss he so reluctantly broke off less than ten minutes ago.

The affection, love, respect, and passion they shared was rare in this era when most married for convenience or by arrangement, or both. Nick and Rose considered themselves fortunate to belong to a close circle of family and friends, all of whom had married for love, despite their diverse backgrounds, and the unconventional way each had met their spouse.

It was something to which Jessica had laughingly drawn their attention the previous year, while celebrating the wedding of Nick and Rose — christening the five couples, the linen and lace clan. Meant as an amusing aside, they all agreed her description to be apt, and it quickly became a moniker they found curiously felicitous.

Such reminiscence was, currently, the last thing on Nick's mind. Gathering Rose into his arms, he strode across the rug to the bedchamber, depositing his wife gently next to the bed, making short work of the buttons on her gown.

Pushing the pale blue silk off her shoulders, Nick scattered butterfly kisses from her lips, down her throat to the slope of her breasts, the hushed swish of the material slithering to the floor, heightening anticipation.

Gently, he walked Rose backwards until her knees hit the edge of the bed and, as one, they tumbled onto the rich coverlet, Nick kissing her anywhere his lips could reach. Grumbling that he was wearing far too many clothes, Rose unbuttoned his trousers, but could not slide them over his hips.

"I cannot... you need to... Nick..." her frustrated tones eliciting a wicked chuckle.

Nick stood and quickly divested himself of the last barrier between them, flinging them over the back of a chair. Rose lifted herself up on her elbows, studying his movements as he stalked towards her, a hunter seeking its prey.

She shivered, the thrill of expectancy quivering through her. In the hearth, a fire crackled merrily, the warm light catching subtle highlights in her silvery hair which spilled over her naked slenderness.

Nick raked ardent eyes over Rose as he joined her on the bed. From her toes to the top of her head, and everywhere in between, Nick drove his wife to distraction with his seductive sorcery, causing her to writhe wildly beneath him. Her uninhibited response as provocatively irresistible now, as it was the first time they had made love, on their wedding night, almost one year ago.

Rose wove her own enchantment, revelling in her husband's body; dearly familiar yet never uninspiring. From his stubble-shadowed jaw, along the strong column of his neck, to his broad chest, peppered with pale scars. Taking the time to trace each one with cool fingers, wresting a guttural groan from Nick.

Her touch, a brand, his desire now all-consuming. Inexorably, her path took her to where his need for her throbbed, her hand curving around the muscle, alternately stroking then massaging, until he quaked with longing.

Capturing her hand, he moved over her, stealing her lips, while his fingers worked their magic until she was begging him to take her. Ignoring her breathy pleas, he continued to push her towards the peak, until at the same instant she thought she might splinter, he nudged her legs gently apart and, with tortuous slowness, claimed his prize.

His name fell from her lips in a ragged scream. Their bodies merged, as they moved with hypnotic cadence, surging towards the cresting wave, exploding together in a maelstrom of euphoria. Limbs tangled, hearts pounding, it seemed hours had passed before the world righted itself.

When he felt able to speak with a modicum of coherence, Nick raised himself up, and cupped his wife's cheek, his thumb grazing the corner of her mouth. His fingers slid around her face to tuck an errant strand of glimmering hair behind her ear, kissing the delicate shell as he did so, whispering his love for her.

The bristles on his chin tickled her sensitive skin, sending a tremor undulating down her spine. She sought his lips, the answering throb deep in her core, declaring their passion was not quite sated.

"Rose, I have an announcement." The formality of his words had Rose widening her eyes, little realising it was the only way for him to stop from sinking back into her. "Tomorrow marks one year since we wed and, in honour of this, I have organised a small token of my love."

Intrigued, Rose shifted slightly to study his face, while Nick revealed, rather circuitously, his surprise.

"My darling wife, we met in the most unexpected of circumstances. From the moment I heard your voice, looked into your incredible eyes — though I assumed I was hallucinating, certain you were an illusion from the realm of the fairies sent to convey me to the after-life, everything I thought I wanted was turned upside down.

"It could never be, we came from two different worlds, yet although I tried to distance myself, you inveigled me, ensnaring me like the sirens of myth. I know I fought your lure, but I am endlessly glad I fell under your spell. You are my reason for breathing. Without you, my life would be hollow and empty.

"On this, the eve of the anniversary of the most wondrous day of my life, I affirm my love. To celebrate, I have organised for us to spend a month in Runswick Bay where a piece of my heart resides, atop a cliff among a field of daisies."

His face was flushed. To admit to such sentimentally was… unorthodox, but Nick held her gaze steadily. A momentary awkwardness was worth it. Rose deserved nothing less.

His wife was silent for long moments, absorbing his words. A romance, a love, neither had looked for or wanted, which survived despite the odds stacked against it.

Her mind drifted back to a little over a year previously, when she found the courage to disclose the whole truth of the five days locked away in Obadiah Matthews' brothel.

Nick, although appalled and horrified at what Matthews subjected Rose to, had merely reiterated how grateful he was they had found her in time, before demonstrating, most effectively, the strength and depth of his love.

Precisely as Grace Elliot had assured Rose, he would.

"My darling husband, thank you for this gift. 'Tis as though you can read my mind, for I too have been recalling those days."

Rose collected chaotic thoughts.

"Nicholas Drummond, you blew into my life on the wings of a storm, crashing through my neat and tidily organised existence with your alluring gaze and your rich voice. I knew, even though you would likely leave as quickly as you came, vanishing in a heartbeat, that to kiss you, however brazen or inappropriate an act, would be *the* most incredible experience. I was right. You were my first kiss and, despite the evil intentions of others, my only.

"Memories of your kiss sustained me through my darkest hours, through the terror haunting me, through the days when I believed I would never be so lucky as to see you again. Mayhap this was our fate, to rescue each other, to suffer the worst, in order to realise the best was right in front of us. I love you with a love so profound it makes my heart swell, my body tingle, and my knees weak, and will do so until my last breath."

Rose had scarcely finished speaking, when Nick seized her lips with an almost frenzied fervour, the smouldering flame flaring into incandescence.

Dinner was very late that night!

It was a cold and blustery day. Two figures, snugly wrapped up in warm winter attire, tramped the last few yards to the top of a cliff. They had arrived in the village late the previous afternoon, and this morning, in spite of the inclement weather, were eager to climb the steep track to their special place.

Rose shucked back her hood. The wind whipped her hair, tearing it from its shining plait. Lifting her face, she breathed in the salty air. This was the first time she had returned to her former home since departing for London eighteen months ago, unaware how much she had missed it, until this moment.

The sea was grey, restless waves reared and billowed, white horses skimming the swell as the breakers crashed on the shore. Clouds scudded across the wintry sky, a pale sun doing little to remove the chill.

January in Runswick Bay was not for the faint-hearted. The awe-inspiring power of Mother Nature, untamed yet nurturing, remorseless yet magnificent, unyielding yet abundant.

Rose loved it.

Nick stood next to her, draping one arm around her shoulder, hugging her to his side.

"I have a gift," he announced, and digging around in the capacious pocket of his great coat, withdrew a small box, handing it to her.

Intrigued, Rose smiled up at him, turning the little box in her gloved hands, and loosened the bright blue ribbon thoughtfully tied around it. Lifting the lid, she husked a breath, gulped, swallowed, and tried to speak.

Nothing came, the words caught in her throat.

Nestled on a cushion of midnight blue velvet, sat a locket. Using her teeth to remove her gloves, Rose lifted out the delicate piece, the gold chain glistening when it trailed over her hand.

Giving the box to Nick, she opened the catch. Each behind a tiny sliver of glass, were two settings. On the left, a miniature of the two of them, taken from the portrait Nick had insisted they sit for when they married. On the right, a dried, deep pink rose petal, on which a daisy rested.

"N-Nick..." she faltered, tears brimming in her glorious

eyes. "How did you...? When did you...? Never..." completely lost for words, Rose stared at him.

"The day I first kissed you, you were making a daisy chain. The way your fingers formed the links, stirred something within me, and without knowing why, as we left, I picked it up. I still have it, well most of it," he grinned, elated at being able to surprise her thus.

"The rose petal is from our garden. From the bush you said was the reason it should be our home. A choice neither of us regrets." He shrugged nonchalantly, his casual attitude not fooling Rose for an instant. "I used two more for cufflinks."

Rose pushed the sleeve of his coat back, spying the beautifully crafted cufflinks, a tiny daisy embedded under clear resin.

"*This* was why you refused to let me fasten them this morning. I admit to being put out. I always fasten your cuffs. Now I understand." She lifted his hand, twisting his sleeve so she could study the clasp in better light.

"Oh, 'tis a skilled man made these. Such artistry." Sneaking a kiss on the inside of his wrist, feeling his pulse flicker beneath her lips. "Thank you, my love. I will treasure this always. A more thoughtful gift I cannot imagine. Please will you put it on for me?"

Carefully, Nick fastened the necklace, making sure the clasp was secure, before lifting her hair out of the way, taking the opportunity to kiss her throat while doing so. Rose brushed light fingers over the delicate locket, the burnished metal cool against her skin.

"Oh Nick," she sighed, "'tis so beautiful." A sudden gust of wind made her shiver. Quickly wrapping her cloak back around her, Nick opened his coat, tucking her against him. Resting her head on his chest, his heart beating under her ear, Rose heard him say.

"How about we revisit that kiss?"

Rose tilted her head. "I think 'tis imperative we do." An impish grin twitching at her mouth.

He bent to kiss her.

His lips, cool and firm, moved sensuously over hers. One hand curved around her nape, fingers entwining into her hair, the other held her flush to his body.

They had come a long way since their first kiss, but it was as sweet today, as it had been then.

Minutes ticked by; their embrace broken only when a large drop of rain hit Nick on the nose. He proposed they hurry home, receiving an answering nod from Rose, neither wishing to be caught in a winter squall.

They turned to head down to the village. Rose grasped his hand and smiled up at him, her eyes gleaming with happiness.

Nick was held motionless by the woman who had captured his heart.

His beautiful wife, no hidden flower. She was vibrant, and tenacious. A blossom of brilliant radiance. Her subtle fragrance teasing the senses.

An evocative bloom, worthy of the name Rose.

ABOUT THE AUTHOR

Rosie Chapel lives in Perth, Australia with her hubby and three furkids. When not writing, she loves catching up with friends, burying herself in a book (or three), discovering the wonders of Western Australia, or — and the best — a quiet evening at home with her husband, enjoying a glass of wine and a movie.

Website: www.rosiechapel.com

OTHER BOOKS BY ROSIE CHAPEL

Historical Fiction

The Hannah's Heirloom Sequence

The Pomegranate Tree - Book One

Echoes of Stone and Fire - Book Two

Embers of Destiny - Book Three

Etched in Starlight - Prequel

Hannah's Heirloom Trilogy - Compilation – e-book only

Prelude to Fate

Regency Romances

The Linen and Lace Series

Once Upon An Earl - Book One

To Unlock Her Heart - Book Two

Love on a Winter's Tide - Book Three

A Love Unquenchable - Book Four

A Hidden Rose - Book Five

The Daffodil Garden

The Unconventional Duchess

Rescuing Her Knight

His Fiery Hoyden

A Regency Duet

A Regency Christmas Double

Fate is Curious

A Christmas Prayer *with Ashlee Shades*

The Lady's Wager

Winning Emma

A Love Impossible

Unravelling Roana

Fairy Tale Romance

Chasing Bluebells

Contemporary Romances

Of Ruins and Romance

All At Once It's You

Cobweb Dreams

Just One Step

His Heart's Second Sigh

The Pomegranate Tree
Hannah's Heirloom - Book One

Hoping to trace the origins of an ancient ruby clasp, a gift from her long dead grandmother, Hannah Wilson travels to the fortress of Masada with her best friend, Max. Strange dreams concerning a rebel ambush begin to haunt Hannah and following a tragic accident, she slips into the world of Ancient Masada.

A woman out of time, Hannah must rely on her instincts and her knowledge of what will befall this citadel to survive. Will she escape, or is she doomed to die along with hundreds of others as Masada falls – and what does any of this have to do with an ancient ruby clasp?

Echoes of Stone and Fire
Hannah's Heirloom - Book Two

Pompeii - a vibrant city lost in time following the AD79 eruption of Vesuvius. Now rediscovered, archaeologists yearn for an opportunity to uncover the town's past. Some things, however, are best left alone - revealing the secrets hidden beneath the stones could prove perilous. Hannah and Max are brought to Pompeii by a surprise invitation to join an excavation team who are trying to uncover the city's long history.

After entering an excavated house that bears a Hebrew inscription, Hannah's two worlds collide, and she falls back through time to ancient Pompeii. A place where her ancestor is a physician to gladiators engaged in mortal combat, where riotous mobs run amok and where a ghost from the past returns to haunt her.

Will Hannah and her loved ones manage to escape the devastation she knows is coming, before the town is engulfed in volcanic ash? Will she ever find her way back to Max the love of her life, waiting not so patiently millennia away? Or will echoes be all that remain?

Embers of Destiny
Hannah's Heirloom - Book Three

AD80 - Hannah and Maxentius must embark on a new journey to Northern Britannia. This harsh frontier is far from the comforts of Rome and danger lurks where least expected; a garrison of soldiers, some unhappy with their isolated posting; local tribes, outwardly accepting of their Roman occupier, but who may still resent the seizure of their lands.

Millennia away, Hannah Vallier finds a familiar item while working in a museum near Hadrian's Wall. It is the pomegranate; carved by Maxentius on Masada. Before Hannah can discuss it with Max, disaster strikes! Believing her husband has been killed, Hannah retreats into the past, her soul melding with that of her ancestor, but with little idea of what they could face. Is the risk from the conquered tribes, or much closer to home?

As rebellion threatens to shatter a fragile peace, Hannah's heart whispers that just maybe Max isn't dead and that he is calling her home. Can she trust her heart, or will she remain caught out of time, her destiny floating away like embers on a breeze?

Etched in Starlight
Hannah's Heirloom - Prequel

Maxentius - a Roman soldier fresh from the battlefields of Armenia, arrives to take command of the military outpost of Masada, Herod's isolated citadel in the Judaean desert. A seemingly mundane posting after years of warfare, Maxentius finds it more challenging to maintain a focused garrison than to face the wrath of the Parthians across a disputed frontier.

Hannah - a young Hebrew physician spends her days dealing with injuries from street brawls, deprivation, disease and loss. As her beloved Jerusalem plunges into chaos; her brother — who belongs to a band of rebels determined to drive out their Roman occupiers — tells her of their plans to storm a desert fortress and steal the weapons stored there, persuading his reluctant sister to go with him.

Masada - following the ambush, Hannah finds and treats three badly wounded Roman soldiers. In the aftermath and against impossible odds, Hannah and Maxentius realise that they are more than healer and captive, their fate already etched in starlight.

Prelude to Fate

For Lucia, staring into the jaws of an horrific death, escape seems impossible.

Rufius Atellus, a veteran Roman soldier, is appalled when he recognises one of the victims about to be executed. Surely this is a ghastly mistake?

A ferocious she-wolf, anticipating a tasty meal, suddenly finds herself under a human's control.

In an unexpected twist, and as danger threatens, the lives of all three become inextricably entwined.

Was it chance brought them together in that theatre of bloodshed, or simply a prelude to fate?

~

Once Upon An Earl
Linen and Lace - Book One

When Fate saw fit to intervene in the life of Giles Trevallier, the very respectable Earl of Winchester, by dropping a female — soaked to the skin and with no memory of who she is or how she came to be there — literally at his feet, no one could have predicted the outcome.

While uncovering her identity, Giles realises he is falling hopelessly in love with his mystery guest, who unbeknownst to him, is succumbing to similar emotions; but, when the heart is involved, a thoughtless word or gesture can thwart even Fate's best-laid plans.

Faced with misunderstandings, whispers of scandal, secret documents and foreign agents, their chance at a happy ever after seems elusive, but fairy tales often happen when least expected, and love — however inconvenient — usually finds a way to conquer all.

To Unlock Her Heart

Linen and Lace - Book Two

Abused by a duke, and shunned by Society, relief seems at hand when Grace Aldeburgh is bequeathed a house in a small village, far from malicious gossips.

Once there, a tentative friendship blooms between Grace and Theo Elliott, the local doctor, who has already resolved to be the man to unlock her heart.

Just when happiness appears to be within her grasp, her erstwhile tormentor once again stalks Grace. After a failed kidnap attempt, the duke's quest culminates in an acrimonious confrontation, and the reason for his venal pursuit becomes agonisingly clear.

Love on a Winter's Tide
Linen and Lace - Book Three

Every day, Helena disappears into a world few acknowledge, helping the poor, downtrodden, and abused. A husband is the last thing she can be bothered with.

Busy managing his shipping line, Hugh Drummond sees no need for a wife, whose only joy is dancing and frivolity. If — and it was a huge if — he ever married, it would be to a woman as capable as he, not some giddy society Miss.

Then, Hugh meets Helena and despite their resolve, fate, it seems, has other ideas. As their attraction deepens however, treachery threatens to tear them apart. Will they uncover the perpetrator in time, or will their love be swept away, lost forever on a winter's tide?

A Love Unquenchable
Linen and Lace - Book Four

Jessica Drummond, a bright and cheerful young woman, rarely gives romance, let alone love, a thought. Long hours working in her brother's shipping office affords little chance of her ever meeting an eligible bachelor.

Duncan Barrington, veteran of the Napoleonic Wars, believes himself wounded in both body and soul. He has no intention of inflicting his demons on anyone, certainly not a beautiful and, in his opinion, irresponsible city lady.

One cold and snowy morning, the plight of a bedraggled puppy throws Jessica and Duncan together and, as a spark of something indefinable yet wholly unquenchable begins to burn, it is unclear who rescued whom.

A Hidden Rose
Linen and Lace - Book Five

After witnessing his mother's grief at the loss of his father, Nick Drummond resolved never to cause someone he loved such distress. Even the happiness of his siblings would not sway him – until he met Rose.

Rose Archer was almost content assisting her doctor father in a tiny fishing village in the north of Yorkshire. To experience the world beyond, a tantalising dream – until she met Nick.

Unexpectedly, the impossible becomes possible, and the renounced – desired above all things, but the shipwreck that brought them together, may yet tear them apart. Will Nick learn to trust his heart, or will his love for Rose remain forever hidden

∾

The Daffodil Garden

Horrifically scarred during the war, William Harcourt - Marquis of Blackthorne - prefers to spend his days in the quiet of his daffodil garden; plants do not pity, turn away, or judge.

Lucy Truscott, whose life is far removed from that of the *ton*, has no idea that by saving the life of a young woman, to whom she bears an uncanny resemblance, her own will be placed in mortal danger.

A chance encounter leads to something more. William begins to trust that Lucy sees the man beneath the scars, while Lucy is persuaded that love might actually transcend status.

Unfortunately, before their courtship has really begun, someone has every intention of ending it - permanently.

∾

The Unconventional Duchess

Refusing to suffer the humiliation of her husband flaunting his mistress at Society events, the newly married Duchess of Wallingstead, Ella Lennox, takes control of her life. She leaves London for the family's country seat in remote Yorkshire.

A woman alone, Ella spends the next four years turning a cold, grim house into a home, and transforming the fortunes of the estate. Not afraid of hard work, she soon earns the respect of those around her with her determination and unconventional attitude.

Out of the blue, the duke arrives. Resigned to another arduous visit, Ella is stunned when it seems he is attempting to court her.

Impossible!

Could her dream of a happy marriage be about to come true?

Everything hangs on a snowstorm, a herd of cows and an uninvited guest!

∼

Rescuing Her Knight
The de Wiltons - Book One

A story, invented to keep a little girl distracted, marks the beginning of another tale. One destined to remain unfinished for nearly twenty years.

Against her better judgement, Kitty de Wilton is persuaded to help Adam Marchmain banish his demons. This requires a subterfuge which, if discovered, might shatter more than the bonds of friendship forged two decades previously.

To Kitty, determined to break through the shield Adam has erected, the risk is worth it.
To see his smile and hear his laughter.
To rescue the knight of her childhood.

Just when a fairy tale ending is within her grasp, Kitty is threatened by the man who murdered her husband. In a cruel twist the tables are turned, and Kitty is the one who needs rescuing.

∼

His Fiery Hoyden
A Novella

Livvy has no respect for the nobility; they let her down when she most needed them. Why should she accede to their demands now?

Philip, Lord Harrington, is stunned to discover the young heir to the dukedom lives a stone's throw away in a ramshackle cottage, and resolves to restore the child to his birthright.

They meet in a clash of wills, but just when it seems Livvy might surrender, the victory Philip desires, may not taste all that sweet.

∼

A Regency Duet
Luck be a Pirate

Luck wasn't something retired pirate Kennet Alexson believed in – good or bad. However, even he had to concede that landing a job at Trentams shipyard, and meeting Lynette Collins, was more than coincidence.

Fortune it seemed, was smiling on him for once.

As Kennet adjusts to life on dry land, his friendship with Lynette deepens into something far more enduring, and what once seemed elusive now becomes possible.

Unfortunately, fate has other plans, and Kennet's good luck is about to run out.

The Highwayman's Kiss
Surrendered Hearts – Book One

Nothing exciting had ever happened to Juliette St Clair. Her days were spent assisting her father or calling on friends, wandering art galleries, taking constitutionals or, and more preferably, escaping into her books. Her evenings her evenings — an endless round of balls, where she preferred to remain invisible.

Until the day she was robbed by a highwayman.

$\sim$

A Regency Christmas Double
Heart Rescued

Four years since Jasper lost the woman he was hoping to marry. Four years since he closed his heart and withdrew from Society. He has no idea his reclusive existence is about to be shattered.

Enter his sister's best friend, Harriet, a flame haired beauty, who needs his help.

Reluctantly he agrees and as they spend time together, it is clear their feelings run deep. Although Harriet affects Jasper in a way no woman ever has, he believes her to be out of his league ~ but it's Christmas and she might just be the one to melt his frozen heart

Catch a Snowflake

Romance often blossoms in the most unlikely of places - but in a ward full of wounded soldiers - surely not?

When Lucas Withers comes face to face with Jemima Parsons - a young woman who blames him for her brother's injury - falling in love is the last thing on their minds. What neither of them anticipated, was the magic of snowflakes.

$\sim$

Fate is Curious
A Novella

Happily, ever after? No such thing! Bereft, following her beloved husband's sudden death, Lady Charlotte Sherbrooke has lost her belief in such romantic nonsense.

Successful shipping merchant, Zacharie Romain, is no stranger to loss; his business can be hazardous. Moreover, his wife died in childbirth and even though it happened a decade ago, he has no mind to expose himself to such sorrow again.

They meet in less than joyful circumstances but, as the year turns and grief diminishes, the woes of a small boy become the catalyst for something wholly unexpected. Can Charlotte and Zacharie trust what Fate has in store or will past heartbreak prevent them from taking a chance on love?

∼

A Christmas Prayer
with Ashlee Shades
A Short Story

An entreaty from a frightened child.

Orphaned and only nine, Caroline Thorne has to grow up before her time. She is doing everything she can to keep what is left of her family together and out of the workhouse but is terrified her prayers are not being heard. Or maybe they are…

A petition from a woman desperate for a family.

A chance meeting with three orphaned siblings, tugs at Elizabeth Barrington's heart strings. Thus far, she and her husband have not been blessed with children and, as Christmas approaches, a plan begins to form - one which might just be the answer to her prayers.

Two Christmas prayers, as different as they are the same.

Will they hear and, more importantly, heed the answer?

∿

The Lady's Wager
Surrendered Hearts- Book Two
A Novelette

Ged Mowbray will do anything to avoid being married off to the suitable prospects his parents insist on parading in front of him.

Melissa Bouchard is under no illusion her sizeable dowry is the attraction to suitors, not her.

An overheard conversation leads to an offer too good to refuse, but what happens when a lady's wager, becomes a gamble on the happily ever after, you did not even realise you wanted?

∿

Winning Emma
Surrendered Hearts - Book Three
A Novelette

Randolph Craythorpe — earl, covert operative, and occasional highwayman — believed his dalliance with Lady Felicity Hartwich would lead to marriage. It did, but not to him! The arrival of an unwelcome guest, however, provides the perfect opportunity to indulge in a little retaliation.

Emma Newbury accompanies her cousin, Lady Charity Anscombe, to London for the Christmas season. Once there, she comes face to face with the three men who witnessed the humiliating aftermath of her father's disgrace — one of whom, to her irritation, has taken up residence in her dreams.

Their infrequent encounters only serve to confuse but,

while winter tightens its grip on the city, what was inconceivable becomes the one thing for which they both yearn, yet bound by Society's rules, cannot admit.

As the snow falls, Randolph begins to understand that to win Emma, he will have to surrender.

~

A Love Impossible
A Regency M/M Novelette

Tasked with investigating a heinous crime, Edward Lindsay travels from London to Dublin — a city which holds too many memories — in the guise of guardian to his sister. He knew it could be hazardous, and relished the challenge, but that wasn't what caused his stomach to tighten as they approached landfall.

Dublin held more than just a murderer.

There was also Aidan.

While attending a party, Aidan Griffen is astonished when he comes face to face with a man who fled Dublin two years previously. A man he has desperately tried to forget.

As Edward closes in on his quarry, a fire, deliberately extinguished, is rekindled. But what of it? Edward and Aidan share a love impossible, and to acknowledge their feelings — more dangerous than confronting a killer.

Is there any hope of a happily ever after?

~

Unravelling Roana
A Novelette

Tired of being ignored by her husband, Roana Dumont, Countess of Brooketon does the one thing guaranteed to get his attention. She runs away... to Venice, leaving behind a set of riddles for him to solve... *if* he feels their marriage is worth saving.

Gideon Dumont, 6th Earl of Brooketon is flabbergasted when he discovers his wife has apparently vanished off the face of the earth. A series of puzzles, the only clue as to her whereabouts.

The question is... will he unravel them?

Chasing Bluebells

A Novella

Once upon a time, somewhere in France, there was a man whose reckless obsession led him down a dark path. One which, ultimately, cost him his life.

That ought to have been the end of it. Regrettably, as is so often the case, those who least deserve it, suffer for the actions of others.

A decade after being sent away, Sebastien Daviau returns to the little village where everything began, hoping to lay the ghosts of his childhood to rest, studiously ignoring the possibility, he might run into Charlotte de Montbeliard.

As luck would have it, Charlotte is the one who runs into him… well his horse. Although the encounter leaves a lasting impression, neither recognises the other.

A name revealed causes a freak accident, catapulting Sebastien's past into his present, and bringing him face to face with a man whose reputation would intimidate the most ardent of suitors.

Can whatever is blossoming between Charlotte and Sebastien survive the challenge imposed, or is their happily ever after about to fade as quickly as the bluebells they loved to chase?

∽

CONTEMPORARY ROMANCE

Of Ruins and Romance

Kassandra Winters has intrigued Gabriel St Germain since he accidentally knocked her flying outside her university professor's office. Her face haunts his dreams, yet he never expected to see her again. So, he is surprised when she appears, as though destined to do so, in the middle of a ruin, and he concocts a plan to win her heart.

Gabriel's old-fashioned courtship touches something deep inside Kassie and, although struggling to believe someone as handsome as Gabriel could possibly be interested in her, she soon realises she has fallen irrevocably in love with him. However, just as Kassie shares everything of herself with Gabriel, her world comes crashing down.

Can their romance survive or will it fall in ruins, like the relics of antiquity that brought them together.

~

All At Once It's You

When Alex arrives in the small village of Rosedale Abbey, to take up a position as a research assistant for a renowned archaeologist, the last thing she is looking for, or expects to find, is love.

Jake was perfectly happy with the status quo. When it came to relationships, he didn't do committed or long term. He called the shots, and if his current flame didn't like it, she knew what to do. A philosophy, which served him well - until he met Alex.

Romance blooms, but even as the untamed wilderness of the North Yorkshire moors weaves its spell, a long-buried secret might yet jeopardise their happily ever after.

~

Cobweb Dreams
A Novella

A holiday on the Scottish isle of Mull was just the break Chloe Shepherd needed, an escape from her boring office job and her complete lack of anything resembling a social life. Romance, it seems, isn't on the cards and, although Chloe dreams of finding her soulmate she is beginning to believe love is like cobwebs — spun overnight, only to vanish in the early morning breeze.

Under sufferance, Dominic Winters makes a flying visit to Mull to check on a rental property owned by his family. He hasn't got time for this — so indulging in a holiday fling is the last thing on his mind.

A lamb stuck in a bog proves a most unexpected match-maker and, while Mull weaves its magic, Chloe wonders whether those fragile cobwebs might be far more stubborn than she thought.

Just One Step
A Short Story

In the aftermath of an horrific car accident, Daisy Forrester travels to Italy - hoping, so far from her memories, she might begin to heal.

Archaeologist, and single father, Adam Willoughby is too busy looking after his young daughter to give romance let alone love, a thought.

Neither expects a chance encounter in an ancient ruin to be anything more, but sometimes, that's all it takes.

His Heart's Second Sigh
A Novella

Reuben Faulkner and Paige Latimer are two happily single people, who have no desire to upset the status quo.

Unexpectedly, they are thrown together, only to discover both want far more than a casual friendship.

Just when things take an interesting turn, Reuben's past catches up with them, and threatens to derail their blossoming romance before it has chance to start.